Frederick Wayland Joyce

The Life of Rev. Sir F. A. G. Ouseley

Frederick Wayland Joyce

The Life of Rev. Sir F. A. G. Ouseley

ISBN/EAN: 9783337332860

Printed in Europe, USA, Canada, Australia, Japan

Cover: Foto ©Raphael Reischuk / pixelio.de

More available books at **www.hansebooks.com**

THE LIFE OF

REV. SIR F. A. G. OUSELEY, BART.

M.A., MUS.D., ETC. ETC.

FREDERICK OUSELEY

AS A CHILD OF 7 OR 8 YEARS OLD

From a picture at S. Michael's College—Artist's name unknown.

Photographed by C. Davies, Tenbury.

THE LIFE OF
Rev. Sir F. A. G. OUSELEY, Bart.

M.A., Mus. D., Etc. Etc.

By F. W. JOYCE, M.A.

RECTOR OF BURFORD, I P., SALOP

WITH TWO CHAPTERS APPRECIATIVE OF
SIR F. OUSELEY AS A MUSICIAN

By G. R. SINCLAIR
ORGANIST OF HEREFORD CATHEDRAL

WITH PORTRAITS AND ILLUSTRATIONS

METHUEN & CO.
36 ESSEX STREET, W.C.
LONDON
1896

TO

ALL CONNECTED WITH

ST. MICHAEL'S CHURCH AND COLLEGE

WHO HONOUR

THE MEMORY OF THEIR FOUNDER

THIS BOOK

IS DEDICATED

PREFACE

Sir Frederick Ouseley's life was one unique in
its way. It was not a great life, as great lives are
commonly esteemed. That is to say, he was not
a man widely famous, nor in all respects successful. Yet, with abilities of a very high order, in
other things beside music, he did a work in his
own generation of real and abiding value. He
was a man who had one set purpose in his life ;
and that purpose, despite certain failures of complete success, he fulfilled.

But this is not all. For it is rather on the
charm of that simple, single - hearted character,
by which he attracted and endeared to himself
all who came near him, that the claim must rest
for bringing any " Life of Sir Frederick Ouseley "
to publication. When he died, he left no surviving relatives nearer than cousins. And yet it is
not an exaggeration to say that his death was
mourned by scores of friends as that of a brother,
and by many hundreds as that of a member of
their own family. It is, then, this strong feeling
of personal affection on the part of numbers of

Sir Frederick's friends which has resulted in the present attempt to portray his life. The wish has been constantly, and from many quarters, expressed, that some permanent Memoir of him should be written.

Otherwise, I may be allowed this opportunity of saying, I should scarcely have ventured on the attempt. For, apart from any personal shortcomings and inexperience of my own in literary work, I must plead also a scantiness of written materials. Sir Frederick kept no diary, and preserved very few letters. In such circumstances it is difficult for any biographer to write either as fully or as accurately as might be wished. None the less, one feels it to be a real privilege, if one may only attempt to describe the life, work, and character of so estimable a man as was my own godfather and my father's lifelong friend. Especially may one hope that future generations at St. Michael's College will welcome this account of their Founder's life. No pains have been spared to make the Memoir as authentic as possible; and, in this respect, my grateful thanks are due to the many kind helpers who have aided in the work. Among these, particular acknowledgment should be made to Sir F. Ouseley's Trustees, for allowing me free access to such papers as were left in their charge; to the present Warden of St. Michael's College, the Rev. John Hampton, for much help in the way of search and revision; to Mrs. F. T. Havergal, for a generous permission to make " unfettered use " of the late Dr. Havergal's valuable records (*a*) ; to Mr. T. L. Southgate, for unstinted assistance ; to the Very Rev. the Dean (G. W. Kitchin) of Durham ; to Canon J. Rich of Chippenham ; to Sir Walter Parratt, Mr. W. H. Cummings, Mr. A. H. D. Pendergast, Mr. Ebenezer Prout, the Rev. J. S. Sidebotham, the Rev. Dr. J. H. Mee, the Rev. V. K. Cooper, the Hon. Mrs. Fitzmaurice ; to Mr. John S. Bumpus, for the use of his valuable Catalogue of Sir F. Ouseley's compositions ; and not least, in the last place, to Mr. G. R. Sinclair, now the talented Organist of Hereford Cathedral, but once a pupil at St. Michael's College, and one of whom that College is justly proud. His Chapters criticising Sir F. Ouseley as a Musician will give this book a value which it could not otherwise claim.

One thing more, perhaps, should be said by way of preface. Ought a son to apologise for introducing his own father's name, so fully as I have felt bound to do into certain parts of this "Life of Sir F. Ouseley"? I can only answer, that such deep affection and such constant intercourse existed between the two friends until my father's death, in 1887, that it would be affectation to ignore the influence which the elder friend must have exercised on the younger. Moreover,

(*a*) *Memorials of Sir F. A. G. Ouseley*, by the Rev. Francis T. Havergal, D.D. This book was chiefly a collection of extracts from the newspapers written at the time of Sir Frederick Ouseley's death. In his "Prefatory Note," Dr. Havergal expressed a wish that what he had collected might be "useful as a basis for some future biography." It is very probable that no "Life" of Sir F. Ouseley would ever have been written if Dr. Havergal had not had the prescience to gather together such materials as he did whilst it was possible to do so.

PREFACE

the general view taken in this book of Sir Frederick Ouseley's character and not a few of the details of his life are derived from reminiscences of my father's conversation.

F. W. JOYCE.

BORASTON RECTORY, TENBURY,
February 1896.

CONTENTS

CONTENTS

CHAPTER I

ANCESTRY, PARENTAGE, AND EARLY YEARS—
1825–1840

THE Ouseleys are said to have been originally descended from an ancient Shropshire family. Their most remote ancestor traceable by authentic documents appears to have been Thomas Oseley of St. Winifred's, Salop, A.D. 1486. One branch of the family formerly lived at Alscote, in the parish of Worfield, near Bridgnorth. In the fourteenth year of Queen Elizabeth, A.D. 1572 (*a*), Richard Ouseley, Oursley, or Oseley, great-grandson of the above Thomas, held, by "grant of the Crown," the estate of Courteen Hall, in the county of Northampton. Three generations later, *circ.*

(*a*) Epitaph on the monument of Sir Richard Ousley, Esq., at Courteen, Northants :—

<table>
<tr><td>[No date.]</td><td>A Sallop's Oseley I
  A ruen *Partrige* woonne—
No birds I had her by
  Such work with her was doonne.
Shee dead, I turtle sought
  A *Wake* in Salsie bred :
Twise six birds shee mee brought,
  Shee lyvs, but I am dead.</td></tr>
<tr><td>SHE—</td><td>But when ninth yeare was come
  I sleapt that was a *Wake* :
So yielding to Death's doome
  Did here my lodging take.</td></tr>
</table>

1650, we find two younger sons of this branch of the family, Richard Ouseley and Jasper Ouseley, emigrating to Ireland. There it is said that the Wellesleys and the Wesleys sprang from the same stock as the Ouseleys. Anyhow, three generations later again, we find the descendants of the above-named Jasper Ouseley still settled in Ireland. To Ralph Ouseley, great-grandson of Jasper, there were born, from his first wife, Elizabeth Holland of Limerick, six children, all in the castle of Dunmore, County Galway. Of these six, the eldest son was William (afterwards Sir William Ouseley, LL.D., a notable Oriental scholar); and the second was Gore Ouseley, born June 24, 1770. He was the father of the subject of this memoir.

At the age of seventeen, Gore Ouseley went out to India to seek his fortune. In course of time he there became attached to the Court of the Nabob Saadut Ali at Lucknow, first as Major Commandant and afterwards as *Aide-de-camp*. In this position he was able to cultivate a good understanding between the State of Oude and the British power. His courteous and winning manners, combined with a ripe knowledge of Eastern languages and customs, stood him in good stead; and gradually he came under the favourable notice of Lord Wellesley, the Governor-General. In 1805, after seventeen years' absence from home, Major Ouseley returned to England (*b*).

(*b*) See Reynolds's *Memoir of Sir Gore Ouseley*, passim.

In 1806 he married Harriot Georgina, daughter of John and Mary Whitelock. In 1808 he was created a Baronet. In 1810 he was appointed Ambassador Extraordinary and Minister Plenipotentiary to the Court of Persia. In this capacity he won the credit of bringing about peace between Persia and Russia. He was resident for about four years at Teheran, and for twelve months in Russia—in Moscow and St. Petersburg. In 1812 and 1814 Sir Gore Ouseley was honoured with the insignia of the Royal Persian Order of the Lion and the Sun, and the Grand Cross of the Imperial Russian Order of St. Alexander Nevsky. The Shah presented him with a magnificent gold-enamelled plate. It contained an inscription, setting forth Sir Gore's virtues in very flowery language. He received many other marks of distinction, and was a noted member of several scientific and literary societies both at home and abroad. On his final return to England from his diplomatic missions, he received from the Crown a pension of £5000 a year. Sir Gore was a man of considerable and varied attainments, and was in great request in society. He was himself musical ; played the violin, besides several other instruments, and was one of the chief founders of the Royal Academy of Music, established in 1822. In 1823 he took a prominent part in the institution of the Royal Asiatic Society of London, and did much to advance the cause of Oriental literature. He himself published an interesting work on the " Persian Poets." In fact, he was a *dilettante* in art, and a man of much culture for those days. During his residence abroad he had had special opportunities for buying up art treasures. It was in this way that his son afterwards became possessor of the beautiful inlaid Persian furniture, and other things, of which he was so proud ; and practically Sir Gore laid the foundation of the fine general library (c) now at St. Michael's College. Among his other accomplishments may be reckoned that of ivory-turning, a pursuit begun, no doubt, as a pastime in Persia, but one with which in his later years — not being so devoted a church-goer as his son afterwards became — he was accustomed to while away the long hours of an English Sunday. He claimed to possess a charm, revealed to him by some Eastern Sheik under seal of secrecy, for curing any venomous snake - bite, and is said to have, on one occasion at least, successfully used it. He had also learned from the same source some system of training the wildest horses.

Lady Ouseley's maiden name was, as above stated, Whitelock. She was born in 1787, being thus seventeen years younger than her husband. One of her ancestors, Sir James Whitelock, was a Judge of the King's Bench in the reign of Charles I. His son, Sir Bulstrode Whitelock, born in Fleet Street, 1605, became M.P. for Marlow in the Long Parliament, and afterwards

(c) Cf. p. 114 *infra.*

4

represented Oxford in the House of Commons. He was one of the Council of State in 1659, and died in 1675. A great-grandson of his, in 1783, married Mary Lewis. These were the parents of Lady Ouseley.

Five children were born to Sir Gore and Lady Ouseley, but only three survived to maturity. When the last of the family, Frederick Arthur Gore Ouseley, was born, in London on August 12, 1825, there were only two other children living. These were both daughters, Mary Jane and Alexandrina Percival. The elder of his two sisters was, at the time of Frederick's birth, at least eighteen years of age. She was not only very musical herself, but was otherwise possessed of excellent abilities ; and it is to her that we owe the interesting account, at the end of this chapter, of her little brother's early years (d).

Sir Gore Ouseley, on his permanent return to England, lived first at a place called Woolmers (c), in the parish of Hertingfordbury, Herts. Not far off from this place was the East India College at Haileybury, of which one of Sir Gore's half-brothers, Colonel Joseph Ouseley, after leaving the Indian Army, was one of the Oriental pro-

(d) Appendix A, p. 17 *infra*. [The reader would do well to read the Appendix here, before proceeding further with this chapter.]

(c) The beautiful tune to No. 424, in *Hymns Ancient and Modern* ("They come, God's Messengers of Love"), was written in after years by Sir F. Ouseley, for the dedication of his Church, and named "Woolmers," from his early home in Hertfordshire. Very appropriately, too, the Hymn was sung at his own burial on April 11, 1889.

fessors. Later on, the Gore Ouseleys settled down at Hall Barn Park (*f*), near Beaconsfield, Bucks.

Of the childhood of their only son, numerous stories are told in connection with his musical ability, besides those recorded in his sister's account. He is remembered as sitting on his sister Janie's knee, "picking out tunes on the pianoforte at three years old." In fact, he could play almost before he could talk. His earliest composition, as taken down and committed to paper by his sisters, is dated November 1828, *i.e.* when he was no more than three years and three months old. When he was four, he played the piano for the servants to dance to. A year or two later he had a serious illness, in the form of a fever, lasting for some weeks. On his recovery from this sickness he composed a piece of music descriptive of how the disease had run its course. All the stages are described in turn, the beginning, progress, crisis, and abatement, and then the relief of convalescence. "*Andante expressivo*—beginning to be a little ill—now I'm very ill—iller than ever—blisters— a little better—not quite well yet—now I'm quite well!" This piece was intended by the youthful composer as a present for Dr. Granville, the kind physician who had attended him in his illness. On this composition a criticism is to be found in

(*f*) This place now belongs to Sir Edward Lawson. It was once in the possession of the poet Edmund Waller, from whose representatives Sir Gore Ouseley bought it.

the *Harmonicon*, a musical magazine of that time, dated May 1833 (vol. xi. part i. pp. 102, 103) :—

Though an abundance of lively fancy is displayed in this, there is nothing in it at all extravagant or ridiculous ; on the contrary, it is strictly *en règle*, and expresses, as well as inarticulate sounds are capable of expressing sensations, all the variety of feeling which would be experienced in the course of a long fever.

The same number of the *Harmonicon* prints a March, composed by the little Frederick Ouseley at the age of six, which is described as "one of the most marvellous productions of this age of musical wonders." The *Harmonicon* goes on to speak thus of

the extraordinary, the unexampled genius of this little boy, now only seven years and a half old. . . . He has received no instructions in music, and, though taught by himself to play with considerable skill on the pianoforte, does not know his notes on paper, and trusts to his sisters for writing down what he composes. He improvises entire scenes, singing to his own accompaniment, the latter often exhibiting harmony the most *recherché*, chords that an experienced musician only uses with caution ; but these are always introduced and resolved in a strictly regular manner, not by rule, for he has learnt no rules, but by the aid of a very surprising ear, and of some faculty which, for want of a better term, we will call intuition. His organ of hearing is so fine that, with his eyes closed, he instantly names any musical sound produced ; and so discriminating is this sense in the child, that, when a note is struck on an instrument, tuned either above or below the usual pitch, he immediately discovers, and accurately states, in what the deviation consists. A chord of four notes being sounded, he named each note exactly, though at some distance from the instrument, and with his back turned to it. . . . Under a French governess and a tutor for Latin, his education is proceeding in the usual manner, music forming no part of it. His intellects are quick, and declare themselves in a countenance remarkable for intelligence and beauty. His habits and amusements are suited to his age, and the activity of his mind does not appear to have operated unfavourably on his general health, which seems to be good, and as well established as is usual with children of his years.

Though music appears to have formed no part of the child's regular educational routine, it is clear that he was encouraged at home to follow up his own natural bent in this direction. A small volume of his early compositions, which is preserved at St. Michael's College, although measuring no more than $9\frac{1}{2} \times 5\frac{1}{2}$ inches, yet contains on two hundred pages no fewer than two hundred and forty-three examples, of which two hundred and nineteen were written before he was six years old (*g*). Some of these were written for his parents, others for friends. His first operetta was composed at the age of seven and a half. The MS. of this consists of fifty-three pages of six lines each. It bears no distinguishing title, but seems to be made up chiefly of hunting and other rustic scenes, the words (in English) having been probably supplied by his father. In 1833, when eight years old, the child composed a more ambitious and much longer opera, with solos, choruses, etc.—the words being taken from the Italian *L'Isola disabitata* of Metastasio. With regard to this composition, the *Musical Library* of September 1834, after remarking on its "manliness . . . as quite unexpected from so youthful a pen," goes on to say :—

There are a few notes which an experienced composer would not have used, but they will serve to convince the sceptical, if any there be, that the author had no professional aid in this production

(*g*) See note at beginning of Appendix A, p. 17 *infra*.

—a work which, from a child of eight years, will hardly fail to be received with astonishment.

Miss Ouseley also records that another capable critic of music, Mr. W. Ayrton, having come to hear this youthful composer play and sing the first song and recitative in his opera, declared that, though he had Haydn's composition on the same words, he considered it much inferior to the little Ouseley's, which seemed to him to be rather the work of an adult, and as sufficient to form the fortune of a composer. Mr. Ayrton said he had been reading Danes Barrington's accounts of Mozart, Wesley, Crotch, and other musical prodigies, but that none of them, in his opinion, approached the phenomenon which he had just witnessed, of extempore playing, guessing chords, and so on.

Various instances are given, too, of the child's extreme acuteness of ear. A celebrated violinist was playing a Sonata in A flat, and for the sake of greater brilliancy had tuned his instrument a semitone sharp. When the performance began, Cipriani Potter, who was in the secret, came to the little Ouseley and asked him what the key was. The answer came out pat, "A." His father, Sir Gore, who was sitting by, vexed at what he supposed to be the boy's mistake, showed him the programme, in which the Sonata was specified as being in A flat. But the child insisted on "A"; and in the end was duly justified for that sense of absolute accuracy of ear which in his case had already begun to attract the notice of musicians (*h*). Another amusing instance is recorded of a certain concert where the *bénéficiare*, or some other great star, was improvising an elaborate piece on the piano. Our youthful composer, still quite in his early childhood, was present, sitting next to a lady friend, Mrs. Henry Davidson. Suddenly the "little imp," as Mrs. Davidson called him in relating the story, looked up in her face, and said: "I wonder how he is going to resolve that discord. It's the discord of the minor ninth, and can be resolved in four different ways." It is only fair to Sir Frederick's character for personal modesty, to add that when this story of his childhood was told to him in after years, his only remark was, "What an abominably disagreeable child I must have been!" The above reminiscence throws an interesting light on the fact before noticed, that this musical child was not taught music in any definite and regular way. His knowledge of the "discord of the minor ninth," and of its four possible modes of resolution, may indeed have been derived from his sister's instructions. Logier was Miss Ouseley's pianoforte tutor; and it was Logier who was one of the first, if not the first, of musical writers who spoke of the "minor ninth," in place of the expression then commonly used, "diminished

(*h*) A somewhat similar anecdote was recorded in the *Pall Mall Gazette* at the time of Sir F. Ouseley's death. But there seems reason for doubting the accuracy of the particular account there given. The above version of the story was told to the Rev. J. Hampton, the present Warden of St. Michael's College, by the late Sir John Goss.

seventh." But in later life Sir Frederick Ouseley used himself to say: "I have never been taught music; all my musical knowledge has been evolved out of the depths of my own inner consciousness" (*i*).

Nevertheless it is quite clear that from the beginning the child was moving in a musical sphere. His precocious genius, coupled with his father's position in society, brought him into frequent contact with some of the most eminent people in the musical world. The following letter, written by the Duchess of Hamilton more than a year after the one quoted by Miss Ouseley (in Appendix A), shows how great and continued was the impression made by the child's performances on one of the first musical amateurs in England :—

A LETTER FROM THE DUCHESS OF HAMILTON.

April 13, 1832.

I have been to-day to hear Sir Gore Ouseley's little boy, and never was I so affected by anything in my life. I can find no words to express my astonished delight when I saw the little fellow, only six years old, sit down to the pianoforte, and commence

---

(*i*) This assertion must, of course, be taken with some reservation. As Mr. Hampton has pointed out, Sir F. Ouseley, when at Christ Church, in his undergraduate days, had regular instruction of some kind from Dr. Stephen Elvey, taking written fugues from time to time for his revisal. He had read every available book on the Theory of Music when he left Oxford ; and throughout his after life he was accustomed to read up every work published on that subject by the learned in different countries. He learnt German, for instance, and Spanish in his later years, in order to read the many works on Musical Theory in those languages. Still it was no doubt substantially true that he had never been *taught* music, except by self-instruction and by what his sister could impart to him.

an extemporaneous performance which baffles all description. His large dark eyes lighted up, his whole soul seemed intent upon what he was about, and yet with all this there was such a genuine childish simplicity. I could not say half of what I feel.

I am afraid this will be thought an exaggeration, but I never was an admirer of wonderful children. I have seen many who had extraordinary execution upon an instrument, but God has given this child an intuitive knowledge of the most hidden mysteries of sound—a creative power perfectly organised that surpasses belief.

Read the accounts of Mozart's infancy and you have read this child's.

I sat down to the piano, and while his mother held him at a distance, I endeavoured to puzzle him by the most intricate modulations, but he not only instantly named the key I was playing in, but followed every change (even when an enharmonic transition rendered it almost inappreciable to the ear) with the rapidity of thought,—he knew it, but he knew not why.

In the course of playing I struck the chord of the sharp 6th—the German 6th as called by some writers, and upon resolving it in the usual way he started up and cried out, " that is the sharp 6th in the key of C minor, and I can *dissolve* it another way." He ran to the piano, and without a moment's hesitation struck the chord, and proceeded to resolve it in a most *abstruse* but perfectly correct manner, and then went on modulating till he brought it back to the original key. He played me numbers of the airs he had written, all distinguished by the exquisite taste and plaintiveness of their character, some marches, loud and lively, with an evident idea of orchestral effect in their arrangement ; indeed orchestral and dramatic effect pervades every note he plays.

I can never forget the impression this scene made upon me. I am not ashamed to say that it affected me to tears.

The little fellow's countenance is a noble one—very delicate, with full dark eyes, and a very prominent and expansive forehead ; there is every promise of genius of the most commanding kind about him.

May he live to be a second Mozart is my sincere wish ; may he live to prove that an Englishman can excel in the most divine of Sciences as he can in all the rest.

Malibran, too, the great operatic singer, came in 1833 to hear the little Ouseley improvise, and sing his opera of *L'Isola disabitata*. So much affected was she by the performance, that she cried almost to hysterics. In the course of the next three years, before her early death in 1836, Malibran used also sometimes to sing with the boy. His voice then was exquisite, and ran to one note higher than hers. Even at this early period he evinced, too, something of that power of mimicry which always to the end of his life lay strong within him, though then it was less often indulged in. When quite a child, he is remembered as having delighted himself in imitating, all too faithfully, the very flat and very nasal singing of a certain lady amateur whose vocal ambitions were in advance of her capacity.

But probably one of the proudest moments of all for this youthful musician would have been when, at the age of six years, he played a duet on the pianoforte with the great Mendelssohn, the very composer with whom in after life his own musical tastes and refined style of composition appear to have been most in harmony. On that occasion Mendelssohn was a guest at Sir Gore Ouseley's house. It would have been perhaps at a later date—or possibly it may have been on this identical occasion—that the *extemporaneous* duet was played, to which the following memorandum refers, written in 1894 by a former friend of Sir F. Ouseley (*j*) in answer to a request for materials for this present memoir :—

(*j*) The late Rev. H. Deane, Fellow of St. John's College, Senior Proctor, and once Vicar of St. Giles, Oxford, who died (like Sir Frederick Ouseley) very suddenly, on July 1, 1894, three days after writing the letter above referred to.

LIFE OF SIR F. A. G. OUSELEY

Clayhill House, Gillingham, Dorset,
June 28, 1894.

. . . I can supply you with many facts about him. What requires to be most carefully ascertained is the story of his *extemporaneous* duet on the pianoforte with Mendelssohn. Sir Frederick told me that he had done it. My old master, Mr. Reinagle, said that he heard it. The odd thing is that the whole subject has perished.

On one occasion King William IV. and Queen Adelaide went to Hall Barn to hear the boy sing; and, at some period or other of his youth, Frederick Ouseley is said to have played duets with H. M. Queen Victoria also at Buckingham Palace.

Of other events in his boyhood, besides those in connection with his musical ability, there are but few reminiscences forthcoming. The life of a boy who never went to school, either public or private, whose father was advancing in years, and whose education was left mainly, no doubt, in the hands of his mother, and the two sisters much older than himself, would naturally be uneventful. I remember, however, his telling me on one occasion how much he used to dread the regular interview which took place once every year between himself and his godfather, the great Duke of Wellington. The contrast between the " Iron Duke " and the gentle, home-trained boy, with his high-strung musical nerves, is a suggestive one. But the godson declared that it was the Duke who was shy and stiff and awkward, and who, whilst invariably kind in his intentions, never seemed to know what to say next on these (to the boy) all-important occasions. On the whole, both godfather and godson appear to have regarded their annual meetings in the light of an ordeal of duty which had to be gone through, and which they were both glad to get over.

More congenial, no doubt, to the boy's tastes were those meetings, above referred to, which he enjoyed from time to time with some of the most eminent celebrities in the musical world. Here is one more reminiscence of this kind which dates a few years later than those events hitherto recorded. The late Sir George Elvey, formerly organist of St. George's Chapel, Windsor, related how he once went to Hall Barn Park to hear the boy play, when he was about twelve years old :—

He sat down to the instrument and extemporised in the most surprising manner. . . . The great basso, Lablache, went to hear the boy play, and was as much astonished as myself. His ear was so quick that I was told, on a grand piano, if a note was out of tune, he would put his ear close to the instrument and point to the wire that was at fault. This he did in the presence of Lablache, who exclaimed, *Le Diable!* Let me also mention that, in my presence, a heap of notes being put down by the palm of the hand, the boy actually named every one of them without seeing the keyboard.

As to what religious influences may have been helping to form Frederick Ouseley's character all through these early years at home, it seems impossible to trace anything very definite. It is noteworthy, perhaps, that his baptism did not take place until within eight months after his birth. He was born August 12, 1825, and was baptized in May, 1826. This would now be considered an exceptionally long interval. But during the first half of the nineteenth century, even in families of professedly church principles, the baptism of infants would seem to have been frequently deferred still longer than in this case. Lady Ouseley, if we may judge by the following extracts from her letters, and by the tender memories of herself always cherished by her son, must have been a woman of gentle and loving character. Her strict ideas of the keeping of Sunday appear to have been little altered by her long residence abroad; and in other ways her old-fashioned piety may have laid the foundations of that devotion to duty, and, above all, that intense love and reverence for the service of God, which marked the future life of her son. In this con- nection, too, we may well imagine the effect which sacred music would exercise upon this youngest member of the Ouseley family. When he was only six years old, one of his aunts, Miss White- lock, found him one Sunday playing the " Halle- lujah Chorus " on the piano at home. " Why, what do you call that ? " she asked. " Oh ! I'm sure I don't know," was the child's answer ;—" it is something the man played to-day on the organ as we came out of church."

APPENDIX A.

ACCOUNT OF THE EARLY YEARS OF FREDERICK A. G. OUSELEY, BY HIS ELDEST SISTER.

THE composer of the airs contained in the following pages (*a*) is the only surviving son of the Right Hon. Sir Gore Ouseley of Hall Barn Park, co. Bucks, Bart., G.C.H., K.L.S., and K.S.A., and of Harriot Georgina, his wife. He was born in Grosvenor Square, London, on the 12th of August 1825, and christened in May 1826, by the names of Frederick Arthur Gore. Sponsors, His Royal Highness Frederick, Duke of York and Albany, and Arthur, Duke of Wellington ; his godmothers, Frances, Marchioness of Salisbury, and Mary Jane Ouseley, his eldest sister.

At the early age of three months he showed not only a very unusual love for music, but even the power of distinguishing particular tunes, listening attentively to every air his sisters played, but more earnestly marking his approbation of Weber's waltz in the Freischutz by various kickings in his nurse's arms, and other strange exertions. When suffering the greatest pain from teething, an air on the pianoforte was sure to stop his crying ; and he probably thus increased his love for music by being indulged in it whenever pain or illness called for its soothing consolation. His ear was constructed in so extraordinary a manner, that long before he could speak he took up airs with his voice precisely in the same key in which they had been played or sung to him, at even a long interval after they had ceased.

At the age of seventeen months he could sing any air to which his ear was familiarised, without any assistance from others, or from the instrument, and on trial it was found invariably pitched in the key in which it was usually played or sung, and every note in perfect tune.

When two years old, his sisters and their governess were astonished to perceive that often when standing on their left hand, while they were playing on the pianoforte, his little hand fell as it were instinctively on the dominants and tonics, and even when they changed the key to puzzle him, he changed his tonics and dominants also without ever making a false chord. From this period may be dated his incipient love of harmony, although the

---

(*a*) The collection of the young Frederick Ouseley's early compositions, — a volume still preserved at St. Michael's College. See *supra*, p. 8.

hands, not being able to cover a sufficient number of the keys, necessarily restricted him to melody, unless when he took the bass part of another player's treble, in which he acquitted himself in a surprising manner.

The first number of the following airs will show that he commenced composing in regular measure and rhythm at about three years of age. This was effected by his voice, whilst he imitated the motions of playing with his fingers on the window. One of his sisters hastened to commit to paper the first part of this Sauteuse, which was all that he had then composed, and when written out, after some interval she begged he would add a second part. This he instantly complied with, and in a surprising manner completed it in the same key as the first part, although some time had elapsed between the two compositions.

Numberless were the instances he now daily showed of the wonderful accuracy of his ear, and as he knew the names of the notes on the instrument (tuned to concert pitch), his ear retained the intervals, so that he could at once tell what the tone was of any noise he heard; sometimes it thundered in G, and the wind whistled in D, and invariably when anyone ran to the instrument for proof of his assertions, they found him quite correct. In the tone of most bells there is a second tone perceptible to an acute ear, which did not escape little Frederick's observation; for one day when walking out with his nurse, Mrs. Barlow, he happened to be near the coach-house when the clock over it struck, on which he said, "Do you know, Ba (as he usually called her), the clock has struck in B flat minor?" The poor woman could not conceive what he meant, but reported it to his mother, who took pains to ascertain the fact, and found to her great surprise, when the clock next struck, that its double tone was in the key of B flat minor.

At Brighton one evening an ambulant band of wind instruments stopped to play under the windows; when they had concluded their first air, his father asked him what key they had been playing in, to which he at once replied, "Why, papa, it is a kind of F, but neither F natural nor F sharp"; and on his father's going to the pianoforte in the next room he found that the child had stated the fact, it being a quarter of a tone too sharp for one and as much too flat for the other. This occurred in 1830, when the child was four years old.

About the same period the Countess de Montalembert begged of Lady Ouseley to give her copies of a few of the little boy's compositions for a very musical friend. That friend was the Duchess of

APPENDIX A

Hamilton, certainly the most accomplished musician and singer ever known amongst English amateurs.

The compositions were copied and sent, and in a month or two the Countess received a letter from the Duchess, of which the following is an extract :—

"HOLYROOD PALACE,
"December 1, 1830.

" I cannot tell you how much I think of the wonderful child, my dear friend. I have been amusing myself putting basses to and making variations upon his delightful compositions, and I should be laughed at could people know how much the occupation affects and enchants me. Dear little darling ! how could he imagine such touching tones at four years old ? And yet why should not the *Soul* triumph at the earliest age ? It is a beautiful proof of its divine nature. Pray tell me what kind of a looking child my *petite passion* is. I quite long to see and to hear him, and were he within any reasonable distance, I would fly to his pianoforte side. He *stands*, I think you said, to play. When did he begin music ? and does other people's performance interest and please him ? I wish there were good likenesses of him, I would ask you to beg, borrow, or *steal* one for me. Oh, what I would give to have such a child ! No wonder Sir Gore and Lady Ouseley worship him ! Does he enjoy good health ? I hope they don't excite his musical feelings too much. I know something about that, and certainly few things produce such an electric effect on the nerves as some combinations of harmony. I have often made myself ill by listening to certain chords. Oh, the dear child ! His image haunts me. I love him for having appreciated you, and I flatter myself we shall prove great friends some day or other. One more question —Is he childish in manner, and does he seem happy ?"

On a further supply of the little boy's compositions being sent to her Grace through the same channel, she writes :—

" I am equally *astonished* and *enchanted* with Sir Gore Ouseley's child's talent. Pray tell Sir Gore I hope and trust I shall one day have the happiness of hearing this second Mozart. Oh, the darling child ! Heaven bless and preserve him."

But although some of the airs sent to the Duchess of Hamilton were simple melodies, yet the dates of compositions in the following sheets will prove that even in his fourth year he had an unusual knowledge of harmony. During the short *séjour* of the family at Brighton, he made several discoveries of harmonies until then new

19

to him ; and although his parents and sisters (from apprehensions of his health suffering, or his head being affected by it) cautiously forbore giving him the smallest instruction in music, either practical or theoretical, further than telling the names of the chords (when he asked them) which he had by himself discovered, he still seemed by intuition to be versed in the most abstruse mysteries of harmony and modulation, so as to excite the astonishment of the most eminent amateurs and professional musicians then in Brighton, who even tried him in modulating from very extreme keys. Amongst the former I venture to mention the name of Mr. Solomon, the famous double bass player (second only to the celebrated Dragonetti); and amongst the latter, that pleasing maestro, Signor Gaboussi, and Signor Borgatta, the wonderful improvisatore on the pianoforte.

To give the reader of these hasty memoranda some idea of the manner in which this inspired child spoke of his harmonies, whilst it at the same time proves the delightful childishness of disposition, so much wished to be found in him by the Duchess of Hamilton, the following dialogue between him and his eldest sister is copied from a memorandum made at the time ; it took place at Brighton in 1830, and is given in his own phraseology ; his questioner was his eldest sister :—

Janie.—" Boy, how did you modulate in going from C to D flat minor ?"

Fredk.—" I took the chord of A flat with the 9th,—you know, Janie, the *minished* 7th."

Janie.—" Why did you first strike the chord of C minor before you went to A sharp?"

Fredk.—" Because I thought it sounded pretty."

Janie.—" Why pretty ?"

Fredk.—" Because there was one note of one chord in it, and one note of the other."

In these last two replies, how clearly he has demonstrated the necessity of what the masters term *combination* in modulating from one key to another (that the chord you go to must have at least one note in common with the chord you go from), dictated by Nature more true even than Art, and couched in the childish but beautiful expressive answer, "Because I thought it sounded pretty." It tends to prove that everything, however artful and abstruse it may appear in Science, originates with Nature, which the handmaid Art develops, dresses, and fixes under laws and regulations, for here Nature, and Nature alone, whispered to a child of four years and three months that he must not jump from one chord to another without having some note as a bond of union common to both.

All this gifted boy's replies bore the same character of simplicity and charming childishness, although always direct to the point. When asked to go from B sharp to C flat, he immediately remarked that they were the same note, innocently giving as a reason, that "there was no black note between them on the pianoforte."

He was one day (in 1831) playing the cadence of D, and after repeating it two or three times he dwelt upon the following

chord of the added 6th  and asked what it meant.

His sister purposely delayed giving an answer, when, after trying both G and E in the bass, he decided, quite unaided, that it was *not* the chord of E minor.

In the course of the year 1831 his compositions, as will be seen in the following pages, assume a character of sweet pathos in the melody, and uncommon harmonies in the bass, much beyond what could have been expected, and, one might perhaps add, beyond the efforts of any other natural untaught genius, who had not completed his fourth year.

In the August of that year Sir Gore Ouseley received a letter, of which the following is an extract, from the celebrated John Baptist Logier, Esq., Professor of Music, and Originator of a System of Musical Instruction which met with merited success in England and Ireland (although more qualified in the former), but most particularly in Prussia, where it triumphed over opposition and obtained royal and ministerial protection and patronage.

Mr. Logier had given instructions when in England to Sir Gore Ouseley, and subsequently to his two daughters, in the theory of music, but at the time this letter was written he was residing in Dublin, where he had for three or four years taught this system in an academy filled with pupils.

[COPY.]

"DUBLIN,
"*August* 25, 1831.

"DEAR SIR,—Miss Ouseley has just sent for my perusal the last production of the young musician. No. 154 in C minor is really a very elegant and pathetic little composition. I had almost said (considering the infantine source from whence these effusions have flowed) that they are *too* plaintive. Whilst I was playing them over, tears involuntarily started into my eyes. The merry little strain, however, which follows immediately after in C major, sets all to rights again. The three pieces which are in minor keys are by far the best which the little musician has written as yet. This proves (if anything were necessary to prove it) how truly this child is gifted with genuine musical feeling. Let us look at bars

13 and 14 of No. 159   What true feeling !

Perhaps I may see more in these two bars than others do ; yet I know what I am saying.

"Excuse these few hasty lines, my dear sir, I could not resist the temptation of giving my opinion of the little musician's effusions, for they have given me real pleasure. May I beg to present my best regards to the little composer, whom I shall soon have the pleasure of seeing.

"I am, my dear Sir,

"Your very obliged humble Servant,

(Signed) "J. B. LOGIER."

This testimony from such an acknowledged good judge proves the proficiency that the little Frederick had made both in his choice of melodies, as well as harmonies, previously to having entered on his fifth year.

The uncommon beauty of the two bars alluded to by Mr. Logier (where breaking off suddenly from harmonic accompaniment the youthful composer indulges in four notes of unison in treble and bass, emphatically pronounced) had already attracted the attention and admiration of the whole *Fanatici* family. In fact, it was as much the introduction of those unisons, as the general elegance of the plaintive air itself, that induced them to send a copy of it to Mr. Logier, without comment. The above letter from that excellent maestro will prove that comment was not necessary.

About a couple of months after he had entered his fifth year (October 1831), whilst sitting on the sofa chatting with his mother and his younger sister, and apparently thinking of anything but music, he suddenly started up and said, "Oh ! I know of such a pretty chord, I am sure it will sound beautiful ; do come and listen to it, Leili." He than ran in his usual playful manner and executed

22

the following chords without the least hesitation. (See examples A and B.)

In the course of this year he furnished numberless proofs, similar to the above, of his wonderful recollection of the intervals between the keys of the pianoforte, which enabled him to invent harmonies at a distance from the instrument ; and he has often dictated to his sisters, from the adjoining room, the component parts of very beautiful chords, which, although often very uncommon, were always correct.

In this, his fifth year, hearing his eldest sister making use of the chord of the sharp sixth whilst modulating, he admired it, and asked her the name of it, but took no more notice of it at the moment. Some three months afterwards he said to her, "Janie, I wish you would play that chord which I admired so much at Woolmers ; I think you called it the *sharp seventh.*" She guessed at what he meant, and told him she would introduce it in the course of modulating, and that when he recognised his favourite he was to call out. She modulated for some time accordingly, introducing the chords of the 7th, 9th, 11th, and 13th ; but the moment the sharp sixth was pronounced, he called out that it was that chord he wanted, and he was then informed that it was the sharp sixth, and not the seventh, as he had from forgetfulness called it. He then played the chord over several times, and, to the astonishment of the family, called out in great delight that it could *dissolve* (as he then called resolve) into another chord. He had been playing the sharp sixth of A flat (see example C). He then said it could go in the chord of C, meaning (see example D), which he played quite correctly. Everyone present was necessarily much surprised at his having made this discovery, and his sister asked him if he could find any other chord into which it could resolve, when, before a minute elapsed, he discovered the following resolution into C sharp by the enharmonic change (see example E). He had been only playing the simple 6, not $7\frac{6}{5}$; and his auditors felt convinced that, had he been playing the latter, he would have found the remaining chord into which he might have resolved it.

Mr. Hingston, the tuner of our instruments, once made trial of Frederick's ear in a manner that he said had hitherto puzzled the most competent musicians. Whilst tuning a square piano, he tuned the wire of one note exactly one note higher than the other wire, and then, sounding three or four notes consecutively, asked the child the name of each note, which was correctly answered until he came to the *untuned* note, which, when asked, he unhesitatingly said, " It is E, but I see D in it," to the great astonishment of Mr. Hingston. He generally tried the instruments when fresh tuned, and found out the smallest fault ; but the tuner deprecated his criticism by saying, " Pray, Master Frederick, don't be severe."

About the same period, as he was sitting between two young ladies, his papa happened to have a bad cold, when he said to them, " Only think, papa blows his nose in G," which occasioned a roar of laughter.

His talent at improvising or extempore playing was extraordinary beyond all description. The thoughts seemed to flow faster than his small hands had the power of executing them, and often has he been observed by the family, after many fruitless endeavours with his two hands to give utterance to the beautiful fancies floating in his brain, to give the aid of his fine and extensive voice to his already overburthened fingers, with happy and singular effect.

Before he completed his fifth year, he sang many beautiful and impassioned melodies, which he accompanied with both hands in the fullest and most varied harmony,—sometimes in triplets, sometimes in *Arpeggio*, — and always introducing false cadences, sevenths, ninths, and other chords the most *recherchés*.

CHAPTER II

In February 1840, or perhaps earlier, at all events before he was fifteen, Frederick Ouseley was sent as a pupil to the Rev. James Joyce, vicar of Dorking. This must have been the boy's first departure from his own home circle. Some who were members of the household at Dorking Vicarage in those days have thus described their impressions :—

> Our recollections of him there are of a good and amiable boy remarkable by his musical genius. . . . His voice was beautiful : he used to sing little Spanish songs. He would play on a comb if no other instrument was at hand. He once became deaf for a time in boyhood, and used to say he never would forget his delight at hearing his father blow his nose in B flat. . . . I wish I could tell you of some of the wonders of his early genius ; but, not being musical, I am not capable of doing so. I remember, all people who did understand music were wonderstruck by his beautiful extempore playing. All the time we knew him at Dorking he was absorbed in music,—so much so that my father [Rev. James Joyce] used to say he ought not to take "Orders," because music would always be the first interest to him.

Nevertheless, humanly speaking, it was probably to the influence of the vicar of Dorking, in the first instance, and afterwards to that of his son, the Rev. J. Wayland Joyce (*a*), that the boy's

(*a*) Father of the writer of this book.

ROUGH SKETCH OF FREDERICK OUSELEY AND HIS 'CELLO

Drawn by James Joyce, about 1841

eventual desire to seek "Holy Orders" was due. Mr. Wayland Joyce was assistant curate at Dorking during most of the time that Frederick Ouseley remained there; and in after life the pupil used freely and gratefully to acknowledge how much he owed to the intercourse of those few years which he spent at the Vicarage. No doubt the rough discipline of a public school is the most wholesome system of education for the generality of English boys. But there are some boys, of exceptional genius and of nervous temperament, for whom an education by private tuition may be the safer course. The boyhood of Frederick Ouseley may well be regarded as a typical instance of this kind. In a private home his musical genius would be allowed a liberty of development difficult, if not impossible, to be found at a public school. It is evident that at Dorking the boy was allowed full scope for the exercise of his talent, and he was left free to develop it in his own way. Meanwhile, though gifted with a marvellous faculty for languages, as proved in his after life, he must have found the grammar of Latin and Greek, with all the other technical details of a classical education, as it was then conducted, irksome enough. I have heard my father (most patient of teachers!) very graphically describe how this youthful musician, when he was preparing for Oxford, would wildly tear his hair and stamp his feet over the Greek plays and his other classical studies, and how there used to follow the inevitable, "It's no use,

Frederick, the thing must be done!" Who that has ever struggled with the dull intricacies of Latin prose, or the doubtful readings of some involved chorus of Æschylus or Sophocles, cannot sympathise? How ill would such subjects accord with those beautiful harmonies which filled this pupil's head, and were pleading for deliverance! It was a case of the old variance between music and letters, between Hortensio (*b*) the musician and Lucentio the philosopher. Hortensio claims that his fiddle is

> The patroness of heavenly harmony :
> Then give me leave to have prerogative ;
> And when in music we have spent an hour,
> Your lecture shall have leisure for as much.

But Lucentio insists on the prior place of letters. Music, he urges, is only to be used as a recreation. If we read far enough we shall learn

> To know the cause why music was ordain'd.
> Was it not to refresh the mind of man
> After his studies or his usual pain?
> Then give me leave to read philosophy,
> And, while I pause, serve in your harmony.

There was a certain loft over the stable at Dorking Vicarage which my father had converted into a private sanctum of his own, apart from the rest of a very full house. As he said, "Any hole, even a cockloft, is worth having, if you can have it to yourself." Here, in July 1842, a small second-hand organ, which my father had bought, was set up and duly opened by Ouseley. It was

(*b*) *Taming of the Shrew*, act iii. sc. 1, *ad in.*

a one-manual instrument with an octave of pedals. The maker was John Avery, 1790. It was chosen, of course, by the young musician of the household, who had already made himself an authority on such matters ; and many a happy hour, no doubt, he spent in discoursing sweet themes and weaving cunning fugues on the keys of the humble instrument.

In 1843, at the age of eighteen, Frederick Ouseley went to Oxford, entering Christ Church as a gentleman commoner. At that time Gaisford, the giant scholar, was Dean. The other members of the cathedral body were then, or thereabout, Dr. Barnes, Sub-Dean ; Dr. Hampden, Regius Professor of Divinity ; and the six Canons—Dr. Pusey, Regius Professor of Hebrew ; Dr. Faussett, Margaret Professor ; Dr. Ogilvie, Professor of Pastoral Theology ; Dr. Clerke, Archdeacon of Oxford ; Dr. Bull and Dr. R. W. Jelf. The Rev. Osborne Gordon was Senior Censor, and the Rev. W. E. Jelf, Junior Censor. The reins of college discipline at Christ Church, as elsewhere, were no doubt more tightly drawn in those days than they have been in later times. Still, on going up to Oxford, the young Ouseley must for the first time in his life have found himself more or less his own master. Music naturally continued to be his chief interest, and must have always hindered any very intense application to other studies. Nevertheless, he was endowed with good general abilities, and he was conscientious enough to feel that he must put them to account with a view to securing his university degree. The amount of classics then required for a pass was not anything very extensive. Three Greek plays, or three books of Herodotus or Thucydides, together with three books of Livy or four books of Virgil, Latin prose and some logic, made up the sum. Ouseley's great natural gift for languages must have made these classical studies easier than they would have otherwise been to him. The possession of a good musical ear is said to be allied with the faculty of learning languages. His marvellous memory, too, must have stood him in good stead. After reading a work over two or three times, when he could bring himself to that amount of perseverance, he could repeat the greater part of it by heart. But it was to mathematics that he chiefly applied himself, under the guidance of Edward Hill, who was then mathematical lecturer at Christ Church, and for whom he always entertained a very high esteem. Ouseley's quarters were in Peckwater while in college; afterwards he lodged at Ringrose's in St. Aldates. There are extant a dozen or so of the letters, all undated, but written to him from home during his first few terms at Oxford. They are, of course, of an essentially private and domestic character; but they illustrate well two points—on the one hand, how exceedingly inexperienced he was in the ways of the world; and on the other hand, how greatly those at home feared lest his natural want of application to books, or rather his impatience of the routine work of reading, should tend to prejudice his studies at Oxford.

It was, indeed, this lack of power to apply himself persistently to the dry details of any study which, throughout his whole life, was probably the weak joint in his harness. There can be no doubt but that he had splendid abilities in many directions besides that of music. But he was restless,—his wits worked too quickly ; like many other clever men, he trusted too much to his own powers of intuition, and the result was that the full powers of his mind were never concentrated long together on one point. Rather, perhaps, one should say that he saw the point of any particular subject quickly enough, sooner than most men ; but he had not the patience to search round it, to master its bearings, and to modify his own first impressions (c).

Here are some extracts from the letters mentioned, the first ones being chiefly from the pen

(c) It should be stated that, with regard to Sir F. Ouseley's later life and work, Mr. T. L. Southgate, no incapable critic on the subject, differs from the view above given. He says : " Ouseley never struck me as being impatient or unwilling to work methodically and steadily to an end." One or two other friends of Sir Frederick have spoken to the same effect. The Rev. J. Hampton, who, as his fellow-worker for over thirty years, had the best opportunities for judging, says : " No man was so patient and persevering when there was particular occasion for it. He has worked ten and twelve hours daily to accomplish many an object upon which he had set his heart. It is true, however, that when he had made up his mind on any topic, he was somewhat hasty in dealing with others who differed from him. In a similar way, when once he had finished off any composition, he would throw it aside, and never trouble to polish or improve it."

On the whole, I still think that the impatience and restlessness of character which undoubtedly marked his earlier years did influence also, to a certain extent, the work of Sir F. Ouseley's later life.—F. W. J.

of the younger of his two sisters, Alexandrina Percival Ouseley. It should be premised that Sir Gore Ouseley's income at this time had been much reduced, presumably by the purchase of the Hall Barn estate :—

Pray remember in trifles that pence makes pounds. . . . Pray do not lose your money when you get it. . . . I hope you are as economical as you can be. . . . Do not let Coe [his servant] be extravagant, and consider well if you really can or cannot do without a thing before you get it. . . . Good-bye, dearest Fred, keep yourself well and in the right path.

The next extract from his sister's letters will show that his standard of hours for reading was by no means a high one :—

I hope, as you began so well on Saturday, you will continue, dear Fred, and steadily resist all inducements not to read *sufficiently*— I do not mean study six hours a day, you know !

The following extracts are from his mother's letters, and reveal how near to her heart her only boy was :—

I have little spirits for anything without having the delight of my dear boy's presence. . . . I trust that you will soon be able to find out if you have any chance of getting into better rooms, and when you think of mounting your "coach." I confess on this last subject I feel more anxious that I can express, as I think it is so important to you ; and I flatter myself it will *regulate* your studies more than anything else can do. I am convinced that you would not be able to bear studying many hours in the day, as some can, and I am quite satisfied that it is not necessary, but that regularity is the grand essential. It requires moral courage to resolve upon devoting certain fixed hours to it ; but if you can but *begin steadily*, I am sure you will find no difficulty afterwards, and that four or perhaps five hours in the course of each day at stated times will be as much as you would require. Your having a private tutor will be a great assistance to you, and a good reason to those thoughtless beings by which you are surrounded for wishing to pass some hours of quiet. Do not, my dearest Fred, delay, but make up your mind at once, for, if you once fall into *old habits*, you will find it far more difficult to fix your mind to study afterwards. . . . I shall rejoice to hear that you are thrown more into the society of Gore Langton, and such as he is, and I long to hear that you have any prospect of getting away from your present noisy Quad.

I am quite rejoiced to think that you have got a good tutor, and I fondly hope you will, by your diligence and attention, make him take an interest in you, and prevent the possibility of your being considered idle or frivolous. Such a character would stay by you for life. For safety I shall divide the check. Mind you put this half-check carefully away at once.

What about Tom Quad? Have you any chance of getting there? I long to hear a little about how you are going on, dearest, and how you continue to like your "coach," what encouragement he gives you about the "little go," and in fact I want to hear all about you. . . . Have you had much music, and do you find time for singing lessons? . . . I know, my dearest Fred, that I need not urge you to consider expense rather more than it might have been necessary formerly, when our means were more than double. Christ Church is a very ruinous place, and far more so than it was formerly, or ought to be now.

The three following extracts may be perhaps worth recording, if only to illustrate Lady Ouseley's old - fashioned prejudice against railway travelling, her strict views on the keeping of Sunday, and her slender faith in the existence, or at least in the merits, of Oxford or Buckinghamshire hair-cutting :—

You will not forget to tell me at what hour the coach will set you down at Beaconsfield. I am very glad you prefer it to the railroad. . . .

I hope we may receive a letter from you to-morrow, as surely there can never be anything wrong in writing to a mother or sister on Sunday. . . .

Have you got a good hair-cutter in Oxford? If so, pray have your hair in good order before you leave it, and it will save you the bore of going to town.

On November 18, 1844, at the age of seventy-four, Sir Gore Ouseley died ; and his only son, Frederick, before he was twenty years old, succeeded to the baronetcy. I remember Sir Frederick once saying that, on the morning when the news of his father's death reached him, he had a presentiment that something was wrong. He had no notion what the exact trouble was ; but a kind of indefinable depression took hold of him. His servant knocked at the door, and, directly the man had come into the room, and before he had spoken, Sir Frederick at once, and without turning his head, said, " You have come to tell me that my father is dead." Sir Gore had indeed been ill for two weeks or more ; but he had not taken to his bed until three days before his death, and it is evident that the son had not been apprised of his father's serious condition. This was the first great shock of the kind experienced in Frederick Ouseley's life ; and, whilst it must have done much to steady his character, there can be little doubt but that it would draw his affectionate heart more closely still to those left at home.

With his fellow - undergraduates he was a general favourite. Good temper and modesty go a long way in any community to ensure popularity ; and these qualities the young Ouseley possessed pre-eminently. Moreover, he was gifted with that rare capacity of appeasing opposition by a spirit of real and unaffected forgiveness. He could fire up on occasions, and speak his mind as well as other men. But he could not bear to

be permanently at enmity with anyone. Throughout his whole life there are numberless instances
which might be quoted of how completely he won
over to peace and friendship men who had once,
in some way or other, been bitterly opposed to
him. There is a pleasing description given of a
certain Baron of Burford (Salop) who lived in the
sixteenth century (born 1535, died 1585):—

For his own delight he had a dainty touch on the lute ; and of
such sweet harmony [? was he] in his nature, as if ever he offended
any, were he never so poor, he was not friend with himself till he
was friend with him again.

Most exactly may this description be applied
to Frederick Ouseley. His simple, childlike
character seems to have endowed him with a
wonderful power of disarming opposition. Here
is an instance, during his undergraduate days,
which will illustrate also the fact that he was not
wanting on occasion either in spirit or in practical
ingenuity. There was a certain fast set among
the gentlemen commoners at Christ Church who
bore a grudge against Ouseley, because he preferred to consort with quieter and more studious
friends (*d*).

So a *Vehmgericht* sat on him, and decreed that he should be
screwed up. Somehow Ouseley got wind of their intentions, and
took measures accordingly. He laid in a stock of cayenne pepper
and some fetid chemical (probably it was assafœtida), and bored
some holes in his oak. No sooner had the enemy commenced
operations than they found themselves half-suffocated with clouds
of pepper, emitted with a hot blower, and then besquirted with the
foul liquid. Having forced them to beat a retreat into the opposite

---

(*d*) Contributed by an Oxford contemporary of Sir F. Ouseley, at the
time of his death in 1889, to the *St. James's Gazette*.

rooms, he promptly screwed them up by means of the very engines they had prepared against himself.

It is only fair to add that this very successful ending to the Ouseley siege appears to have been partly due to the aid of a certain faithful ally, who also helped him to carry the war triumphantly into the enemy's camp. Thereupon "the assailants capitulated; and thenceforth Ouseley lived on friendly terms with the 'fast' set, though he was never intimate with them."

Some of the Christ Church friends with whom he was most intimate were—John Rich (e), H. Milman (f), R. M. Benson (g), G. F. Boyle (h), H. P. Liddon (i), G. W. Kitchin (j), T. Vere Bayne (k), Herbert Murray (l), E. R. Hampden (m), A. C. Wilson, — Pennell. The present Dean of Durham, the Very Rev. G. W. Kitchin, characterises the young Ouseley of those days as

Absolutely guileless,—indeed, a little more guile would often have served him in good stead. His good nature made him popular, in spite of certain peculiarities of appearance which might otherwise have made him rather a "butt."

Canon Rich, with whom Frederick Ouseley was closely associated both at Oxford and in later

(e) Now Vicar of Chippenham and Hon. Canon of Bristol.
(f) Minor Canon of St. Paul's.
(g) Father Benson of Cowley.
(h) Afterwards Lord Glasgow.
(i) Afterwards Canon of St. Paul's, etc.
(j) Now Dean of Durham.
(k) Afterwards Senior Censor of Christ Church
(l) Now Governor of Newfoundland.
(m) Afterwards Rector of Cradley, near Malvern.

years, has given many reminiscences of his friend.
He thus describes him in his college days :—

> He was of very cheerful disposition, though at times given to
> a fit of despair when things went wrong : he was very full of fun,
> and his excitable impetuosity often made him more funny.

This description may be supplemented by the following graphic picture drawn by the hand of another of Ouseley's contemporaries at Christ Church : (*n*)—

> He was always ready to play to us, and I can see him now,
> jumping from side to side on the music stool ; for he never sat still
> a minute, and his thin legs were never quiet directly he began to
> get absorbed. Most of his playing was extempore, and it was our
> frequent amusement to make him play two airs at the same time,
> say, "God save the Queen" with the right hand, and " Rule
> Britannia" with the left, which he did with the greatest ease, and
> many variations.

Needless to say, this young undergraduate musician made the most of his opportunities in organ-playing at Oxford. Dean Kitchin recalls how, in his Christ Church days, he was one day walking down "The High," when he saw in the distance, coming towards him, a man with his open palms extended in the air over his head, like a praying dervish, and running at a good speed. As the man approached, he saw that it was Ouseley. He stopped him and said, "Why, Ouseley, what on earth is the matter?" "I have just obtained permission," replied the breathless enthusiast, "to play on the organ in Magdalen Chapel, and this is the only way in which I can

---

(*n*) Contributed to the *Globe* newspaper at the time of Sir F. Ouseley's death in 1889.

keep my hands cool for playing, by preventing the blood running into them!" And then he rushed on his way. But Ouseley's music in those days was not all instrumental, nor was it always solo work. He and others used on summer evenings to gather in the beautiful hall-staircase at Christ Church, with its groined roof and single supporting pillar, and entertain the College generally, and " Tom Quad " in particular, with glees of various kinds. The staircase (o)

has remarkable acoustic properties ; a chord sung clearly will often continue to vibrate for a few seconds : therefore to stand by the central pillar and shout an *arpeggio* was a favourite pastime of the men. But Ouseley completely beat all competitors at this fun, because, owing to his use of *falsetto*, he could produce an *arpeggio* nearly three octaves in compass.

He was also often busied, even in his undergraduate days, with organising concerts in Oxford of a more ambitious character. Thus, under his supervision, Handel's *Samson* was performed in New College Hall. One who took part in the oratorio recalls, forty-four years later, how "Ouseley took the alto solo, and executed a shake, in falsetto, on the words ' abyss of woe.' " On another occasion he got up the *Messiah* in the Town Hall at Oxford, for the benefit of the Irish sufferers in the famine of 1845. He also composed a glee, "Sweet Echo" (*p*),

(o) *The Character and Influence of the late Sir Frederick Ouseley*, an Address delivered on December 2, 1889, before the " Musical Association," by Sir John Stainer, and published by Novello, Ewer, & Co., p. 31.

(*p*) Dr. J. H. Mee sends the following note (November 1895) :— " ' Sweet Echo ' was written for the Oxford Musical Society. I came across the original copy, with dedication and date, some six months ago, in a quantity of music that I rescued from the refuse cart of a contractor."

the proceeds of which were to go to the same object. Undergraduates at the university have a character in certain quarters for ignoring all the world outside their own circle and their own small "set." The "set" in which Frederick Ouseley moved at Oxford was certainly not of this character. Here is another reminiscence apropos of the thoughtfulness and sympathy then shown even by these young undergraduates at Christ Church for the sufferers in Ireland. A friend of Ouseley's, who stayed with him for a week in 1846 (his last year at Oxford), says :—

He took me to wine at places every evening. At Lord Dufferin's, G. F. Boyle's (*q*), and J. S. Pakington's (*r*), there were only biscuits and wine. He told me that they, as well as himself, did this, that they might give what they did not spend on the extravagant desserts, which were then the custom, to the Irish Famine Fund.

From the same pen we get also the following record, which proves that Ouseley, at the end of his Oxford career, was no mean scholar, or at least that he had studied his Horace to good effect :—

One other fact only dwells in my memory, viz. his readiness in "capping" Latin verses in Benson's room. It came to his turn unexpectedly to give a line beginning with X ; he gave—*Xerius amnis* ; and, the same thing happening again a few minutes after, he gave *Xanthea Phoceu* in an instant.

At the same time, this well-conducted son of *Alma Mater* seems to have been not altogether innocent of that very common failing of most university students, viz. the habit of practical joking. Canon Rich recalls how he once found

(*q*) Afterwards Lord Glasgow.   (*r*) Afterwards Lord Hampton.

that someone had been "making hay" in his rooms, Ouseley being the culprit; and how, on another occasion, they both conspired, together with a third friend of kindred spirit, to produce the following musical effect. A concert was being given in the Oxford Town Hall by the "University Amateur Musical Society." The three conspirators were thus armed—Ouseley carried a gong, the loan of which he had obtained for this particular occasion from the then Junior Censor, Mr. W. E. Jelf, with whom he was somewhat in favour. The Censor, on his part, had annexed the gong from another undergraduate, who, in his judgment, had been making too much noise with it. Rich carried a pair of cymbals (so-called),—they were really two round pieces of thick bell-metal, and the noise they produced was indescribable. In the hands of the third performer, C. Webber, was borne a good-sized tin tea-tray. Behind the orchestra in the Town Hall was an uncovered, but hidden passage. Here the trio concealed themselves, and then, without any warning, in the *fortissimo* part of the "Wedding March," came in with a tremendous crash. Canon Rich thus concludes his reminiscences :—

Dear old Dr. Stephen Elvey, who was conducting, was at first as indignant as he was astonished ; but, when he found that the audience were highly amused and pleased with the effect, he took it all in good part, and I am not sure that he did not himself *encore* the performance (s).

(s) It must have been to recall these happy memories, as by way of echo, that Sir F. Ouseley was known now and again, in after life, when delighting some evening party with a skilful performance of the "Wedding

Here, too, perhaps, may be best inserted one more vivid description given by Canon Rich of his friend in those and in later days :—

Of his extraordinary musical gifts I was many times the auditor, as I often went with him to different organs. He was most remarkable in power of extempore fugue-playing. Given the subject, the treatment seemed to be at once mapped out in his imagination. He would ask me, "Give me a subject." I would give him half a dozen or more notes. He would say, "Yes ! that will do very well,"—or perhaps, "No ! that will not do ; if you change this note to so and so, then I can do it." As he went on he would say, "Now I am augmenting it in the bass" ; "Now I am diminishing it in the tenor ;" "Now I am inverting it in the treble ;" "Now I am diminishing in the alto, and inverting it in the bass," and so on. Thus, with his running explanation as he played, he gave me an insight and an interest in a fugue which otherwise I should probably never have had, and which, I am glad to say, I have not lost.

Throughout his whole life his extempore playing was indeed Sir F. Ouseley's most wonderful gift. Not only could he play fugues in this way, but sonatas, fantasias, and any other kind of music. These extemporaneous effusions would always be in strict form, worked out elaborately and often most originally. And yet, if required to do so, he would adopt the style of any of the great masters (*t*).

Meanwhile, as may well be imagined, the Oxford influence of religion was not being lost on a character like that of Frederick Ouseley. His years at college, 1843–1846, corresponded with what may be called the crisis of the

March," to spring up suddenly from his seat, at the point where the cymbals come in, turn round with his face to the audience, and sit down with a crash on the keys of the piano.

(*t*) Cf. pp. 116 ff. *infra*.

"Oxford Movement." In 1841 Newman had written the famous Tract XC., and in 1845 he left the Church of England for that of Rome. The author of the "Christian Year," though no longer the Oxford Professor of Poetry, was still a name of power in the university. And all the while Pusey was one of the canons of that cathedral within whose walls young Ouseley was a daily worshipper. Dr. Pusey's condemned sermon was preached on May 14, 1843. No one of any sensibility, much less Ouseley, with his strong religious instincts, could have lived through these years at Oxford without being influenced one way or another by the "Movement." On him, one of its chief effects would naturally be to intensify that devotion to Church worship which was the dominant note of his whole after life. Already in his earliest Oxford days we can see that the Services of the Church were to him something more than mere compulsory attendance at a college chapel. Years afterwards he himself recalled with pleasure how delighted he once was, on a certain Sunday at Christ Church, when his friend G. F. Boyle came to him and said (*n*) : "Ouseley, we are both of us unwell, and have neither of us been able to attend chapel to-day ; let us read part of the Church Service together."

But music was the special gift with which God had endowed him. And so it was in this direction that the spirit of worship found its

(*n*) Havergal's *Memorials*, p. 40.

chief expression in his case. From the beginning to the end of his Oxford career, as undergraduate hardly less than as professor, Ouseley sought to elevate music, and sacred music in particular, to a higher place in the university life than it had hitherto occupied. And yet for a gentleman-commoner at Christ Church to take up a line like this could then have been no easy task. Not only was the whole cathedral body, from all accounts, an eminently unmusical one, but all the traditions of the place were against him. There is a story told of a certain canon of Christ Church about that time who was asked by one of the (minor canon) chaplains to be kind enough to undertake a Service for him. The potentate's only answer is said to have been this : " Sir, I would have you to know that the distance between a canon of Christ Church and a chaplain is immeasurable " (*v*).

Whether the story be true or not, it very aptly illustrates the kind of spirit against which Ouseley, in all his efforts for the cause of music at Oxford, had to contend. Nothing daunted, however, this young gentleman - commoner persevered in the cause he had at heart. Not only did he seek by his position and influence to lend dignity to a then despised branch of art,

(*v*) It is said that the same canon, finding a lady on one occasion kneeling in the cathedral out of Service hours, and engaged in private prayers, touched her on the shoulders, saying : " Come, come, Madam, no more of this nonsense." This story in turn recalls that of the Westminster Abbey verger who, protesting against some pious effort of the same kind, informed a private worshipper that his intended act would be an insult to the Dean and Chapter.

but he took an active and laborious part in its exercise. During his last year at Christ Church, Dr. Marshall, the cathedral organist, resigned. Ouseley immediately offered his services as honorary organist, an offer which the Dean and Chapter were only too glad to accept. He made himself responsible for the whole of the musical work of the cathedral, and, until Dr. Corfe was appointed some months later, is said not to have missed a single service. But his relations with the stern Dean were not always of so smooth an order : (w)—

Just before the Ter-centenary of the foundation of Christ Church, Ouseley called on the Dean to ask his permission for a concert in the Hall as an item in the celebration. It must have required considerable courage to make this request to such an imperious magnate, as concerts in College Halls were unheard of in those days. "Concert, Sir," said the Dean, with unusual brusqueness,—"certainly not, Sir, certainly not ; and besides, Sir, there's no precedent for it." But Sir Frederick begged to remind the Dean that there *was* such a precedent, as a concert had formed part of the Bi-centenary celebration. "Leave the room, Sir,—leave the room," was the only reply of the (at times) somewhat peremptory magnate. But he asked Sir Frederick to dine with him the next day, when his habitual kindness and courtesy had returned.

One other characteristic anecdote is related of Dean Gaisford's dealings with his musical alumnus : (x)—

Ouseley once, on the last day of a vacation, was at Swindon Station, when, through some mistake, the last train for Oxford had departed. Knowing he could not keep term unless in Christ Church before midnight, he spent £25 on a special train, and just saved it. Next day he called on Gaisford to explain the unusually

---

(w) Havergal's *Memorials*, p. 40.   (x) *Ibid.* p. 45.

late hour, and told him what he had done to save the term. The Dean said, in his dry way, nothing but, " You did wisely, Sir."

In 1846, at the age of twenty-one, Sir Frederick Ouseley graduated as B.A. At one time he had been supposed to be safe for a mathematical first class. But either from the interruptions caused, first by his father's death, and afterwards by an illness of his own at a critical time; or from that innate want of application on his part to really hard study, which has already been referred to, the idea of his seeking honours was eventually given up, and he only presented himself for a pass degree. The authorities were, however, so well pleased with his papers that they granted him an " Honorary Fourth." There are some who maintain that music and intellectuality do not go hand in hand. Perhaps it would be nearer the truth to say that music is really one branch of intellectuality, but that where a choice has to be made between the study of dry books or figures on the one hand, and the charms of music on the other, the latter very naturally take precedence. This was certainly the case with Frederick Ouseley in his college days, as in all his after life. Dean Kitchin's verdict on the point is as follows :—

He had wonderful abilities as a linguist and as a mathematician, but his passion for music prevented the full development of the sterner pursuits.

CHAPTER III

FOR the two or three years after he left Oxford,
Sir Frederick Ouseley appears to have spent
his time chiefly with his mother and sisters in
London, at 39 [?] Lowndes Street. But he paid
frequent visits also to my father, his old friend and
tutor, the Rev. J. Wayland Joyce, at Burford,
Salop, to which parish Mr. Joyce had recently
come as Rector. It was in this way that Sir
Frederick first made acquaintance with the neighbourhood of Tenbury and the Teme Valley, where
some years later he built St. Michael's Church and
founded the College, and where so large a part of
his own after life was to be spent.

My father used to relate a story of this date in
illustration of the fact that Ouseley, excitable as
he was by nature, and "full of nerves," could yet
be not only as plucky, but as collected as anyone
else in a case of emergency. On September 16,
1846, they were driving together from Burford to
Ludlow in a dogcart behind a somewhat uncertain mare. When within two miles or so of
Ludlow, they met the mail coach. H.M. mail

was too much for the mare, and she first shied and then ran away. It is a hard thing, of course, to sit still when you are yourself driving a runaway; but it is a very much harder thing to sit still when you are being driven behind one. On this occasion my father had the reins, and, seeing the likelihood of an upset, he said : " Now, whatever you do, Fred, don't move till I give you the word; and then jump as quick and as far as you can." Ouseley sat perfectly still. When eventually they ran into the ditch by the roadside, and when, being just on the balance to go over, my father called out, " Jump!" he jumped clear off, alighting like a bird unharmed on the top of a thick-trimmed hedge. My father often declared that he had never in his life seen anything so neatly done, and so absolutely in the nick of time.

At this period, besides paying constant visits to Burford Rectory, and some to Oxford, Sir Frederick Ouseley was already beginning to travel about, as for years after he loved to do, trying many of the best known organs in England. Meanwhile he was reading for his ordination —whether under any definite and regular tuition, does not appear. At one time, indeed, my father was credited with having "prepared him for ordination." This, however, could hardly have been the case; for his visits to Burford at the period in question, though very frequent, lasted usually no more than from a week to a fortnight at a time. But what was said of him in after life

—"Ouseley is the man to spot heresies"—is a proof not merely of his natural theological ability, but of the fact that he had studied theology to some purpose. He once told Mr. Hampton that, at the time of his reading for "Holy Orders," he had worked very hard, that the argument of Paley he knew by heart, and that sometimes he would read fourteen hours a day. This brought him to the head of the list of candidates, and he read the Gospel at his ordination.

In 1848, at the age of sixty-one, his mother died, four years after the death of her husband. Lady Ouseley suffered from a weak heart. The day before her death she had been out driving, and there had been an upset of some kind. Though she received no actual bodily hurt, she had been very much frightened. That same night she sat up suddenly in her bed and died. What the loss of a mother, so attached to her only son as she had been, must have meant to him, with his affectionate nature and his child's heart, it is easier to imagine than to express. In the *Life of George Herbert of Bemerton* (1593–1633) are recorded these solemn and memorable words, as spoken by him, when a youth of seventeen, to his mother—a mother to whom, as he afterwards acknowledged :—

> " I owe all learning, earthly and divine "—
>
> For my own part, my meaning, dear mother, is in these sonnets to declare my resolution to be, that my poor abilities in poetry shall be all and ever consecrated to God's glory.

If the words "sonnets" and "poetry" be exchanged into "music" and "the glories of harmony," we may imagine Frederick Ouseley to have made some similar vow, perhaps in his mother's hearing, early in life. Anyhow, his whole after life was a fulfilment of such a resolve, and in his case, as in most others of a like kind, no little share of the credit of the son's work should be doubtless attributed to the mother's influence.

In 1849 (apparently on Trinity Sunday, June 3), Frederick Ouseley was ordained deacon by the Bishop of London (Dr. Blomfield), being licensed to a curacy under the Rev. W. J. E. Bennett, vicar of St. Paul's, Knightsbridge. Sir Frederick had previously, as a layman, together with Sir John Harington and others, sung in the choir of that church. The new curate's work lay almost entirely in serving the daughter parish of St. Barnabas, Pimlico. At the beginning of his curacy the church itself of St. Barnabas was not finished. In a kind of choir college he lived with the Rev. Lawrence Tuttiet and some others. Services were held in the schoolroom ; and together they worked the district assigned to St. Barnabas. Later on came two other fellow-workers, the Rev. Henry Fyffe and the Rev. G. F. De Gex, both his lifelong friends in after years. The church was consecrated on St. Barnabas Day, June 11, 1850, the Bishop of London preaching on the occasion. The music, as well as the ritual, at the new church was of an advanced order for those days, and Ouseley appears to have been busy with choir work especially, besides taking part in the general routine of a London parish. But, before the year 1849 was out, more serious matters were already beginning to occupy his thoughts, and to cause him great anxiety as to the position of the Church of England. Although now only in his twenty-fifth year, he had a mind naturally clear, and capable of grasping great principles. The logical training which Oxford then supplied to all her sons led many of them in those days to consider exactly where they were standing as ordained Ministers of the Established Church. "What was meant by the 'Royal Supremacy'?" "How far was that doctrine or principle to be carried?" "What were the true relations of Church and State?" "And was it a fact that the rights and liberties of the Church were being encroached on?" These were the questions which many thoughtful men amongst the English clergy were beginning to ask themselves. And Frederick Ouseley, thrown as he was now into personal contact with some of the leading men in the "Oxford Movement," came quickly to close quarters with these difficulties, as will be shown by the letters which follow.

Perhaps some apology should be made for publishing a correspondence which, on the one hand, is broken (for several of the letters are not forthcoming), and, on the other hand, may be regarded as in some details overfull. But there are so few letters of Sir Frederick's extant on subjects of general interest, such as this one, that,

at the risk of being prolix, I have thought well to
include almost the whole of this particular correspondence between himself and my father, on both
sides, so far as it has come into my hands. The
correspondence has lso an interest of its own, in
showing how very serious at that time were the
perplexities of many of the English clergy, steer-
ing their course, as they were driven to do, between the Scylla of Erastianism and the Chary-
bdis of secession. Some of Sir Frederick's friends
were accustomed, in later days, laughingly to call
my father "Ouseley's Pope." If this was only
meant in the sense of my father being a father
and adviser to him, so far as an elder friend can
take that position towards a younger one, then Sir
Frederick would have been the first to give him
the title, and my father would no doubt have felt
proud to bear it. But if the saying was in any
way intended to imply that the one friend was the
keeper of the other's conscience, or that he defined
his faith for him, the phrase was entirely misleading. Sir Frederick's own views on most subjects,
more especially on matters of theology, were, even
in his earlier years, definite and clear-cut, not to
say dogmatic. And my father, though the elder
of the two by thirteen years, would have been
the last man in the world to presume to be his
younger friend's superior, at all events in quickness of intelligence. Nevertheless it is plain, from
so much of this correspondence as can be found,
that my father was most anxious at the time as to
what turn events might take. He had serious

fears lest Ouseley's impetuosity, combined with those occasional fits of despondency which appear to have troubled him all his life through, should lead him to take some over-hasty step of secession. And so the elder friend very naturally used all the influence which his seniority of age, his wider reading, and his riper experience gave him, to insist on the true position of the Church of England, and the spiritual rights of her Ministry.

F. A. G. O. TO REV. J. W. JOYCE.

ST. BARNABAS, *Jan.* 23, 1850.

MY DEAR WAYLAND,—Most truly and sincerely do I congratuate you on the happy event you informed me of in your last letter. You judged rightly when you said you counted on the interest I take in you and yours—indeed, I should be a beast did I otherwise.

We are full of trouble here. Mr. Bennett, Mr. Dodsworth, Archdeacon Manning, Mr. Maskell, Dr. Pusey, Archdeacon Wilberforce, Henry Wilberforce, and Mr. Keble—(and Mr. Marriott)— have been putting their heads together on the subject of the Royal Supremacy. On this point the whole question of State aggression in all its branches turns—"Is the Queen's decision, through her Council, on appeal, or otherwise, binding on our consciences, in matters of doctrine, by virtue of our oaths (at ordination) of supremacy and allegiance?" The opinion of counsel learned in the law having been taken, it appears, by the decision of Sir J. Dodson and two others (one civil, another common, and another counsel lawyers), that it *is* so binding; and moreover, since every oath is binding *ex animo imponentis*, the decision is retrospective, and these congregated divines have each and all *unanimously* decided that they *cannot* longer serve the Church, save *under publick protest*. Mr. Bennett, accordingly, at a large meeting of his parishioners yesterday held, told them that if they would support him by pledging themselves to use all lawful means to relieve his conscience of the imposed load, either by memorialising or petitioning the Powers that be, he would remain their pastor; but if not—*si secus fecerint*—if they should not think it worth while to bestir themselves for him, then he must retire into lay communion, or leave the English Church. His conscience would not permit him to serve at God's altar with "a lie in his right hand." The parishioners present unanimously agreed to take it up, and are determined to fight for their pastor to the last gasp. So we are all right, at least *pro tempore*. I think the sense of justice natural to the English character, and that desire that all should have right of conscience, and liberty of will, which forms so essential a characteristick of the Publick Mind, will revolt [? against] the unjust oppression and force the State to remove or alleviate the burthen. God grant it ! If *not*, *I*, with others, have determined first to *protest*, and then to serve the Scotch, or American, Church—either as a missionary under *their* Bishops, or otherwise. In this case England shall see our face no more. A long voluntary expatriation is the only thing left.

Pray write—I am in terrible depression of spirits on this account. Your row is bad enough, and may *help* : but ours strikes at the *root* of everything ! Do tell me what you think.—Yours ever affectionately, FREDERICK A. G. OUSELEY.

I left my hood behind me. Will you send it next time anyone is coming here from your parts, who will bring it *uncrumpled*.

REV. J. W. JOYCE TO F. A. G. O.

BURFORD RECTORY, *Jan.* 25, 1850.

MY DEAR FREDERICK,—Your letter has distressed me beyond measure. I wonder not that you are depressed in spirits. The [? array of] names of clergymen you have sent, so much my betters, who are inclined to view the Queen's decision (either by herself or Council) as binding on their consciences, in matters of doctrine, of course staggers me. For the lawyers' opinion I care less. In *ethical* matters a moderate divine is a far better judge than a first-rate lawyer. So peace to them ! Considering the names of the clergymen contained in your letter who take this appalling view of their ordination oath, you may deem it presumptuous in me to declare that I cannot readily agree with them. So for your comfort (if it please God) I will make a brief essay on the other side.

The point is, are we bound in conscience by our oaths to accept the Queen's or her Council's decisions in *matters of doctrine?* I answer, No. (1) As regards the oath in the Ordination Service, as printed in the Prayer Book, it is *omni exceptione major*. No fault can be found with it. It only asserts that no *foreign* Prince, etc., must interfere with our National Church. It only asserts the principle of the independence of this National Church in [? which] we are all agreed. (2) Then comes the question of the 1st Article in the 36th Canon. This will require more thought, and a comparison of other declarations and other documents must be here admitted, that we may arrive at its true meaning. We subscribe (we *don't swear*—I merely mention this *as a fact*, not to endeavour to shield ourselves under a paltry distinction between an oath and a subscription, both equally binding on a truthful man—we subscribe) to this : "That the King's Majesty, under God, is the only Supreme Governor of this realm, . . . as well in all *spiritual or ecclesiastical things or causes* as temporal." The succeeding words are only an exact repetition of the allegiance oath in the Ordination Service. Now, my belief, and firm belief, is that, when this was compiled, those who drew it up meant to express an exclusion of *foreign* jurisdiction. My notion is that the nation had been so much vexed by Italian interference with the temporalities and discipline of this National Church, that it was thus sought to exclude such annoyance for the future.

This, however, is but opinion ; let us go to more direct argument. Does the expression "spiritual or ecclesiastical things or causes," in the Canon, signify *questions* of doctrine, or questions wherein *liberty of person*, [? or] enjoyment of temporality, *is involved?* I answer only the latter. That it does not mean questions of doctrine I shall endeavour to prove by concurrent declarations and authorities and considerations. You are wrong in saying that an oath is binding *ex animo imponentis*. A promise is binding "as the promiser thought the promisee accepted it." Treat the question before us in a similar manner. "An oath is binding *as the taker thought the proposer meant it* :" not as the taker meant only, for he might make mental reservation ; not as the proposer meant, for he might in his mind unduly enlarge the obligation ; but *as the taker thought the proposer meant it.* Now, I venture to say that neither Mr. Bennett, nor Mr. Dodsworth, nor Archdeacon Manning, nor Mr. Maskell, nor Dr. Pusey, nor Archdeacon Wilberforce, nor Mr. Keble, nor Marriott, nor you, nor I, ever dreamt that the subscription to the 1st Article of the 36th Canon meant that the Queen was to be a judge of doctrine, or could propound new doctrine, or could take away old doctrine. And why have we all good and sufficient reason for not thinking so?

Because Queen Elizabeth expressly declared "that she would have her loving subjects to understand that nothing was by the oath of supremacy intended but only to have the duty and allegiance that was acknowledged to be due to the noble Kings, King Henry and King Edward, and was *of ancient time due to the Imperial Crown of this realm—i.e.* under God to have sovereignty and rule over all manner of persons born within these realms, either ecclesiastical or temporal, whatsoever they be, so as no other foreign power shall or ought to have any superiority over them" (Strype's *An.* i. 159).

Because the 37th Article speaks the same sentiment in plain language (which read). Not a word do we hear of doctrine, but of *causes* and *persons.* "Causes" does not mean questions of doctrine, as is plain to my mind from the context in which it occurs always being the same. That Article plainly declares that "we only give that prerogative" (by the oath of supremacy) "which we see to have been given always to all godly princes in holy Scriptures by God Himself." Surely there are instances enough of God's anger against those who usurped priestly functions to satisfy us here.

Because King James I., in his address prefixed to the Canons (containing the very passage from which all the presumed difficulty arises), does virtually refer all doctrinal questions to the Church duly represented, desiring that it should "confer, treat, debate, consider, consult, and *agree* of and upon such canons, orders, ordinances, and constitutions as they should think necessary, fit, and convenient for the honour and service of Almighty God, the good and quiet of the Church," etc.

Because—and this is really the point—the Royal declaration at the beginning of the Articles states :—"We are Supreme Governor of the Church of England" (*i.e.* over *causes* and *persons*, not *doctrine*), "and if any difference arise about the external policy concerning the Injunctions, Canons, and other *Constitutions whatsoever*" (here's doctrine at last!) "*thereto belonging,* THE CLERGY IN THEIR CONVOCATION IS TO ORDER AND SETTLE THEM, . . . That out of Our Princely Care that THE CHURCHMEN MAY DO THE WORK WHICH IS PROPER TO THEM, the Bishops and Clergy, from time to time in Convocation, SHALL have Licence," etc.

Now I know that my ethics are right : An oath (or subscription, the same thing to a truthful man) is binding in the sense in which the taker thought the imposer meant it. The imposer's intention is plainly set forth in the foregoing Royal declaration. This is to my mind satisfactory. My view is also strengthened by the other considerations—"over causes and persons" (see Bingham). *I.e.* in *courts* for deciding *liberty of person* and questions of temporality, the Queen is supreme ; but I know of no other supremacy.

Indeed, previous Sovereigns (Queen Elizabeth and King James) have disclaimed it ; the Royal declaration before the Articles disclaims it ; and, until a fresh claim is set up and actually conceded by the Convocation to our present Sovereign of a power, which I never thought belonged to her, and which I never *intended* at my subscription to consent to, I shall not think myself bound *in foro conscientiæ* to consent to any dictum or doctrine which she or her Council may promulgate.

I must protest against leaving the Church because she is bullied. In the time of Trajan and the Antonines, what would have become of her if the Saints had left her Altars? In the time of Julian, what would have become of her pure doctrines, if her priests had deserted her on account of the Imperial heresy? I can't believe that you or others will desert because she wants your help. I can't believe that, just as the hour of battle begins, your places will be empty. I can't believe that, at her cry for a stout heart, you will be deaf or cowardly. I can well believe, if you thought you had sworn to that which you don't hold, that you would think it right to retract. But I cannot think, if rightly viewed, that you [? can so judge the matter]. If your version of *ex animo imponentis* is the lawyers' gloss, I boldly say they are wrong, absolutely wrong in ethics. Divines, be assured, in such matters, as I said before, are better judges than they. It is rather our province than theirs.

Now, I pray you, let me hear at once. As I have given you so long a letter, I *claim* of you to let me know if my counsel has quieted your mind. . . . I am most anxious about you.—Your ever affectionate,

J. W. J.

P.S.—In consulting all the authorities you will see that "*persons*" and "*causes*" are always united. These are legal terms, and are used in the *second intention*, as referring to 'jurisdiction in Courts. In ancient times a clergyman, though convicted of murder or felony, could not be sentenced or executed by the temporal judges or officers, but was delivered to his Ordinary, and by him committed to prison, and after some time admitted to compurgation, by which he was generally acquitted, etc., etc. Before Henry VIII., the Clergy swore obedience to the Pope ; and they held that if the commands of Prince and Pope varied, they ought to obey the Pope. It was against this state of things that the terms "*causes and persons*" were directed. See *Vade Mecum*, p. 28. The author of the foregoing, Johnson of Cranbrook, fought out this very question in Geo. 1st's time. He said that—"The King was supreme only

in his *Courts*, and that he knew of no Supremacy besides." I am
convinced, my dear Fred, that this is the true view. It is a matter
I have considered much and long, as perhaps you may gather from
so ready a reply.

J. W. J.

F. A. G. O. TO REV. J. W. JOYCE.

ST. BARNABAS COLLEGE,
Monday, February 4, 1850.

MY DEAR WAYLAND,—You have doubtless wondered why I
have so long delayed writing to you in answer to your very kind
and well-written letter on the important question of State-
aggressions and Church-slavery. When you consider, however,
the necessity of carefully substantiating and verifying all one's
facts, ere one should venture to enter into the discussion of such
delicate points ; and when you reflect how little spare time I have
for such investigations, I feel confident you will acquit me of any
carelessness or neglect in the matter, and give me credit for
sincere and laborious search after truth : for truth after all is the
object. We must not stop to consider to what practical results
(painful or harrowing though they may perhaps be) such discovery
may lead us. We must shut our eyes to everything but one great
question, *i.e.* should the State enslave the Church—she not protesting, but tacitly acquiescing—are conscientious men justified in
continuing to minister at her altars ? Now, I do not propose to
enter deeply into this discussion to-day, inasmuch as Mr. Bennett
has embodied the whole in a couple of sermons, the last of which
was preached yesterday, and which will be published immediately.
A copy of them I will send to you as soon as ever they are out ;
and they will explain the whole matter in a much clearer way than
could be effected by anything I could write. Still, their remains a
good deal which I feel inclined to say to you, only it is difficult to
know how and where to begin.

I laid your letter before Mr. Bennett, who, after reading it
attentively, said that for the most part it was just what he should
have written three months ago. But he perceived you had not
studied the Acts 23, 24, and 25 of Henry VIII. By the first of
these the *temporal* power of the Pope was transferred to the King.
So far, so good. But the King kept Cardinal Wolsey by him, and
styled him " Pope's Legate." Accordingly the Clergy did so too.
But lo ! the King turns round on them and says, " By so styling

him you "acknowledge foreign jurisdiction." So he brings a *Præmunire* to bear against them: they protest: the King (cunning beast!) says, "Well, I will let you off if you will acknowledge me sole spiritual head of the Church." Well, the Clergy fought long against this: but, finding the King inexorable, they said they would do so, only with this proviso—*Quantum per Christi legem licet.* To this, after much demur, the King consented; and *the Clergy submitted in full Convocation.* The King then passed it through Parliament (25 Henry VIII.), and it became law, called the "Clergy Submission Act" (see Collier, Burn, Blackstone, Burnet, Massingberd, etc., etc.). This has *never been repealed*, and the law has been *always* interpreted to include headship in doctrine. (Witness various subsequent Acts of Parliament.) And now every lawyer tells you that you have subscribed to the 36th Canon, Art. 1, in this sense.

And then, as to the question of *ex animo imponentis*, Mr. Bennett says you are wrong. Suppose a man were to say, when pressed to pay a sum he had in writing agreed to pay, "I won't, because I did not think, when I signed the agreement, that it was ever meant I should have to pay,"—would not he be laughed at and forced to pay? Especially if he voluntarily came forward to sign the agreement, as we voluntarily came forward at our Ordination to subscribe the Canon (for no one compelled us to be ordained). Moreover, the disclaimer of Queen Elizabeth in her "Injunctions," and King James's declaration at Hampton Court, only exonerated those monarchs from the charge of sacrilegious usurpation. But (*O si sic omnes!*) it did weaken the force of Henry VIII.'s *unrepealed law*, whereby it was in the power of the State (*de jure civili*, though not *divino—de facto*) to assume such a tyrannical posture of aggression whenever they choose. And now *they have done so:* they *are doing so*: and we must protest, and in the event of defeat we have but to go—ὃ μὴ γίνοιτο.

As for the Preface to the Articles, and Article 37,—standing *alone* they would be quite satisfactory: but, coupled with the above deplorable Statute, they are worth nothing. They do not annihilate it; but it nullifies them.

As soon as Mr. Bennett's Sermons are out, you shall have them. Now adieu!—Ever most affectionately and faithfully yours in Christ,

FREDERICK A. G. OUSELEY.

FIRST CURACY

ST. BARNABAS, *Monday, February* 18, 1850.

MY DEAR WAYLAND,—At last Mr. B.'s Sermons have issued from the press, and I send you a copy. I think the matter is therein so fully set forth, that any observations of mine would be quite superfluous. There is one point, however, wherein I differ from you, which is barely noticed in the Sermons, and that is the question whether or no an oath is binding *ex animo imponentis*. I decidedly say, *It Is.* Otherwise there could be no security at all. I have not time to argue the point. But I *will*, if you please.— Yours ever affectionately,

FREDERICK A. G. OUSELEY.

REV. J. W. JOYCE TO F. A. G. O.

BURFORD RECTORY, *March* 2, 1850.

MY DEAR FREDERICK,—Thank you many times for the copy of Mr. Bennett's Sermons, which I read with intense interest. I should have acknowledged them before, but that I meditated a letter to you at the same time on some very important points, which I had not been able thoroughly to master in such sort as to submit my conclusions to paper. I may now state that one principal point in my enquiry has been the *animus imponentis* in case of a *juramentum assertorium*. I maintain my first opinion which you contradict, that is, my first opinion with a shade of modification. And though I am bound in truth and justice to confess this very slight shade of difference (hereafter to be explained) in my opinion, yet I maintain with increased confidence that the opinion of the gentlemen learned in law who stated absolutely that an oath *assertorium* is to be interpreted according to the *animus imponentis* is positively untenable and in direct contradiction to the opinions of the authorities on the subject. You well less wonder at my boldness when you proceed a little further into the matter.

The *animus imponentis* advice from the learned Counsellors is an echo from Dr. Paley, *Mor. Phil.* cap\. 21, 22, which he has not sufficiently guarded, and which is *in opposition* to his *own* views as elsewhere expressed. *E.g.* look at his *Mor. Phil.* cap. 16 sec. 5 : "Promissory oaths are NOT binding where the promise itself would not be so." Then compare this with *Mor. Phil.* cap. 5, sec. 6, § 2 : "When the promise is understood by the promisee to proceed on a certain supposition, and that supposition turns out false, the then promise is not binding." See also cap. 17, *ad fin.* : "His" [the Juror's] "obligation depends upon what HE apprehended *at the time of taking the oath* to be the design of the law in imposing it, and no after requisition or explanation by the Court *can carry* the obligation beyond that." This is a plain proof that Dr. Paley himself did not hold those views absolutely which the unguarded dictum in cap. 21, 22 might lead a reader at first sight to father upon him. But I grudge spending so much of your time on an authority which, if admitted at Cambridge, *we* always hold in slight esteem !

So I must take you on a journey to an armoury of earlier date, furnished by more able workmen, and arm you with some of the brighter and more trustworthy weapons beat out on their anvils.

Now the great treatise on the subject is by the learned Sanderson, of whom it has been said that "Everything he wrote was gold." I might quote multitudes of his *dicta* to my purpose ; but I shall only give one or two which satisfy me in opposition to the opinions of those "learned in law" whom you quote. *De iuramenti obligatione* is the book I refer to. *Juramentum* is divided into *assertorium* and *promissorium*, p. 13. At p. 23 he speaks of oaths partaking of both characters. Such is the oath before us. Then at p. 31 : "Requiritur ab homine jurante ut omnino faciat secundum id quod egressum est ex ore suo : Ut omnino faciat, id est ut tunc temporis bonâ fide intendat facere, et postea bonâ fide quantum in ipso est conetur facere secundum id quod egressum est ex ore suo : id est, secundum *eum sensum quem verba ab ipso prolata juxta communem et receptum morem loquendi apta sunt ingenerare in mente audientium.*" Now I am at a loss to conceive any principle more opposed to the absolute *animus imponentis* principle than this, except anyone should maintain the contradictory of the *animus imponentis*, which would be absurd. The converse of it, that of the *animus jurantis*, would only be on a FOOTING with that of the *animus imponentis*—both equally wrong. You must bear in mind that an *undue enlargement* of the obligation *in animo imponentis* is as subversive of the whole fabric of morals, both in nature and in degree, as is the *undue restriction* of the obligation *in animo jurantis*. Now please weigh that sentence, because in it is contained the whole pith of the argument.

Hear Sanderson exactly to the same point :—"Neve sensum aliquem juramento a nobis præstito, aut ejus alicui parti, affingamus, proprii commodi aut utilitatis causâ, quem non quivis vir alius *pius et prudens* ex ipsis verbis facilé eliceret." Now, having myself read Hooker, *Eccl. Pol.* viii., *passim* ; Hickes, on *Priesthood* ; Sanderson, *Reg. Suprem.*, *passim* ; Lowth, on *Church Power*, pp. 433 ff.; and Collier,—all men *prudentes et pii*,—I find that they do *not* elicit from the Oath of Supremacy any such notion as that the Juror is bound to take Queen's decision in doctrine. On this head, if you are still heterodox, be pleased to read Lowth, cap. 6, secs. 5 and 6 ; and consult Henry VIII. 34 & 5. 1, where you will read even in statute law that recourse must be had to the Catholic Apostolic Church for the decision of controversies. By the way, if the 6th chapter of Lowth had been well got up by Badeley and Adams, they would have proved to the Privy Council that, whatever authority they may have in maritime cases, and suits simply respecting temporalities pertaining to spiritual persons, their claim to decide on doctrine is not grounded on a true interpretation even of statute law.

Sanderson, again, p. 77, speaks directly of the Oath of Supremacy itself in these terms : "Juramenta homagii ; Juramentum Suprematus Regii ; et similia ; quatenus obligent." . . . "NON tamen pariter obligari ad omnia ea observanda quæ sunt dubii aut controversi juris, præsertim cum soleant fere, qui potestate præditi sunt, funiculos agrorum extendere, et ultra lapides clientium salire, nec jurium suorum finibus contenti esse." These expressions are somewhat pertinent to these times. Hear Sanderson again, p. 111,—"Error circa substantiam rei quæ uit propria jurandi causa irritam facit promissionem et obligationem tollit."

And now, if you won't think me a very Dædalus, I must allure you on another flight, whither you may follow without fearing an Icarian fall. We must travel to the 313th page of *Puffendorf, de officio Hominis et Civis*," etc.:—"Nec obligabit juramentum ubi constat eum qui juravit factum aliquod supposuisse quod re verâ ita non se habebat, ac nisi id credidisset non fuisse juraturum." And again, p. 286 : "Ubi error contigerit circa ipsam rem de quâ convenitur, factum vitiatur non tam ob errorem quam quia legibus facti non fuit satisfactum." And then he proceeds to say that the party injured may either retract his contract or compel the other to supply the deficit.

These quotations, which might be multiplied far beyond the proper limits of a letter, convince me that the principle of a *jura-*

mentum assertorium and *promissorium* (*mixtum*), being absolutely binding according to the *animus imponentis*, is untenable.

I can explain how a mistake has arisen among the lawyers. Bear in mind that they are the worst metaphysicians in the world; and for this reason—With very few exceptions they consider Acts of Parliament to be ultimate principles. Now there are two kinds of oaths under the head *promissorium* with which they are conversant. *One* is technically called the *voir dire*, and is thus put to the juror :—" You shall true answer make to all such questions as shall be put to you. So help you God." The *other oath* is the *oath* of a witness sworn *in chief.* Thus :—" The evidence which you shall give touching the matter in question shall be the truth, the whole truth, and nothing but the truth." In the latter of these two at least I grant you the full, *absolute, unrestrained* principle of the *animus imponentis.* This is the oath to which the lawyers are used (as indeed I have good reason to know), and in their metaphysics this is the rock on which they have in your case split. Trust not their interpretation of a vast question in morals when grounded only on one subdivision of a subject which extends itself to an indefinite number of ramifications.

The truth is, an oath *assertorium* is to be interpreted, neither according to the *animus imponentis,* nor according to the *animus jurantis* (in technical language the two parties are called *deferens* and *jurans*). Both interpretations would be equally improper. As to *one* side, so to the *other*, the obligation might in such case be unduly enlarged or unduly restricted. But *an oath assertorium is to be interpreted according to the plain sense of the terms, as prudent and pious men would interpret, ὡς ὁ φρόνιμος ὁρίσαι.* Now it requires but to read Sanderson, Hickes, Lowth, Collier, Hooker (all *prudentis et pii*), on the subject, and to couple with this the declaration of the Statute, Hen. VIII. 24. 12. 1 ; Hen. VIII. 34 & 5. 1 ; Queen Eliz. injunctions ; the 37th Article ; King James 1st's Preface to the Canons, and the Royal Declaration at the beginning of the Articles ;—and surely, then, we must conclude that the oath *assertorium* of supremacy, as expounded by the Sovereigns themselves, by the Church, and by men *prudentis et pii*, does not bind us to take the Queen's judgments in *doctrinal* matters. . . . —Believe me, as ever, your affectionate friend,

JAMES WAYLAND JOYCE.

FIRST CURACY

F. A. G. O. TO REV. J. W. JOYCE.

ST. BARNABAS COLLEGE, *March* 8, 1850.

DEAR WAYLAND,—In awful haste one line. I gave Mr. Bennett your letter and questions. The latter he forwarded at once to Mr. Kenyon, a copy of whose reply I enclose. You do not say your opinion of Mr. B.'s Sermons. Have you read Keble's Tract, Maskell's Tract, Sewell's Sermon, and Dodsworth's Sermon, all bearing on the point at issue? Pray write again. Your letters really keep me alive : they breathe a healthy, country air, uncontaminated by the feverish dust of our excited London atmosphere of polemicks.

Would to God we had some shadow of hope for the English Church? But I fear the lukewarmness of her prelates, and the Erastianism of her children, will smother her.

I am in wretched spirits just now. I sometimes fear I shall go mad. Sleep has, I think, forgotten the abode of my eyelids ; and, unless matters assume a better aspect, I know not what will become of me.—Believe me ever most truly and affectionately yours,

FREDERICK A. G. OUSELEY.

F. A. G. O. TO REV. J. W. JOYCE.

[*Not dated, but probably March* 1850.]

MY DEAR WAYLAND,—Many thanks for your *very* kind and considerate letter. With regard to Church matters, it seems to be agreed upon now by all hands that a great general move must be made. The Church must now speak her mind. If she agrees with the Committee of Privy Council, then she stands self-convicted of heresy. But if not, then all may be well. . . .

With regard to your kind invitation, I wish I could accept it. Alas ! I am not my own master. My flock have a prior claim on me. Perhaps in a month or so I *may* get a holiday. If so I will assuredly come to you. I am now rather better in health than I was a week ago. My doctor tells me it is all the *mind*—not the body—that is the *causa mali*. . . . —Believe me ever affectionately yours,

FREDERICK A. G. OUSELEY.

F. A. G. O. TO REV. J. W. JOYCE.

ST. BARNABAS, *September* 28, 1850.

MY DEAR WAYLAND,—The usual excuse, want of time, must be mine. I know I ought to have written ; but I had neither time nor spirits. I am in a great perplexity. I *must*, according to the invariable and tyrannical rule of my Bishop, take Priest's Orders at Christmas. But I cannot and will not consent to do so at St. Barnabas, as it is only my being in Deacon's Orders which saves me, as you know, from doing many things sorely *against my con-science*. It is therefore essential to get away ; but I am loth to do so without something definite to go to—*not a curacy*, because of the scandal it would give against Mr. Bennett, who has enemies enough ready to take hold of any pretext to defame him. Bennett himself is quite willing I should go at Christmas ; and I am also sure it is necessary both for my health and happiness to do so. Can you advise me how to act ? Of course, I must not take a holiday till then, but will make a point of coming and seeing you as soon as I can get away.

Pray write to me about this.—In haste, yours ever affectionately,
FREDERICK A. G. OUSELEY.

On Sunday, November 10, 1850, the " No Popery" riots began at St. Barnabas. Mr. Bennett was a man of energy and ability. He had already infused a good deal of church life into his parish, and had gathered round him a goodly number of staunch supporters. But neither his doctrinal views, nor the elaborate scale (as it was then considered) of his ritual, were at that time generally popular. It would appear, indeed, from the above letter [the one dated September 28, 1850], that Sir F. Ouseley himself was not in entire harmony with all the doings at St. Barnabas, and that he was thus placed in a dilemma between his bishop's rule and his own conscience. It is known, for instance, that he disapproved of some of Mr. Bennett's ritual observances, and especially did the musical curate object to the introduction of Gregorian chants. But when at last an organised opposition broke out, loyalty to his vicar and to his other fellow-workers would naturally make him the more anxious to take his share in their troubles. He himself had brickbats thrown at him in the streets. The following letter, written to his former college friend, the Rev. John Rich, gives a graphic description of the disgraceful riots which then took place, continuing for several successive Sundays :—

F. A. G. O. TO REV. JOHN RICH.

Nov. 20, 1850.

YOU have doubtless read in the papers accounts of the outrageous attack which was made by the mob on St. Barnabas' Church last Sunday. But as the accounts in some of the papers are incorrect, it is possible that you and others may have been misled as to the facts of the case. I write this to tell you how it all happened, both because I know you will take an interest in the matter, and because I am anxious the truth should be widely known.

On Sunday (November 10), just as the Non-Communicants were about to retire, a great hissing was heard in the Church, with loud cries of " Popery," etc. This was, of course, stopped, and the Service proceeded ; but a multitude of men had collected outside, prepared to make a rush had any sympathy been evinced within. A great crowd collected in the evening, but we avoided all disturbance then by omitting the Service at 7. Mr. Bennett remained at St. Barnabas to defend his family and property if necessary, and sent me to preach for him at St. Paul's, at 6. When I returned at 8.30, I found the crowd, gathered in knots of men, threatening what they would do next Sunday. I had been insulted and threatened the night before in the street, and Mr. Bennett too had received several threatening letters. We had every reason to be certain of a more violent attack on Sunday, the 17th ; so we took every precaution to be prepared for it, nor were they superfluous. The 8 A.M. and 9 A.M. Services went off quietly; but at 10.30 A.M. the mob began to collect, but luckily our own congregation were seated in time. Nothing in the Church happened before the Sermon, but during it a prodigious yell was heard without, which frightened some of our people much. The Church was crammed to suffocation, and a body of staunch friends were stationed up the body of the nave to prevent any attack on the chancel. When the Sermon was concluded, and the Non-Communicants prepared to retire, a violent rush was made by the populace outside; and doubtless, had they succeeded in their attempt, our beautiful edifice would have been dismantled, and our lives endangered. We know that was their object; but it pleased God to defeat their sacrilegious intention. The well-affected within were too strong for them: 100 policemen succeeded in quelling the mob without, sufficiently to let the congregation retire. The organist, by my direction, played "Full Organ" the whole time, to drown the row, which had no small effect in preventing the disaffected from communicating with one another. In about forty minutes the Church was at length cleared. It was truly gratifying to see the very large number of Communicants who remained to thank God in this way for His Almighty protection.

F. A. G. O. TO REV. J. W. JOYCE.

ST. BARNABAS COLLEGE, *November* 22, 1850.

MY DEAR WAYLAND,—Many thanks for your kind letter. I have given up *all thoughts* of the living about which the question of Simony arose, as indeed I have of *all* livings at present. I must go abroad for a year, *at least.* My health requires it, and many other motives incline me to it.

You will doubtless have read accounts of our fearful *riot* here last Sunday. Next Sunday it will be worse. We are prepared as for a siege. It keeps Bennett faster to us; for it makes him obstinate. For a true account of it all, I refer you to the *Morning Chronicle,* the only just paper. The Church of England is in an awful state. I see *no* hope, and am thoroughly disgusted with everything. In short, I am quite ashamed of my country. I abhor all the popular principles of the day, and shall never be happy till on some distant shore I forget that I have been an Englishmen. . . . Pray write: a letter from you always does me good.—Ever yours affectionately,

FREDERICK A. G. OUSELEY.

At the close of the year 1850 Mr. Bennett resigned the living of St. Paul's, Knightsbridge, and Sir F. Ouseley resigned his curacy at St. Barnabas. The following letter would seem to have referred to some unwarranted report that his resignation of the curacy meant secession to Rome. A reference to the end of his letter (a), dated January 23, 1850, will show with what justice he might repel the charge, and be indignant with those who would not accept his disclaimer :—

39 (or 37 ?) Lowndes Street
[Not dated, but probably January 1851].

My dear Wayland,—I have written a letter to the editor of the Daily News, and another to the editor of the Morning Chronicle; and neither have been inserted. What shall I do next? It is a monstrous thing to tell a vile lie against a man, and then ignore his confutation of it. I really do not know what to do. Shall I write an advertisement? They must insert that.

As regards Dorking—Fyffe objects to go so far from London. He is going to take a large house near, but not in, London.

I have altered my travelling scheme. I intend now to go straight to Lisbon, where I intend to spend a week, then by sea to Cadiz, then up the Guadalquiver to Seville, then to Granada, etc. etc., from Barcelona to Marseilles, from Marseilles to Genoa, etc. etc.

What think you of this? I lionised A , two days ago, all over St. Barnabas, and played the Organ for him, and then took him to the temple and played that Organ too, all which he liked much.

Pray remember me to all your circle, and believe me yours ever,

F. O.

(a) Cf. p. 53 supra.

CHAPTER IV

EARLY in 1851 Sir F. Ouseley left England for a
tour through various parts of the Continent, and
did not return until the close of the year.   Meanwhile, in order that the choir of St. Barnabas, with
its educational advantages and its college traditions, should be kept together, he made generous
arrangements for its migration to Lovehill House,
Langley, Bucks, a few miles from London, on
the Great Western Railway.   Here, under the
superintendence of his friend, the Rev. Henry
Fyffe, was formed the nucleus of his future
school.

The following extracts from a series of letters,
written to my father from abroad, will explain
themselves.   They are interesting not only as
describing Sir Frederick's travels, but also as
showing how, in that one year 1851, when he had
leisure to think and to observe, his views, both
political and ecclesiastical, were becoming fixed in
that one stereotyped form from which they never
swerved in after life.   Like many other conscientious men, he thought out his views once

and for all, and then set himself to do the work of life on those lines :—

GENOA, March 21, 1851.

MY DEAR WAYLAND,—Many things have happened to me since we last met. I have seen strange people, strange places, strange things. I know more of the world than I did. Yet I hope you give me credit for not thinking the less of old friends. However, to make it the surer, I write this, both because I fancy you will like a letter from me, and also because I want to get one from you when I am at Rome, where I hope to be in Holy Week. I have several times wished you had been with me ; and never more so than when I went over the splendid Cathedral at Seville. But I will begin at the beginning and trace out my travels *ab initio*.

The first place I came to was Lisbon, where I stayed ten days. My good friend De Gex is travelling with me ; so we took a private sitting-room, hired a pianoforte, and made ourselves as happy as we could. But still we found Lisbon a horrid place : every kind of dirt is thrown out of window, and the whole place stinks abominably. But the worst thing is the state of the Church—despoiled and impoverished by a semi-infidel Government—the priests not a whit less corrupt for their poverty, most of them open fornicators. Nothing can be at a lower ebb than religion in Portugal : their monastic establishments are all secularised, the greater part gone to ruin, some turned into barracks, or secular schools, or tobacco-factories. The only places worth seeing in the ecclesiological line are Cintra and Mapa—the former celebrated for its scenery and old Moresque Castle, and the latter for the enormous palace and quondam Franciscan Monastery erected there. We went all over it. The best thing about it *now* is its chime of 114 bells.

The next place we anchored at was Cadiz. Nothing can be more striking than the first view of this city as you approach it from the sea. The houses being all white and semi-Moorish, it has almost the appearance of alabaster. It is a very clean, nice, town : but dull, I should think, for a long stay. We only stayed there five days, and then steamed up the Guadalquiver to Seville. Here indeed we were enchanted, first by the splendid old Gothick Cathedral, and then by the Museum, the Alcazar, the Alamedo, and Giralda tower. The Cathedral is pure, unspoiled Gothick : every window full of beautiful stained glass : every side chapel containing some beautiful painting, many by Murillo. The Organs, too, of which there are two, are splendid. But I did not hear them to advantage ; for, being Carnival time, they were busy in the Chancel

69

all day ; so I could not try them, and in Service the Organist used hardly anything but the trumpet !

Our next halting-place was Gibraltar. It was a comfort to come to an English town again, and I was very fortunate, too, in having an introduction to the Governor, Sir R. Gardiner, who treated us with marked civility. We stayed there nearly a fortnight, which I am sorry for, as there is nothing there but what may well be seen in three days. But we gained one thing by it, an expedition to Tangiers in a war - steamer. This was most interesting, as you may suppose. We were fortunate, too, in being there on a market-day, and so seeing more of Arab customs and habits than we other-wise should have done. The Moors are but half-civilised : they are barely civil to an European. We were told if we ventured out unguarded into the interior, we should certainly be murdered. However, we *did* so venture, and here we are at Genoa, safe and sound—*sit laus Deo !* . . . Adieu.—Ever yours most affectionately,

FREDERICK A. G. OUSELEY.

---

59 VIA DEL BABUINO, ROMA,
May 9, 1851.

MY DEAR WAYLAND,— . . . With Rome I have been woefully disappointed. Of course it is full of objects of classical and anti-quarian interest : but it is not in this point of view that I speak of it. It is Rome ecclesiastical which has disappointed me. I cannot tell how disgusted I am with Romanism in its headquarters. What I have seen here has quite made up my mind that even if my own Church were to apostatise—which God forbid !—yet it were better to trust to uncovenanted mercies than join a Church so corrupt, so false, so self-seeking and self-deceiving, as the Church of Rome. The lies which one would have to believe, the lies one would have to preach, the utter abandonment of one's own reason which would become necessary, would soon make one an *infidel. Ita sit !* You are more sanguine about the prospects of the Church of England than anyone else I know. I wish I could look forward as hopefully as you do. As far as I can see, the fearful persecutions at St. Barnabas seem only to be a sample of what may be expected to ensue all over England. . . . No good thing can prosper in Church or in State. . . . All we can do is to pray for the peace of our Jerusalem fervently, incessantly, and trust to God's mercy to make this a temporal chastisement for our sins, and not root us out utterly! You see, I am as yet none the happier for my travels. Absence only rivets the thoughts more on what we leave behind. It is a mistake to suppose it can make us *forget* our home troubles. But enough of this, you will say.

Oh! how wretchedly disappointed I have been with the musick in Rome! On Palm Sunday there was a beautiful Mass of Palestrina's; and during Holy Week I heard beautiful Misereres and Lamentations by Palestrina, Bai, Allegri, and Baini; also on Easter Day a very fine Mass by Siciliani—all first-rate composers. But these Romans can't sing their own musick! They have fine voices (Basses and Tenors, that is), but the (? Alte) Trebles are *execrable*. With the exception of the above-named things, and a Greek Mass I heard one day by Baini, I have not heard a note of musick worth a straw since I arrived in Rome! I have, however, tumbled on my legs in the way, for I have made the acquaintance of 3 good musicians—Fontemaggi, organist of St. Peter's; Bovieri, director of the Sistine choir; and Abbate F. Santini, who has one of the best collections of MS. musick, of an ancient Church style, in the world. By means of these three worthies I have been able to make very extensive and valuable additions to my own private collection of classical musick, already not a contemptible one. So that I hope ere long to be spoken of—*monstrari digito praetereuntium*—as the possessor of a most enviable musical MS. library. There are no good Organs in Rome, which annoys me much. The only really good one I have met with since Seville is at Catania in Sicily. You would be amused if you could see how hard I have been reading up Horace, Livy, Pliny, and Tacitus. But I was determined to be well *au fait* of all the objects of antiquarian interest here, so I have mugged pretty hard. . . .

With regard to a living, . . . my final plans must be *in nubibus*. Much depends on the events which are coming on the Church: much depends on my health, which is very indifferent just now: much, too, depends on a sort of offer I have had of a precentorship at Winchester which is expected soon to become vacant. Still, in spite of all this, I may, after all, settle down into a country parson. If so, I had rather be near you. You see, I have scruples about hiding my musical talent under a bushel. I think I clearly ought, if it be possible, to devote it to God's service in His Holy Church. Now, in a regular country living this is impossible: for a large town living I have neither health nor strength. A precentorship is more the thing: but it has its drawbacks, and they are of no small weight. So, on the whole, I am pulled all ways: I know not whither to turn.

Pray do not omit to write to me to Florence. I like to hear of you and yours. I cannot tell you how interested I am in your proposed restorations at Burford. But, whatever you do, sink the floor to its former level. Your nave wants height, and your windows start too low now, in consequence of the ill-advised raising of your floor. Be your roof what it may, the nave will never be perfect without this, not even if all open-seated and the windows mullioned and coloured : *verbum sat.* . . . I assure you I think much of all my old friends. No one knows the full value of friends at home till he becomes a wanderer like me. . . . —Believe me to be ever yours most sincerely and affectionately,

FREDERICK A. G. OUSELEY.

———

VENICE, *July* 4, 1851. HOTEL DANIELLI.

MY DEAR WAYLAND,—Here I am at length at the Sea-city—a sort of "amphibilious" place, with which I expect to be much pleased ; although I can hardly judge yet, having only arrived this morning.

Your letter, which I got at Florence, pleased me much. You are almost the only correspondent I have who can speak cheerfully on ecclesiastical or political matters. Everybody else inundates me with most doleful productions, which would suffice to make me despair even if I were not naturally inclined to do so. But I try to persuade myself to think as you do, hoping even against hope. God grant that some day I may find cause for more than a vague hope ! But, alas ! the times are very bad indeed. Do not, however, think from this that I am going to Romanise. No ! I have seen quite enough to take away any hankering of that kind ; and, unless I were convinced that the Papal Supremacy was of Divine right (which is impossible, as you truly say), I never can or will become a member of the Roman Communion. But still I cannot but see the shortcomings of the English Church, and that I grieve over.

What a beautiful road is that between Rome and Florence ! We came by Siena, passing Lake Thrasymene. I found several Organs, too, worth trying. The tone of the mixture stops in the Italian Organs is generally good, especially in the old ones ; the new ones excel in their reed stops. I think they are in this respect above the average, but the diapasons are always weak both in new and old instruments. The great point of inferiority, however, is in their arrangement and mechanism ; it is always execrable, the compass almost invariably from F in alt. to CC *short octaves.* A more vile compass can hardly be conceived, especially when you remember that short octaves in *the Pedals* is a barbarism never perpetrated in more enlightened countries. I have got in my writing-book *descriptions raisonnées* of all the best Organs I have tried, which you shall see some of these days.

I like to hear your accounts of English Polemicks. I fancy I see you now sitting midst piles of huge tomes, while I am lying half-dead with the heat at the bottom of a Gondola ! But pray write me accounts of all your researches, as, although I am not studious enough to enter into them myself, yet the results interest me beyond measure. As far as regards Convocation, it would only be a bear-garden now, and might possibly lead to authorised heresy (*a*). It seems to me to be a dangerous thing. I fancy, after all, that the Puritan party in the Church are very strong. The accounts I read in *Galignani* of their meetings to alter the Book of Common Prayer seem to prove it ; and they are the Government favourites too, which is a strong point. Now, I contend that they would very likely prevail in a Convocation just now ; and who knows what might be the result? Who knows what alterations they might make in our Sacramental Services and Ordinal? Who can tell how many pious and hard-working High Churchmen might be driven thereby to seek shelter in another Church? These are no trifling dangers. Have you duly considered them? It strikes me our state is this—we have no acting or energetic head ; the only one we can have is Convocation ; we cannot get on without it. But Convocation will probably ruin us : therefore we must either be *starved* or *smothered.* But enough of this ! . . .

If you write me soon, direct *Poste Restante, Geneva.* I will not give you a later address, both that you may have no excuse for delaying to write to me again, and also because my *route* is most uncertain.—Believe me, as ever, most truly and affectionately yours,

FREDERICK A. G. OUSELEY.

The book of *descriptions raisonnées*, referred to in the above letter, appears now (1896) to be lost. But it is evident from the recollections of friends that Sir Frederick visited a very large number of the best known organs in Europe.

(*a*) Cf. p. 158 *infra.*

He went about trying organs everywhere, and the "natives" used to come and ask when the English gentleman was going to play. Canon Rich recalls, as one of Sir Frederick's observations, that "he thought the organs in different countries were very expressive of the characteristics of the people. German organs were like the English, round, full-toned; French, noisy and reedy; Italian and Spanish, mellow and soft."

At this time Sir Frederick Ouseley had almost made up his mind to build a church, and take charge of a district to be assigned to it, at Ludlow. Eventually this scheme fell through; but the following letter shows how clearly he already had before him the project which he afterwards carried out to completion in the building of St. Michael's :—

LUCERNE, *September* 1, 1851.

MY DEAR WAYLAND,—I have begun two letters to you which have come to grief, for lack of time; but I really must not delay any longer sending you a letter . . . to speak a little of the Ludlow affair in which you have so very kindly interested yourself. I have determined to undertake it. It is, I think, a very feasible project, and I am tired of a roving life. But there are difficulties still. *In primis*, I *cannot afford* to build the Church and endow it too. My income will not do it, and I cannot touch my capital : it is locked up in Chancery. . . . What I have in my thoughts is a Church in the 14th Century style, with Collegiate buildings adjoining, for residences for myself, two Curates and Choir, and Cloisters, too, enclosing a private portion of the Cemetery. Now, this plan is expensive, and so I can only accomplish it by degrees. I will give £1000 every year towards this building, if anyone else will help me in any degree proportionably—*che né pensate?* Then as to the Service. I must have *daily choral Service: my choir must be a model choir* : and I will *not* give up anything if I once commence. . . . Anyhow, I am ready for any preliminary personal measures at Christmas. If absolutely necessary, I will come home sooner ; but would rather not, for I have many Churches to see and many Organs to try. The Freyburg Organ I tried a short time ago, and it delighted me. It is undoubtedly the best I have ever yet seen or heard. There is also a very fine one at Berne just put up ; and I am going to try one in a few days at Winterthur which is said to be better still. So you see my hobby still bears me well. I will give you a detailed account of all my organising experiences when we meet.

Fancy my having the good luck to tumble upon a lot of Christ Church men reading with my old and good double first friend, Kitchin. . . . —Believe me, as ever, yours affectionately and faith-fully,   FREDERICK A. G. OUSELEY.

MUNICH, *September* 26, 1851.

MY DEAR WAYLAND,—It is a great comfort to me to have a correspondent in England like yourself, always able and willing to enter into my views and feelings, and to sympathise with my doubts and perplexities when they arise. I only wish I was able to express to you half the sense I have of the very great kindness you show me in your last as in all other letters. I think I like the Ludlow scheme more and more. The only difficulty I foresee is *money*. You see, my funds are rather reduced just now, in consequence of all I disbursed at St. Barnabas both toward the Church and Choir. . . . Perhaps, however, I may find my affairs better than I expected on my return—*Speriamo!* . . . I will not do without daily choral Service. I have no talent for teaching, no powers of preaching, and no health for hard parochial work. But God has given me one talent ; and that I am determined to devote to His Service, and offer it up to adorn His Church. I should never forgive myself, if I did otherwise ; my conscience exacts it of me, and you may tell Hampden(*b*) so if you like, or think it expedient. . . .

I wish you could see the beautiful Churches the ex-King has built in this town. Were it not for the Lola Montes Extravaganza, he would be called a great man—not a dotard, or worse, as he now is ! In the matter of coloured glass, the Munich windows are of course quite splendid. Still, I infinitely prefer the old Mozaick glass, which you see in Strasburg, etc.; it is darker and richer, and I think more ecclesiastical in its general effect, which is of more

(*b*) The then Bishop of Hereford.

importance in my opinion than excellence of detail. . . . Believe me ever yours most truly and affectionately,

FREDERICK A. G. OUSELEY.

I shall and will be home by Christmas Day.

———

DRESDEN, *October* 21, 1851.

MY DEAR WAYLAND,— . . . I shall be, I trust, once more in England — *post tot tautosque labores* — by the first week in December ; and, as soon as ever I shall have seen a little of my sisters, I intend, if it be convenient to you, to run over and see you : albeit it must be only a very short affair, for Fyffe requires my assistance at his place on Christmas Day, and I have promised to go and look after my *protégés* there, which is of course a duty as well as a pleasure. . . .

I am quite out of conceit with English Chorister boys. I think every Precentor and Choir Master ought to come and hear the boys here, both in the Roman Catholick and in the Lutheran Church. I never heard anything equal or approaching to the excellence of their voices. The intonation is so true, and the style so tasteful and refined, and the quality so rich and full and round, that it leaves nothing to be desired. I wish I could *catch* a Saxon lad and *import* him ! But I fear this is impossible. I assure you, I am "all agog" about this matter. And then I heard, the other day, old *Schneider*, the best living Organist, play on one of the best Organs in Europe ; and I really have not had the heart to touch an instrument since, so unapproachable does his excellence as a fugue-player and accompanist appear to be. So I have had two musical snubs, the first a *national* snub, and the second an *individual* one ! De Gex says he thinks a book, yclept "the snubbed one," might be written, so much amused is he at my mortification and envious feelings. . . . The English Aldermen are to fête Kossuth . . . Why, these are the very men who preach against war, and armies, etc., etc.: and now they are doing their best to embroil us with Austria ! Upon my honour I am nearly driven mad by these evil times in which we live. It is enough to arouse every latent feeling of indignation to hear all the foreigners say of my country, and not be able to confute or gainsay one word of it ! . . . Of all the towns I have been in, I like this the best, and I only regret being forced to leave it so soon. But Fyffe needs my presence so much that I must be back, and should be sorry not to see Paris first, and try the Dutch and Flemish Organs . . . . —Yours very faithfully and affectionately,   FREDERICK A. G. OUSELEY.

———

BERLIN, October 28, 1851.

MY DEAR WAYLAND,— . . . I think in my last letter I told you about the boys' voices at Dresden. Well, at Leipzig, at the Thomankirche, they are well nigh as good. I wish I could capture one! I am quite certain I shall never care for English Cathedral trebles again. I assure you it is worth any musician's while to come to Dresden or Leipzig from any part of the world, if it were only to hear these boys. You never in your life heard anything approaching to it. The best boy's voice I ever heard in England was at Windsor, a great many years ago, when Foster, now Organist at Wells Street, was a chorister there (c). But these Saxon fellows beat him hollow : he can't come within a mile of them. I suspect they are chosen from a somewhat higher class of Society than our own choristers usually are ; and this is perhaps the cause of their more refined style.

In my humble opinion it is very desirable indeed to raise the position of our English Choir boys. *Now* they are too often mere rabble, and what refinement of style can one fairly expect from such materials? Of course, I know there are exceptions, and that not only choristers taken from a higher grade do exist, but that also cases do occur where even those of the lowest rank do by their own individual labours and talents overcome their disadvantageous circumstances, and attain no small excellence. —— is an instance : —— is another. But still, as a general rule, I must say the usual system is radically bad. Now, my choral scheme will tend, maybe, by God's blessing, to improve this state of things. I hope also that by instituting a model choir I may supply another great deficiency, *i.e.* Choir *men*, brought up as Choristers, who shall know how to be reverent and devout in Church ; singing not for their own sake, but for God's glory ; not to earn a scanty pittance, or gain a musical reputation, but to promote the solemnity and impressiveness of the Choral Service of our National Church. This is what a Choir man ought to be, and

———

(c) Mr. John Foster, when he grew to man's estate, developed a very beautiful alto voice, and was appointed, in or about the year 1856, a Lay Vicar at Westminster Abbey, which position he still holds (Nov. 1895).

what he hardly ever is : and nothing but an improvement in the education and training of Choir boys can ever bring it to pass. This, then, is one main object I have in view. But yet further, as some chorister boys will become professional musicians, so others may wish to be *ordained*. Now there is a great lack of good *chaunting clergy* in the Church of England. No man can be so fit to perform the Priest's part well, in a Choral Service, as he who has been brought up as a Chorister boy. But alas ! too many of those who have been so brought up have proved themselves afterwards but too unfit for their Holy Profession. The common education which our Choristers have hitherto received being anything but a good school for piety and devotion. Now this deficiency I hope my scheme will materially tend to remedy, under God ; and I cannot but feel sanguine that when the objects thereof are known, I shall gain the countenance and support of the good and the charitable.

I do not like Berlin ; so we go, on Thursday the 30th, to Hanover, and on the 31st to Cologne, where we stop a week ; then quickly through Holland to try Organs, etc. . . . —Believe me ever yours affectionately,

FREDERICK A. G. OUSELEY.

———

LOVEHILL HOUSE, LANGLEY, BUCKS,
Feast of St. John the Evangelist [*December* 27], 1851.

MY DEAR WAYLAND,—I have been so engaged since I have been in England that I could not fix any time to propose to pay you my promised visit. But now I write to say that I can come any day after January 7th, on which I have to get through some very unpleasant business with my lawyers in Lincoln's Inn. I do so long to have a chat with you again, and to talk over old times and present times and future times, and Church matters, and *my own* Church Schemes, last but not least. It would be forestalling to say much in *this*, but I am still anxious to get work, only *not yet*. I had rather wait till next Christmas and read quietly, for reasons I will tell you, and which I think you will acquiesce in. I still hold good for Ludlow *eventually*.

Bennett has come home furious at all the evils he has seen among Papists abroad, and is going to belch forth a sour pamphlet on the subject. He has been appointed, *I believe*, to the Vicarage of Frome, in the Diocese of Bath and Wells.

78

Direct to me *here*, please.   All our old choristers are here, under
the able superintendence of my late fellow-curate, Fyffe ; and it is
with these materials that I hope to form a nucleus for my projected
institution and College. . . . —Believe me to be, as ever, yours very
truly and affectionately,   FREDERICK A. G. OUSELEY.

From the date of the above letter right on to
the very end of his life, one chief object seems
now to have occupied Sir F. Ouseley's time and
best energies, viz. the serving God with his *one
talent* (*d*), as he called it.   From this time onward
his scheme for the improvement of choral music
in the Church was the one great end of his life.
Undoubtedly he did much valuable work for the
Church of a more general kind as well, but for the
most part it all centred round this one department of sacred choral music.

Near the house at Langley a temporary chapel
had been fitted up, converted from a stable loft ;
and here twice a day a regular Cathedral Service
was rendered.   Of the domestic arrangements of
this choir colony, we have a suggestive description
in the following reminiscence, written in after years
by one of Ouseley's friends : (*e*)—

My friendship with our dear friend Ouseley lasted for a great
many years, and was intimate.   But what I know of him is, I
fancy, only what was equally well known to the hundreds whose
lives were brightened by his unbounded kindness and cordiality.

I have a pretty keen remembrance of one occasion when (at
Langley) I arrived one Sunday evening, after a fatiguing day in
London, to take part in a devotional performance, in the chapel, of
the entire *Messiah* — nothing omitted, and standing throughout
the three parts.   It began, I think, at 8 p.m., and certainly did not
end before midnight.   Then he took us up into his own room, and,
rubbing his hands, said, "Well, I think we must want some

<hr>

(*d*) Cf. p. 75 *supra*.   (*e*) Havergal's *Memorials*, p. 59.

refreshment." The refreshment was strong green tea ! Of course, an absolutely sleepless night followed, especially as the room was an exceedingly cold one. At daybreak, however, I was just drifting into unconsciousness, when a long single file of boys, in their night shirts, passed through the room on their way either to lavatory or oratory, I forget which. The next day was the prize-day for the school, but, as might be expected, Ouseley was disabled by head-ache, and commissioned me (a stranger to the place) to represent him and conduct the ceremonies ! I well remember, too, the misery which he suffered from the possession of that gorgeous, but perilous, heirloom, the Persian enamelled plate (*f*), of pure gold, which he used to hide under his coat, and bring down with whispered cautions to show to his friends.

(*f*) Cf. p. 3 *supra*.

CHURCH OF S. MICHAEL AND ALL ANGELS, OLD WOOD, TENBURY: LOOKING EASTWARDS.

Photographed by R. C. Morris, Tenbury.

CHAPTER V

Foundation of St. Michael's Church and College—Appointment to Professorship of Music at Oxford—Priest's Orders and Appointment to Precentorship at Hereford—Consecration of St. Michael's—1852–1857.

On Sir F. Ouseley's return from his foreign tour, the proposed scheme for a new district in the parish of Ludlow, to be assigned to him, appears to have fallen through. He also had it in his mind about this time to restore Buildwas Abbey, near Ironbridge (Salop). Many who have visited that beautiful old ruin would fain wish that another Ouseley might arise in the Church, and carry the idea into execution. But early in 1852 a third opening offered itself in the same neighbourhood, in the parish of Tenbury. Tenbury is a small market town in the extreme north-west corner of Worcestershire. It belongs to the diocese of Hereford, and lies within a mile of where the three counties of Shropshire, Herefordshire, and Worcestershire meet at the junction of the rivers Teme and Ledwyche. In 1852 the population of Tenbury was but small, as it remains to this day. But the parish was a scattered one, and the new district was to comprise portions also of the parishes of Leysters and Middleton-on-the-Hill. It might have been thought that the offer to build and endow a church in any district, by a man of Sir F. Ouseley's character and position, could have met with nothing but welcome, on the part of churchmen at all events. Yet it is a fact that this scheme too all but fell through, partly, no doubt, from that natural dislike to novelties which distinguishes purely agricultural neighbourhoods, and partly, perhaps, from real fear, existing in the minds of some, that Ouseley would prove to be a " Puseyite "— a name which in those days was spoken with bated breath. The then vicar of Tenbury, the Rev. John Churton, was at first unfavourable to the scheme ; and it is clear, from what evidences remain, that it required the combined efforts of the brothers Miller of Bockleton (of whom more anon), as well as my father, the Rev. J. W. Joyce of Burford, to conciliate the opposition. At last, however, the tide turned. Bishop Hampden approved the scheme, and engaged to assign the district. In June 1852 Sir Frederick bought some land adjoining the "Old Wood" Common, and nearly two miles from Tenbury. In August Miss Harriet Rushout, of Burford House, died, leaving, amongst other charitable legacies, one of £600 towards the proposed new church. Before the year was ended Sir Frederick had settled on the site, not only for the church, but also for a college for his school. Throughout 1853 the plans were being prepared by Mr, Henry Woodyer of Guildford, the architect; and on May 3, 1854, the foundation-stone of the new church was laid.

To many who have since visited St. Michael's, the question has often naturally suggested itself—What would have been the future of Sir Frederick Ouseley's institution, and of his own career, had he built the church and college near London, as was at one time proposed, or at least within easier reach of some large centre? Some of his friends strongly urged him to do this, and he did indeed, at the outset, make a definite proposal to found his establishment near Oxford; but Bishop Wilberforce, who had at that time been driven into a condition of extreme caution, felt constrained to decline the offer of one whose name had been so closely connected with St. Barnabas, Pimlico. Had St. Michael's been built near some large town, with all the advantages of good railway communication, it is quite likely that the school, at all events, might have more materially prospered. But undoubtedly the whole place would have lost one of its chief charms, and that which no one more thoroughly appreciated than its founder, from the beginning to the end of his work, viz. the simplicity of its rural surroundings. On the one side, the rough, open, breezy, common, with the blue Clee Hill and the Ludlow Vinhalls in the distance; on the other side, the lovely scenery and peaceful quiet of a typical Hereford-

shire parish, buried in the richest foliage,—all
these combine to give St. Michael's a character
and charm of its own. There, before your
eyes, as you pass through this scene of primitive
English life, springs, as it were, out of the very
ground a lofty church with a noble pile of
college buildings by its side! St. Michael's has
been characterised as (a)—

The one real development of the æsthetic principle that England
is yet able to boast, . . . emphatically one of the loveliest architectural efforts of the century—the *chef-d'œuvre* of an architect
pre-eminently capable of grasping the spirit of the Middle Ages.

This description may be somewhat overdrawn.
But few could pass St. Michael's Church and
College, springing up suddenly as they do in
this sequestered spot, without delight and admiration. And certainly,—whatever may be thought
of the exact architectural merit of the buildings,—
anyone with an eye for beauty of purpose, seeing
in them a living expression of the faith of their
founder, may well take heart for the future of
the English Church. Far beyond any artistic
appreciation, however, such as that quoted above,
Sir Frederick himself would have been likely to
welcome what his friend Canon Rich said to
him one day in later years, when on a visit at
St. Michael's : "This is the first collegiate church
founded in England since the Reformation." The
fact had never struck the Founder himself before.

In 1850 Sir F. Ouseley had taken his
Bachelor of Music degree at Oxford. At that

(a) *St. Stephen's Review*, October 1883.

time some of the authorities in the university had remonstrated with him. Not only did they point out that it was unfitting to take a lower after a higher degree, a Mus. Bac. (in 1850) after M.A. (in 1849); but they seem to have urged that a man of his rank and position should scorn to take any musical degree at all. Sir Frederick, however, knew his own mind even at that time, and viewed the dignity of art from a higher standpoint than that which was then commonly prevalent (*b*). The wider experience gained in his travels abroad would, of course, tend to strengthen his own views on the matter. Accordingly, in 1854, he proceeded to the degree of Doctor of Music, his exercise for the occasion being the oratorio, "The Martyrdom of St. Polycarp" (*c*). The band and chorus consisted chiefly of his personal friends in the university, the soloists being Miss Dolby, Mr. W. H. Cummings, Mr. John Hampton, and Mr Weiss. Great was the composer's delight when, at the last moment, the unmusical Dean Gaisford walked into the "Sheldonian" to be present at the performance

(*b*) On Hallé's arrival in London, immediately after the Revolution of 1848, and in consequence of that event (which drove all the aristocratic patrons of art away from the French capital), he was much struck by the not merely inartistic but absolutely anti-artistic feeling of a considerable section of the English public. For a man to be able to play the piano was looked upon as a sign of effeminacy, and even of vicious tendencies; and Hallé once told the present writer a sad but amusing story of a clergyman who came to him for pianoforte lessons, and before visiting him always threw off his clerical garb to put on the dress of a private gentleman, in the hope that his "slight sin 'gainst *bonos mores*" would thus escape detection ! We have improved since then.—*St. James's Gazette*, October 28, 1895.

(*c*) Cf. p. 115 *infra*.

of the Mus. Doc. exercise. Thus did Sir F. Ouseley continue to use his influence, as when he was an undergraduate, to popularise music in circles where it had hitherto been banned as either an individual craze, or as a mere professional drudgery.

It is said that the present fashion of the Oxford Doctors of Music wearing velvet caps is entirely due to the fact that Sir F. Ouseley, as a gentleman-commoner, continued to wear his velvet cap when he took his Mus. Doc. degree. Other Doctors of Music, seeing this, followed his example, some of the earlier imitators being very much "chaffed" by their contemporaries. Now all Doctors of Music wear the velvet cap, but it is no real part of the Mus. Doc. academic dress.

Early in 1855 Sir H. R. Bishop, the Professor of Music, died; and the Proctors, unsolicited, offered the vacant post to Sir F. Ouseley. Hitherto the office appears to have been little more than a sinecure. Evidently the authorities regarded it cheaply. The following is a copy of the certificate of Sir Frederick's appointment, written on a very common sheet of paper, scarcely worthy of the great university and of one of her professorships :—

UNIVERSITY OF OXFORD.

These are to certify that on this day, namely, the eighth day of May, in the year of our Lord God, one thousand eight hundred and fifty-five, the Reverend Frederick Gore *Ouseley*, Baronet, Master of Arts and Doctor of Music of Christ Church, was duly elected to the office of Professor of Music in this University, vacant by the death of Sir Henry Rowley Bishop, Doc. Mus.

As witness our hands this day and year above written,

JOHN MURRAY HOLLAND, *Senior Proctor.*
ARTHUR F. STOPFORD, *Junior Proctor.*
EDWARD ROWDEN, *Registrar.*

On Trinity Sunday, June 3, 1855 (six years to the day, it would seem, after his ordination as deacon), Sir F. Ouseley was ordained priest by Bishop Hampden in Hereford Cathedral. Two days later he was installed as precentor. Thus within the space of one month, besides receiving his Priest's Orders, he had been appointed to two public offices of more responsibility than pecuniary worth. How much emolument Sir Frederick reaped as precentor of Hereford—an office he faithfully served for the remaining thirty - four years of his life—may be gathered from the following note, in which Bishop Hampden offered him the appointment :—

EATON PLACE, LONDON, *March* 1, 1855.

DEAR SIR FREDERICK,—The Precentorship in Hereford Cathedral is now vacant. I wish to ask you, if it is an office which you would like to fill. The Ecclesiastical Commissioners have appropriated to themselves the revenues of the office, whatever they may have been. *Stat nominis umbra*, I fear, is all that can be said of it now. Still, I think it important that that should be preserved, and worthily embodied in some living Person. All, however, I ask at present is, whether you would like the sort of thing. You will know generally what the duties are of a Precentor, and that he has an assistant in them under the name of a Succentor, who performs them in the absence of his chief. . . . —Yours faithfully, R. D. HEREFORD.

Meantime, whilst the horrors of war were going

on in the Crimea, the church on the peaceful Old Wood Common was slowly rising upwards. By August 1855 the foundations were got out for the college, and in January 1856 the roof was on the church. Sir Frederick, who had all the while been backwards and forwards to Langley, Slough, superintending the work there, now took a house, Spring Grove, on the "Old Wood"; and this was made the headquarters for the first batch of boys when, later on, they arrived from Langley. At this period he was staying on and off at a rectory near Tenbury, and he is remembered as being then in the best of health and spirits. He would run, as hard as he could tear, up and down the rectory stairs, singing the up scale or the down scale, according to his destination. As the staircase contained seventeen steps, it would well include the two octaves, which would be essential for his vocal practice. He was fond also of singing, among other songs, in alto voice, the air out of *L'Allegro*, "Let me wander not unseen," playing his own accompaniment.

The dedication of the new church and college was to be to St. Michael and All Angels, and accordingly preparations were made for a grand Consecration Service on Michaelmas Day, September 29, 1856. The day fell on a Monday that year. Though the morning was cold and wet, the weather gradually improved, and a fine day succeeded. The event caused the greatest interest for many miles round. Every lodging in Tenbury and its neighbourhood was engaged.

The roads were lined with carriages and " carriage-folk," from far and near; so that only a limited number of those who came could gain admission to the church itself. Some of the London musicians who were present made their first acquaintance with Herefordshire mud. The choir was, of course, a mixed one, gathered from various sources; but it comprised representatives from several of the chief musical centres in England. There were fourteen trebles, including C. J. Corfe, now bishop in Korea, and Arthur S. Sullivan, the now celebrated composer, who was then one of the "children" of the Chapel Royal at St. James's Palace; four altos, including Sir F. Ouseley himself; twelve tenors, of whom one was Mr. J. Hampton, the present Warden of St. Michael's, and fifteen basses. A long procession of clergy and laity was marshalled by Colonel Rushout (afterwards Lord Northwick). At 11.30 A.M. Bishop Hampden met the Founder, signed the consecration deed of the Church, and consecrated also the beautiful set of vessels, presented by Miss Georgiana Rushout of Burford, for the celebration of the Holy Eucharist. The prayers were intoned by Sir Frederick, and the Lessons were read by the vicar and curate of Tenbury. Dr. George J. Elvey, the organist of H.M. Chapel Royal, St. George's, Windsor, presided at the organ (d). The service was

(d) This instrument Sir Frederick himself had planned. Great complaints were made of its incomplete state on the day of the consecration. The facts were, that the organ itself had been finished in the factory at least two years before it was wanted, and had been pronounced perfect as

"Rogers in D." The anthems were Boyce's "I have surely built Thee an House," Elvey's "O praise the Lord of Heaven," and Goss's "Praise the Lord." In the middle movement of the latter, Arthur Sullivan sang the treble, and the principal bass parts were taken by Mr. H. Barnby, of Armagh Cathedral choir, and afterwards of Windsor. Bishop Hampden preached the sermon from Ephesians iii. 10 and 11. There were between three hundred and four hundred communicants. Afterwards the churchyard was also consecrated in due form, the whole time of the various functions extending over four hours. A luncheon then followed in the scarcely finished library of the now growing college; and the day ended with the first of those many evening services which have since been offered up from the "Old Wood" Church of St. Michael and All Angels.

The following account of the church, as it was then seen, may be taken as approximately accurate. The account appeared in the newspapers at the time of the consecration, and was probably written by the architect himself. At all events, it is likely to have passed under his eyes, as well as Sir Frederick's, before publication, and so has an interest and accuracy of its own :—

The Church of St. Michael and All Angels is middle pointed in style, and cruciform in plan. It consists of a choir of three bays,

---

to tone and mechanism. But when the organ arrived at St. Michael's, the architect insisted upon some change in its position, which resulted in what the builder prophesied would be serious mischief. It was on this account that the organ could not be got ready for the consecration day.

with a polygonal apse, north and south transepts, and nave, with three large and one smaller bay to the west. There are lean-to rests to the choir and nave, beneath a lofty clerestory, communicating by moulded and corbelled niches with the transepts. The sacrist or vestry is on the south side, adjoining the south aisle. A vaulted passage leads from it round the south transept into the south nave aisle. There is a lean-to north arch. Excepting the aisles, porch, and vestry, the church is groined and vaulted throughout in wood. The ceiling over the choir is treated with colour slightly, but over the apse more elaborately. The pavements are entirely composed of Messrs. Minton's tiles, disposed in different patterns, more richly towards the east, that within the altar railing of minute tessaræ in geometrical figures. The altar-table, under an elaborate canopy, surmounted with a gilt metal cross, stands in the chord of the apse. It is not yet finished, but when completed will have a gorgeous appearance. The stalls and other choir fittings are of oak, the choir-boys' desks being of wrought-iron. A lofty iron screen, with folding gates, divides the choir from the nave, and screens of the like material [? are] in the double arches leading into the choir aisles. The former screen is surmounted by seven candlesticks (in which seven wax candles were placed on the day of consecration). The screen was coloured ultra-marine, and decorated with gold. The south transept will be entirely filled by a magnificent organ of 56 stops, by Flight. It was so far advanced in erection as to be used on the day of consecration. The pipes already in position were richly decorated in diaper pattern. When completed, the pipes will be projecting, and spreading out in front in Spanish form (fan-like shape). The north transept will be used as a baptistery. The font, on a cross-shaped platform and steps, is circular in plan, carved with foliage, and inlaid with green Egyptian marble, surmounted by a rich oak canopy or cover, 22 feet in height. Contiguous to the font is a well, with stone canopy, and arched recess, with stone desk for the registery. The pulpit, which is placed on the north side of the nave, adjoining the screen which divides it from the chancel, is also of stone, and is ornamented with several exquisitely carved figures. At the opposite end of the screen is the lectern (a brazen (e) eagle). The nave will be filled partly with open and movable benches, and partly with

---

(e) Like so many of the lectern eagles made in our generation, the one at St. Michael's was not a conspicuous success. A good old Herefordshire dame was once taken to St. Michael's for a Sunday evening service. When asked her experiences, she answered, "Oh yes, I got a good seat; right up anunst the turkey!"

church chairs. The choir and apse are lighted by nine two-light windows, filled with stained glass, containing figures of angels. The east window represents our Blessed Lord seated in majesty, St. Michael kneeling at His feet, with the usual symbols in allusion to the dedication. From the ceiling of the chancel a number of lamps are suspended, in which camphine will be used. . . . The communion plate and altar vestments are the magnificent gift of Miss Rushout of Burford House, as also is part of the stained glass. Various other offerings to the church have been made by friends of the founder. The church and college, contiguous to and in connection with it, are built with sandstone dug upon the site, grained, and chased with Bath-stone. The roofs are covered with Delabole slating, and a blue stone from the Forest of Dean has been used for the several columns and shafts. The gables are surmounted by crosses, and the western is pierced for two bells. Mr. Woodyer is the architect, and Mr. Chick his clerk of works ; Messrs. Wheeler of Reading are the contractors ; and the undermentioned tradesmen have been employed, viz. Messrs. Woochaffe and Lukes, carpentering and glazing ; Mr. Fisher, decorating ; Messrs. Minchall and White, carving ; Messrs. Hardman, stained glass ; Messrs. Filmes and Mason, ornamental iron-work. The fontcover was executed by the Wood Carving Company in the Belvedere Road, Lambeth. The communion plate was manufactured by Mr. Keith. The length of the church is 114 feet, the chancel being 43 feet 6 inches, and the height from the ground to the cross, 74 feet. The width, including the transepts, 67 feet. The nave is 22 feet wide (with the aisles, 45). From the apex of the ceiling to the ground is 45 feet. The nave and aisles are intended to accommodate 600 persons, although they would evidently hold more. There are two bells placed outside the west front, immediately under the cross (*f*).

Although Sir Frederick's noble gift to the Church generally, and to the neighbourhood of Tenbury in particular, was welcomed warmly in most quarters, yet there were no doubt many, both of clergy and laity, in the diocese of Hereford at that time, to whom his known, or at least his suspected, views on Church matters carried no small amount of alarm. That significant paren-

(*f*) *Worcestershire Chronicle*, October 1, 1856.

thesis—("in which seven wax candles were placed on the day of consecration ")—was evidently inserted in the architect's structural description of the church, above quoted, by the *Worcestershire Chronicle's* reporter. The insertion reveals to us, perhaps, how serious to the popular mind of 1856 was the very moderate amount of ritual (as we should now count it) which then prevailed at St. Michael's. Seven wax candles (? unlighted) at the top of a chancel screen!

There is, however, further and more substantial evidence forthcoming on this point. At the time of the building of St. Michael's, there were living at Bockleton, a few miles off, two brothers named Thomas and John Miller. They were both clergymen, doing duty alternately at the churches of Leysters and Bockleton ; but Thomas, the elder, was also squire of the Bockleton estate. No two men in the neighbourhood were better known ; none were more highly respected. They were old-fashioned English gentlemen, bachelors both, and thorough Churchmen. Their memory is still green in the parish they once served so faithfully. John Miller, the younger of the two brothers, was a man of great ability. He had been Bampton Lecturer at Oxford in 1817 (*g*), and had been the friend of Keble, both in the university and in after years. Keble, indeed, held him in the highest reverence, alike for his piety and his wisdom. He used to call him " Hooker," as being the most judicious of all his friends. Both Keble

(*g*) Lock's *Biography of John Keble*, 2nd ed. pp. 6, 7.

and Wordsworth used to stay with the Millers at Bockleton (*h*). John Miller, with all his spirit of religious seriousness, was exceedingly witty and full of fun. A friend called on him one day, and found him suffering from a bad toothache. His cheek was puffed up to twice its usual size. " I am so sorry," his friend said, "to have come in on you just now." "Oh no!" said the sufferer ; " I am *doubly* glad to see you."

To such a work for the Church as Sir F. Ouseley had now embarked on, the Millers would of course be among the first to wish "God speed." But the following letters read together will show that the gradual development of Sir Frederick's scheme was not only causing alarm in certain quarters, where alarm might have been expected ; but that it had now begun to create misgiving even in John Miller's mind. Such letters as these of his would be worth reproducing, if only as samples of the perfect literary style in which men of the old Oxford School then wrote to one another. They well illustrate, too, that judicious caution which Keble noted as the characteristic of his friend. It should be premised that, in the interval between the consecration of St. Michael's and the writing of these letters, Thomas Miller, the elder of the two brothers, had died. The

(*h*) A mile or so from St. Michael's, across the fields, on the Leysters road, is a spot whence may be seen one of the most beautiful views in this beautiful district. On a ferny bank lies a large stone, called the " Poet's Stone." It bears the initials W. W. But they are cut deep, and evidently by a mason's hand. It is said to have been a favourite walk of Wordsworth when he came to Bockleton. The buildings of St. Michael's now form a striking feature in the foreground of the view.

Deanery of Burford, in its two divisions of East and West, comprises some thirty-five parishes :—

REV. JOHN MILLER TO REV. SIR F. A. G. OUSELEY.

BOCKLETON, *March* 13, 1857.

DEAR SIR FREDERICK,—Before the Church of St. Michael and All Angels was completed, it was felt that a work of such disinterested munificence and piety had a strong claim to some expression of acknowledgment and respect on the part of the neighbourhood. Of course this term had need to be defined ; and therefore the limits of the Deanery of Burford were assigned, in the first instance, as being the Ecclesiastical Division in which the Church is situate.

The day of Consecration, however, gave many others an opportunity of witnessing your noble work, and a consequent desire to take part in an offering so justly due. It was then suggested, that probably the contemplated tribute could take no form more acceptable to yourself than that of placing at your disposal such means as might be raised towards adorning the west window of the Church in a manner corresponding with those in the Chancel.

As treasurer of a subscription entered into for this object, with sanction of the Bishop, and of the other Ecclesiastical authorities of the Deanery, it is now my duty to hand over to you (clear of all deduction) an amount of two hundred and seventy pounds, together with a detailed list of the contributors. And I trust it may be as gratifying to yourself to accept this expression of goodwill, as I feel sure, from manifold evidences, it is to them to offer it to your acceptance—with every earnest wish that your good work may prosper, and that you may live long to witness and rejoice in the fruits of it.

I venture to add, personally, that it was a great satisfaction to one who zealously promoted this offering, by a liberal example in the outset, to know that the desired means had been secured, although his valuable life has not been spared to see the project carried into execution.—Believe me, dear Sir Frederick, faithfully yours, JOHN MILLER.

———

95

LIFE OF SIR F. A. G. OUSELEY

*Private and needing
no notice.*   BOCKLETON, *March* 14, 1857.

DEAR SIR FREDERICK,—It seems advisable to accompany the *official* note, which travels with this, with a few private explanations; in respect of one of which I shall trust entirely to your kindness for not misconstruing me.

First let me say, with great pleasure, respecting the contributions generally, that you could not have wished for anything more agreeable than the prevailing spirit in which they were given. In sending you one note for special illustration of this, I am only doing justice to an entirely disinterested subscriber, on whom there was no claim at all. He does not reside within the Deanery, and I was not aware of his having been present at the Consecration; until an accidental mention of such fact, at a late day, and of the delight he had taken in it, led me to write to him: and lo! the result.

It seems well to let you see an answer in a very different tone, where there was special ground of claim upon the writer. The name is suppressed, but the copy is true; and I have subjoined a fragment of what I wrote in reply, that you may see how little *sympathy* I have with this correspondent, though there may be some agreement between us in *opinion*. And here it is that I need your indulgence.

I should feel, then, that my own part in a crusade (*i*), which I rejoice to think has proved so successful, might be misunderstood by you if I did not honestly confess myself largely dissentient from what I cannot but think the hyper-ritualism of St. Michael's; and also, that the whole scale of the establishment is something altogether different from what we had any conception of here, when the subject of a site was first broached. Hence it has been a main object with ourselves throughout (I speak as if my brother was not lost) to conciliate just forbearance towards what is unquestionably a startling innovation in these parts, and obviously open to unkind constructions. And it seemed desirable to show, by holding out the right hand of fellowship, that your work was not regarded with fear or jealousy by persons of such old-fashioned pattern and notions as ourselves; nor yet by the Bishop, or by any officials of the Deanery. But *we* have all along regarded the extent of your plan as a great local mistake; and I would fain express an earnest hope that you will be careful not to damage a good cause by any such

---

(*i*) The "crusade" appears to have been the attack on the contributors.

form of excess as might possibly lead to unthinking resistance. I should not think it becomingly respectful to say more than this ; but I cannot feel it consistent with perfect sincerity to say less. Not to have felt respect for your noble generosity would have been cold-hearted indeed. . . . —With kind regards and every good wish, believe me, dear Sir Frederick, very sincerely yours,

JOHN MILLER.

[No. 1 Enclosure, referred to in above Letter.]

——, A NEIGHBOURING LAYMAN, TO REV. JOHN MILLER.

Dec. 1856.

MY DEAR SIR,—With many thanks for your kind letter and circular, I beg to say I have great pleasure in giving the enclosed ten pound note in aid of the stained window proposed in St. Michael's Church ; and I am very glad to find you are going to present a small tribute of respectful acknowledgment to Sir Frederick Ouseley—whose noble generosity I, in common with everyone in this neighbourhood, must ever most highly appreciate. And I sincerely wish him health for very many years to see his good work prosper.—Believe me, etc.,

[No. 2 Enclosure referred to.]

—— TO REV. JOHN MILLER.

Dec. 1856.

DEAR SIR,—I am obliged by the favour of your letter, which has placed me in some difficulty. Not knowing whether St. Michael's is intended to carry out the ceremonial practices and principles of St. Barnabas, Pimlico, I am unwilling, by subscribing, to give countenance to anything of that kind, at the same time that I duly appreciate the earnestness and sincerity of Sir F. Ouseley.—I beg to remain, etc.,

FRAGMENT OF REJOINDER TO ABOVE BY REV. JOHN MILLER.

After mention of the cordial sanction received in every way, and at every step (as believed), of the Bishop of the Diocese, I wrote :

7

"I cannot think, under such circumstances, that we who subscribe to the window make ourselves in any way responsible for—
still less, that we acquire any right to object to—the mode of performing Service."

"I will not give up anything, if I once commence" (*j*) — such had been Sir Frederick's
determination before ever his foundation was
established. He had no doubt seen ritual
troubles enough at St. Barnabas, and would wish
for no more. On the one hand, it would seem
that he had not been in absolutely full accord
with everything that had been done there (*k*).
He did not go all lengths with Mr. Bennett,
nor, indeed, with his own sisters, probably,
as to the vital importance of particular ritual
points. But, on the other hand, he had long
cherished a high ideal of how all that was offered
to God should be of the best possible kind. He
had founded St. Michael's at a time when the
standard of Church worship in England was de-
plorably low, and his heart's desire was to raise
it. Some men, by their very natural strength of
will, manage to carry all before them within the
range of their own personal influence. Others,
conscious that they do not possess this natural
will-power, have to fall back upon the bases of
their own principles. Sir Frederick belonged to
this latter class. He could be as resolute as anyone on points of principle which he had once
thought out; and the resolution of never giving
up anything that he had once begun was faith-

(*j*) Cf. p. 74 *supra*.　　　　(*k*) Cf. p. 64 *supra*.

fully adhered to in the future history of St. Michael's. It was undoubtedly the wisest course a man of his disposition could have taken. Any irritation which may have been caused at first, by the "ceremonial practices and principles" of St. Michael's, soon gave way before the genial influence of his simple character, combined, as it was, with transparent honesty of purpose. St. Michael's ceased before long to be regarded in the light of a "startling innovation," and became with all classes a favourite institution, of which the neighbourhood is justly proud.

This may perhaps be the best place for noting, what is an undoubted fact, that, from the outset, Sir Frederick himself regarded the foundation of St. Michael's as to some extent a restitution, on his part, of Church property. Whether through the purchase of the Hall Barn estate, or otherwise, it does not appear ; but he certainly believed that some temporal advantage had accrued to his patrimony from a sacrilegious source. There is evidence that he often thought and spoke to his friends in this sense, by way of justification, as it were, of his munificent contribution to God's service from his own private means. One can well imagine how, to a heart like his, sensitive in the highest degree to all instincts of honour and religion, such a manifold restitution as he made must have been a real relief as well as a great joy. Some people would call this superstition. Others of us prefer to regard it as simply honourable dealing in the highest relations of life.

CHAPTER VI

SIR FREDERICK OUSELEY'S best friends could
never have claimed for him that he was a good
man of business. In truth, he lacked many of
those practical qualities required for developing
with success such an institution as St. Michael's.
One most valuable faculty, however, he did
possess even in this direction, namely, the faculty
of keeping a single end in view. From the time
when St. Michael's was first founded, down to the
day of Sir Frederick's death, he had before him,
as his one chief aim in life, the improvement, in
accordance with his own high ideal, of Church
worship in England. The work he did for the
Church was indeed manifold; but nearly all of it
tended towards this one object.

The noblest passages in *Paradise Lost* are said
to have been composed whilst Milton's daughter
played to her father on the organ. And Dr.
Pusey, in one of his University sermons,—that on
Dominus Illuminatio Mea (Ps. xxvii. 1),—speaks
of "the almost spiritual properties of harmony."
Music, with its wondrous power over the soul of

man, is, he says, "the echo, as it were, of the harmony of all creation." No doubt Sir F. Ouseley felt all this in his own person to the highest degree. But his work in life was to make other people feel it, and to make them feel it in connection with the Church (a). In his view, the highest form of music was sacred music. The highest purposes to which musical gifts could be applied were those of divine worship. But if music be the common language of the world,—the language understood by all, or nearly all, people, and if beautiful Church music does make most worshippers more conscious of the presence of God,—then to what higher use could a musician like Sir Frederick have devoted his "one talent" than to the improvement of choral worship?

In accordance with this guiding principle, the Services of the Church always took the first place at St. Michael's. Alike from a devotional and a musical point of view, Sir Frederick sought to make those Services of the highest order. Hence he always insisted on the strictest punctuality and regularity in all things connected with them. Everything else had to give way to their regular and careful performance. To him a Service was a Service always. It was not a cut-and-dried musical performance for the congregation to listen to. It was an actual offering up of prayer and of praise to God. Moreover, proportionate to his recognition of this truth was his own intense enjoyment of the Service itself. Undoubtedly, to

(a) Cf. p. 79 *supra*.

many minds the expression of such joy might at times naturally present its ludicrous side. But there is surely another side to the question. Although the dancing of David before the Ark was a ludicrous, if not a contemptible, sight to Michal, yet it was Michal's judgment which was at fault in the matter. We English are proverbially cold-blooded, unemotional, in our religion as in other things. All the more may we be thankful that there are worshippers still left in our midst who can now and again, forgetting themselves and their fellow-creatures, remember only the divine Object of their worship. Sir Frederick Ouseley was one who could, and often did, so forget himself. And, though his direct influence with the simpler poor may sometimes have been weakened for the moment by an un-English ecstasy, yet even in this way he taught them definitely one much-needed lesson, *i.e.* that there is such a thing to be found as enjoyment in the worship of God.

It may well be imagined how, to one who thus loved the sacred Services of the Church, every part of the building, too, with all its various ornaments and furniture, would be very dear. In the account of St. Michael's Church, quoted above (*b*), it has already been noticed that a special well had been dug beneath the Church floor, for baptismal use only. The whole appearance of the Baptistery, with its raised font and lofty font-cover, as also of the Altar, with its striking canopy, or baldachino, testifies to that prominence which

(*b*) Cf. p. 91 *supra.*

the Church of England assigns to her two great Sacraments. As Sir Frederick had given to God's glory, and continued to give, of his best, so nothing touched him more deeply than the gifts he occasionally received from friends for the adornment of St. Michael's. For many of these he had to thank his good friend, Miss Rushout of Burford; and it was to her, as their most generous benefactress, that he wrote as follows, some ten years after St. Michael's was founded—on a certain occasion when a present of a beautiful Lenten altar cloth had been made to the church *by every member of the college :*—

I was, of course, immensely gratified, for it showed such good feeling towards myself, besides the higher motive, which I appreciate even more. No one has a greater right than you to be the first to know of any good done to us here ; for no one has been— no one can ever hardly be—so great a friend to us as you have been. So I beg you to rejoice with me—as indeed I know you will—and pray for all those who have joined in this work—for you *know* how we always think of you in our prayers.

Among other treasures belonging to St. Michael's, and well worth a close inspection, is the altar-book, or missal, handwritten throughout and marvellously executed. It was the work of the late J. C. Büdinger, for a long while a member of the choir, and master of the parish school. He was a wonderful penman, and copied and wrote out a vast quantity of music for Sir Frederick at various times.

It was, however, the organ which would naturally attract most attention on the part of those who visited the Old Wood Church. As might have

been expected, Sir Frederick Ouseley was not
easily satisfied in the matter of organ-building ;
and probably some of his greatest disappoint-
ments must have been connected with the early
failures to procure an instrument worthy, not
merely of that particular Church, but of his own
high ideal of a model service and choir.   The
original organ, of fifty-six stops, was built, as has
been already mentioned (c), by Flight of London.
After ten years or so this was reconstructed, and
enlarged to the number of sixty-five stops, by
Harrison of Rochdale.   The instrument still
proving unsatisfactory, it was added to and re-
built by Willis of London, in 1873–74.   Some
further improvements have since been made.
Organ-building on the scale of Sir Frederick's
tastes must have been very expensive work ; but
with his devotion to high aims, he grudged nothing in the cause of sacred music.   In his later
years the front pipes, instead of projecting, as
they used to do in the fan-like Spanish form,
were placed upright in the ordinary way.   There
were good reasons, no doubt, for the change, but
not a little was lost to the eye in artistic effect.

As a preacher there can be little doubt but
that Sir F. Ouseley might have done, from the
mere human point of view, a great deal more than
he did.   He had several of the chief gifts which
make an attractive preacher, using the word
"attractive" in its highest sense.   To begin with,
besides his clear, high-pitched voice, he had an

(c) Cf. p. 91 supra.

exceptionally clear and logical mind. This enabled him, to a certain extent, to make deep subjects plain to the simplest people. Some of his sermons were models in this respect. He had also a wonderfully retentive memory. He could write a sermon, as indeed any other production of his pen, and could then, with a very slight effort, learn it by heart. It has been said that, though he usually preached written sermons, he could, on occasion, preach "extempore" with telling effect. More probably these "extempore" sermons attributed to him were, like most others so - called, only "extempore" to the extent of being delivered, *ex ore*, without paper. At all events, he has been known at times, when the pulpit was ill-lighted, to set aside his MS., and trust to memory alone to complete his subject. He had also one other preaching gift, the greatest, perhaps, of all, and one of the rarest, namely, that he could at times entirely forget himself. Some one, for instance, who once heard him preach on Galatians vi. 14,—*God forbid that I should glory, save in the cross of our Lord Jesus Christ, by Whom the world is crucified unto me, and I unto the world,*—recalls the wonderfully rapt and transformed look with which his whole face was lighted up as he unfolded the great secret of St. Paul's life—that same secret which went so far to inspire his own. It is manifest that a man with gifts like these must have had no little power of drawing, not only the attention, but the hearts of his hearers. Nevertheless, it should be acknowledged that, in this matter of preaching, as in most other branches of his work, Sir F. Ouseley lacked that power of sustained application which can alone ensure the highest permanent results. Whilst all preachers are variable, men of Sir F. Ouseley's temperament are likely to be most so. Moreover, he laboured under one other disadvantage in this respect. His own view of the place of preaching in the Church Services was not a high one. To him, as might be expected, Worship was the great object of all church-going. And so, in his view, the sermon took not only a second place, but one very far behind the prayers and the praise and the music. "What was the Text?" is a question often asked in connection with some Churches. The proverbial question asked by most absentees from St. Michael's used to be—"What was the Anthem?" (d).

The population of the Old Wood parish is about 600. The church itself, though in the diocese of Hereford, stands actually in the county of Worcester. But, looking westwards, it is almost within a stone's-throw of Herefordshire,—Cadmore brook being the boundary,—and a large part of the parish lies in that county. Sir Frederick, partly by reason of his many outside engagements, and partly also from his own gentle and conceding nature, could never have been all that is sometimes associated with the idea of a model parish Priest. For that idea involves to a certain extent

(d) Two examples of Sir F. Ouseley's sermons will be found in Appendix B ; see *infra*, pp. 123 ff.

the quality of masterfulness, a quality of which he
was wholly devoid. Nevertheless, he was the last
man to forget that, as vicar of a country parish, he
held the charge of the souls therein. The parish
was worked and visited on a settled system, he
himself taking one side, and his valued fellow-
worker and assistant curate, the Rev. J. Hampton, taking the other. Any parishioner in sickness,
or in trouble, appealing to Sir Frederick, as many
a one did, might be always sure of a ready hand
and a tender heart. His people loved him in no
ordinary sense of the word, regarding him, it
would almost seem, rather as the child than as the
father of the parish. Nothing, perhaps, could
better describe the feeling cherished towards him
by his simpler parishioners than the title "St.
Frederick" once given him by one of the Old
Wood dames. Quite likely it may have been only a
slip of the tongue, or, maybe, a mistaken estimate
of the worth of an English baronetcy, but it conveyed a real impression which existed with regard
to the Founder and first Vicar of St. Michael's.

As Warden of a College, with accommodation
for thirty boys or more, Sir Frederick's duties
were no doubt defined clearly enough in its statutes
and constitution by his own hand. He never
took part himself either in the regular educational
course of the school, or even in the musical instruction of the choir. He had not the patience,
even if he had any of the other qualities, requisite
to make a good teacher. But the college duties
which he had reserved to himself were neither

forgotten nor neglected. He always considered himself as responsible, in the last resort, for the general management, discipline, and tone of the place. He had strict notions about manners, and his influence with the boys in this respect was most marked and wholesome. The school was once described as one combining (*e*) "the manners of Eton with the enthusiasm of Leipsic." Certainly Sir Frederick did his best in both directions. He was fond of "taking out the boys," that is, of taking out one or two of them at a time for a walk, or when he went to call on some friend in the neighbourhood. In this way he would get to know each boy individually. He was happy with boys; and they, seeming to catch his spirit, were happy with him. Needless to say, he was not a little proud, too, of those who were the ripening fruits of his own planting and his life's work. It was also his invariable custom, when the boys were of age to be confirmed, to prepare them himself with regular instruction for the sacred "laying on of hands." Nor did he lose sight of them when they left St. Michael's. He was a voluminous correspondent, not in the sense of writing long letters, but in the sense of writing many, and to many people. Especially was he always eager to keep in touch, through pen and ink, with old St. Michael's boys; and the letters he wrote to them formed no small part of his heavy correspondence. He loved his boys with more than a mere general feeling of affection.

<hr>

(*e*) *St. Stephen's Review*, October 1883.

The following reminiscence (*f*) illustrates with what thoughtful tenderness he still studied their feelings, even when they had left his charge :—

Once, having just received a letter from an old St. Michael's College boy, which was merely an outcome of affection, and contained nothing of importance, Sir Frederick, who was in a few minutes about to start for Oxford, sat down immediately to write an answer, saying to me, " I *never* leave a boy's letter unanswered : it is not fair to their good nature, and I do not know when I may have time to write if I don't do it at once."

This was one secret of that individual remembrance of his boys, which was the more striking in his case, because, even during their school days, he was often called away from their midst by his other duties, and because also he took no practical part in their daily education. None the less, he was the real Warden, as well as the real Founder, of his College,—honoured by all, loved by all. Familiarly known as "the Bart."—or, as one valued member of the staff (not of English extraction) used to term it, "the Chevalier,"—he drew all hearts in the College to him by his guileless, affectionate disposition. He was the College Orpheus, if the simile may be pardoned by those whom he drew after him with no stronger force than the sweet music of his own life and example. A good many years ago one who had been a choir boy at St. Michael's somehow came to grief in England, and enlisted as a private soldier. In that capacity he went out to one of the South African wars. Entering the Cathedral at Cape

(*f*) From the pen of the Rev. V. K. Cooper, once Headmaster of St. Michael's, and now Precentor of Durham.

Town, the first bars of music he heard were from the "March" out of *Polycarp*, played as a voluntary. What thoughts must that familiar "March" have then recalled of him who wrote it, and of the far-off St. Michael's where, as a choir-boy, Private —— had often heard it played!

St. Michael's has often been spoken of as a mere musical school. To Sir Frederick himself it was of course primarily, and by its very constitution, a place of religious education, his "one talent" (*g*) of music being made a leading feature in the service of religion. Since Sir Frederick Ouseley's death, one (*h*), keenly alive to all educational instincts, has visited St. Michael's in his official capacity, and has paid tribute to the indelible influences of a religious training such as that which is there afforded. Having spoken of the beautiful choral Services daily rendered at St. Michael's, and of the memories which such Services would awaken in the boys' after lives, he said :—

This, then, is my closing word. Your school is a favoured one, and you enjoy many privileges belonging to it. Amidst such surroundings, and under such influences as prevail here, it is easier for you than for most others to grow up, through a happy boyhood, to a strong, and pure, and reverent Christian manhood. And we, your elders, as we look on your life, or share in your worship, pray that you may not be found unworthy of this beautiful home of your early days, in which its pious founder intended that you should be trained, each and all of you, to be loyal and faithful servants of God, and of His Holy Church. These walls stand here in the

---

(*g*) Cf. p. 75 *supra*.

(*h*) Bishop Percival (of Hereford), preaching on Acts vii. 48, 49, at the St. Michael's Commemoration Service, on October 3, 1895.

midst of your daily life, and witness to your souls, as they are a witness to all who look on them, that you recognise a place and times, in which it is your duty to draw near to God in a peculiar sense, in order that you may live nearer to Him at all times and in all places. So it comes to pass that your share in the Services of this House is a gift of great price to you ; it sinks into your growing life as the sign and seal of a Holy Presence.

Sir Frederick took sadly to heart all the worries and anxieties inseparable from such an institution as he had founded. He is remembered on one occasion to have suddenly appeared in a neighbour's house in a grievous state of distress, having had to give notice to one of his staff. He came in, sat down, flung up his hands, and said : " I won't go back as long as he is in the place." Here, too, is another typical pouring forth of his woe, in a letter written to an Oxford friend, at a time when nearly the whole staff of St. Michael's College was rendered *hors de combat* :—

MY DEAR ——, Certainly my name should be connected with the " —— Memorial Fund," and I am obliged to you for naming it. I feel, however, I can't be as liberal towards it as I could have been last year ; for, like all landed proprietors, I have had severe losses of late, and am retrenching in every possible *personal* way, so as not to injure my College. Still, of course, I will contribute *something.*

We have had such a wretched Christmas. I was down with bad Influenza for a whole week. —— has had a narrow escape of rheumatic fever, and is still very seedy. —— kept his room for a week, and is now away for a couple of days to recruit. —— was so bad that I have had to play the Organ for him. Most of the boys had bad colds, and there was more barking than singing in Church. Twice we have had to have a monotoned Service, and no Anthem. We could not have our annual Concert for the Farmers, nor could we have our children's treat, because of the prevalence of whooping-cough in the parish. So you see we have been in a bad way indeed ! And when you add to all these miseries, the anxiety consequent on a change of Headmasters, and the fact of my having had to dismiss a page-boy at a moment's notice for gross negligence, you will agree that I have had a very bad time of it. . . . —Believe me always very sincerely yours,

FREDERICK A. G. OUSELEY.

This mention of the negligent page-boy—the last drop in the Warden's bitter cup—recalls the fact that it was the domestic part of college life for which Sir Frederick was least fitted, and which he naturally found most irksome. If it were not pathetic, it might well furnish a comedy to trace out some of the various experiences in household management through which the first Warden of St. Michael's passed at one period or another of his lifetime. And, indeed, much as he fretted about the troubles at the time, he himself was usually only too ready, when they were over, to view them from their comic side. Another of his pages once gave notice to leave, on the ground that he had "no time to think." And in the case of a third youth, whose general duties lay in the line of "Day & Martin," but who on this occasion had been accused of poaching, the Warden used to give a graphic description of how he himself sat, as Rhadamanthus, on the kitchen dresser, hearing the evidence for and against the culprit. By the way, this youth was of a particularly staid and serious character. He was only known to laugh twice in the course of each year — at cider-making and at pig-killing! The truth is, that, as has been said already, Sir Frederick was no man of business ; yet he was too conscientious to ignore those duties which he felt devolved on him as the head of his own establishment. Fortunately, throughout his whole life at St. Michael's, he had the ever-present aid of his friend, and his now successor in the Wardenship, the Rev. John Hampton. He, in all practical matters, whether as Choirmaster, Curate, or Sub-Warden, proved an invaluable helper. To him especially must be attributed not only the splendid choral training of the boys, but also the loving care with which the whole place has been always kept—Church, Churchyard, and College grounds alike.

Amongst the treasures prized at St. Michael's comes first, of course, the magnificent musical library, said to be the most valuable and extensive private collection in England. The collection is lodged in what used to be called Sir Frederick's "study," and is thus described : (i)—

It contains nearly 2000 volumes, mostly rare full scores and treatises, including, among other things, the old Palais Royal collection, with the French Royal Arms on the covers, consisting of scores of operas, motets, etc., by Lully, Colasse, Destouches, Lalande, Campra, and many other French composers now forgotten. There is also a very large collection of MS. Italian sacred music of the Palestrina schools, copied from the magnificent library of the late Abbate Santini of Rome. Then they possess a very valuable MS. of Handel's *Messiah*, partly in that immortal composer's own autograph, and partly in that of J. C. Smith. It was from this copy that Handel conducted the work on its first performance in Dublin, and it contains various readings and curious annotations in Handel's own handwriting. Amongst the autographs in this library may be mentioned a large collection of curious fugal music, original and selected, in the handwriting of Dr. Crotch ; a full score of Spohr's Symphonies, and autographs of Orlando di Lasso,

____

(i) Sir George Grove's *Dictionary of Music and Musicians*, vol. ii. p. 423.

8

of Benevoli, Blow, Croft, Bononcini, Travers, Boyce, Arnold, Mozart, Paganini, and Mendelssohn. Probably the only copy in England of Eslava's *Lira Sacro-Hispano* is in this library, which also contains copies of all the treatises of Galorius, including the earliest and rarest one, published in Naples in 1480.

This library also contains the forty-part song by Tallis. Besides these musical treasures, Sir Frederick Ouseley and his father had collected between them a very fine general library as well (*j*). This consists of French and Oriental books, with numerous works on theology, archæ-ology, and topography, and is arranged in the large library of the college.

As to Sir F. Ouseley's musical writing and composition, although his pen worked probably by fits and starts, yet it never seems to have lain wholly idle for long. One of his earliest pro-ductions, after settling down at St. Michael's, was, in conjunction with Dr. E. G. Monk, at first the organist at Radley College, for many years after-wards organist of York Minster, to arrange and point the Psalter for chanting. This work was undertaken in a thoroughly practical and painstaking way, and has probably formed the basis of the various improved Psalters since published. The general plan having been pre-arranged, the two musicians worked together at frequent meetings, for several years, either at Tenbury, Radley, or York. Their aim was to steer between the two extremes of "syllabic" and "polysyllabic" pointing.

Together also with Dr. Monk, Sir Frederick

(*j*) Cf. p. 4 *supra*.

edited, later on, the popular collection of *Monk and Ouseley's Anglican Psalter Chants.* He likewise contributed several tunes to *Hymns Ancient and Modern,* besides giving much general advice, in connection with that far - famed book, to its editor, Sir Henry Baker of Monkland, near Leominster, who was his own neighbour and intimate friend. Sir Frederick's larger musical works (*k*) comprise his two oratorios (*l*), *St. Polycarp* and *Hagar,* two string quartettes, two organ sonatas, three andantes, some forty preludes and fugues, a large number of anthems and services, besides several glees, madrigals, and songs. He also edited the cathedral services and anthems of many of our old English masters. His educational treatises on harmony, counterpoint and fugue, musical form and general composition, were published by the Clarendon Press, and became standard works, passing into two or more editions. They are all scholarly and accurate works, and they are written throughout in his usual lucid style, alike of language and thought. He was also a contributor to Sir George Grove's *Dictionary of Music and Musicians,* begun in 1879; and rendered invaluable service to the cause of general musical knowledge in England by editing and supervising Præger's translation of Dr. Emil Naumann's

(*k*) See Appendix D, Catalogue of Sir F. Ouseley's Compositions, by Mr. J. S. Bumpus.

(*l*) *Hagar* was produced at the Hereford Festival in 1873, and performed in 1874 at the Crystal Palace. *St. Polycarp* was performed at the Hereford Festival in 1888. Cf. p. 85 *supra.*

History of Music, the translation being one of Cassell's popular serial editions. He wrote three chapters for this work,—" Early English Music," " Music in England in the Middle Ages," and " Music in England after the Reformation,"— which, though naturally sketchy, formed an excellent conspectus of the progress of the art in this country, and served to show the importance of English music, rendering a measure of justice to our too much neglected native composers, more especially to those who had written for the Church.

Besides making these more solid contributions to musical literature, Sir Frederick was very fond of devising all kinds of musical puzzles.

"All students," he said, "should make it a rule to write at least one canon every day ; I did so myself for twenty-five years, and I have never had occasion to regret it."

Only four nights before his death he was amusing himself, before going to bed, by composing a strict canon, 12 in 6 (*m*). No doubt he kept his hand in constant practice of this kind in order to preserve that wonderful faculty in fugue and counterpoint with which he had been naturally endowed. For in his day he was accounted the best extempore fugue player in England. Sir Herbert Oakeley, Professor of Music in the University of Edinburgh, one of Sir Frederick's oldest friends, was of opinion that (*n*)—

No living British organist surpassed Ouseley in this now rare art. . . . He would treat a fugal theme in its various contrapuntal

---

(*m*) Cf. p. 225 *infra*.　　　(*n*) Havergal's *Memorials*, p. 58.

possibilities, introducing "inversion," "augmentation," "stretto," etc., if either device were feasible, and never abandoning legitimate style. I know of very few published fugues by Englishmen better than some of his improvisations.

Indeed, it was said by the late Sir George Macfarren, the Cambridge Professor of Music, that after Ouseley's death this particular kind of performance, in its highest sense, would have to be considered almost a lost art.

Mr. T. L. Southgate also bears the following testimony to Sir F. Ouseley's remarkable powers of this kind :—

When seated at the organ or pianoforte, a never-failing inspiration came to him, such as perhaps rarely happened when he sat down to write quietly; a flow of melody, all the resources of harmony, a classic and refined feeling, joined to the profound scholarship which resulted from a complete mastery of counterpoint and the constructive side of music, were all present. He could play with ease in any style or form of composition desired. The art of extempore playing seems to be a dying art in our day, and particularly so as regards the severe type of organ music, *i.e.* the fugue and sonata styles. Perhaps the fugue form, over which this master seemed easily to triumph, used to astonish his listeners, who were capable of appreciating this lofty species of scientific music, the most. Indeed, it has been said that these marvellous improvisations were really not played on the spur of the moment, but were studied in advance, easily stored in his memory, and then played when the occasion required. But there seems to be no truth in this conjecture. Over and over again, friends were asked by Sir Frederick to give him a subject when seated at the instrument. Once, when I was staying at St. Michael's, Sir Frederick gave us several evenings of extemporisation, sometimes at the organ in the Church and sometimes at the pianoforte in the drawing-room. For these feats I was told off to write fresh subjects; and I purposely made some of them particularly cranky and difficult to treat strictly, or to develop according to the customary devices. But nothing seemed to baulk this learned and ready player. Subject and answer, augmentation and diminution, episode, the working of the second subject

with the first, inversion, stretto, pedal point, the "knot," and
coda came out from his richly-endowed brain and ready fingers
with ease. On one occasion I supplied a theme in C sharp
major, previously thought out and made especially troublesome to
work. Sir Frederick looked at it as he put the music paper on the
desk, and frowned a little. When the performance was over, he
said quietly, "What a villainous task you set me,—but," he added
with a little smile, " I don't think I disgraced myself"; and that
was indeed true. One noticed that after such feats the player
often showed a considerable amount of exhaustion, and would do
no more work until he went to bed.

But musical curiosities of every kind had
always a great fascination for him ; and some of
his cleverest compositions are oddities of design
and construction,—musical epigrams, as it were,
or sometimes musical mazes, yet always true to
the strictest lines of classical law. Such were his
set of fugues on the Oxford chimes, with which
he used often to charm his musical friends on the
pianoforte. Some of these, it is feared, are now
lost for ever, but Sir John Stainer possesses two
of his fugues in autograph on the Magdalen
chimes. Other productions of Sir F. Ouseley's
pen were the canon that could be sung backwards,
upside down, and as it appeared on the reverse
side of the paper when held up to the light
(Haydn also wrote something of this kind); the
chant modulating up a semitone at each repetition,
written at the request of a man who wanted to
cure his choir of singing flat; and the clever
twelve-part chorus, " War, Wine, and Harmony,"
written at Cambridge, by the Oxford Professor of
Music, to show what the sister University could do.
It is said that this chorus was written one night

when someone had said that Oxford musicians could not do eight - part work. The leading Oxford musician was put on his mettle, and came down to breakfast next morning with his *opus* in his hand.

Sir John Stainer has given the following description of some of the Ouseley canons in his possession : (*o*)—

I have, I am glad to say, preserved a considerable number of these, and I have brought them here to-day for you to see and examine. Here is a *Gloria Patri* in Canon, 4 in 2 at the under 5th and 8th. Another is 3 in 1 at the under 7th and 8th, a most troublesome thing to construct. On the back of one of these slips I find an ingenious little canon sixteen bars in length, in three parts ; the second part answering the first by inversion, while the third part is the first part by augmentation. One page of MS., contains four ingenious canons, which evidently gave him as much amusement as trouble to construct : the first is 3 in 1 at the under 5th and 11th ; the second, 4 in 1 at the under 6th, 11th, and 16th ; the third, 3 in 1 at the under 17th and 19th by inversion ; the last is 3 in 1 by double augmentation. At the bottom of the page he wrote : " A page of the driest possible music, to console those who suffer from the effects of moist weather."

It is quite true that they are dry musically, but as specimens of his skill and patience they are most valuable. When he had brought a difficult canon to a successful issue, he used to burst out laughing, and clap his hands for joy like a child. He has also written across the top of the canons I have just described : " Heavy artillery discharged on the night of Dec. 20th, being St. Thomas's Eve, in defence of a fortress closely besieged by envy and malice, and garrisoned by yᵉ Oxford Professor." Along the side he wrote : "The notes on this page were made to establish the reputation of our Cathedral dignitaries by one of their own body, who hopes to put cavillers to flight—i.e. *qui inimicos* fugare *sperat*," which, of course, might mean—"hopes to make his cavillers write fugues."

(*o*) *The Character and Influence of the late Sir Frederick Ouseley*, an Address delivered on Dec. 2, 1889, and published (1890) by Novello, Ewer, & Co., in the *Proceedings of the Musical Association*, p. 35.

Sir Frederick was also an omnivorous reader on all musical subjects : (*p*)—

His knowledge of music was almost universal, and extended from St. Ambrose to Wagner. He was a most accomplished linguist, and in his magnificent library of upwards of 2000 volumes (besides enormous quantities of full scores and other music), there was only one book which he had not read through. This was a Spanish treatise on harmony, of Brobdignagian proportions ; but at the time of his decease he had perused 1700 pages of it.

The following appreciation of Sir Frederick as a musical scholar was written by Mr. T. L. Southgate, in the *Musical Standard* of April 28, 1889:—

His ripened knowledge, profound scholarship, and grasp of every phase of the history and science of music, were astonishing. There seemed no department of it that he had not investigated, no difficult problem that he had not probed and formed a judgment upon. His extensive knowledge was ever at the service of those who asked him for information ; he could add something more to the laboriously - acquired knowledge of every student. A good classical scholar, he was also a great linguist and reader ; consequently no work on music appeared to have escaped his observation. He seemed to have read everything. The curious treatises of the old Greek philosopher-musicians were as familiar to him as the obscure writings of the mediæval monks, the learned works of French, Italian, and Spanish writers of a bygone age, and the last new theory of harmony by some aspirant who fondly fancied he had solved all root difficulties, and placed harmony on a basis that the merest tyro could understand and appreciate. He knew them all, and his logical and critical powers enabled him to judge these works at their proper appraisement In the literature of music proper he was just as well read. He was acquainted with the various works of the great masters, and yet could go back beyond these, century after century, describing early counterpoint, the gradual growth of the art through the many ages, until it was firmly settled on its present basis, showing just where each departure and fresh advance took place, quoting and playing from the store of his wonderful memory passages and pieces culled from all times

(*p*) For the following quotation, and for some of the matter on the preceding pages, see Havergal's *Memorials*, pp. 14, 45, and 60.

and schools, to illustrate his discourse. Nothing seems to have escaped his notice,—he had read deeply, and he forgot nothing.

As to his method of composition, like most other great musicians, he had a wonderful power of "thinking in music." He used to say that when composing he had it all in his mind before putting it down on paper. This faculty of mental composition could not be better described than in the following reminiscence furnished by the present Bishop of Wakefield (Bishop Walsham How), formerly rector of Whittington, Salop, who stayed more than once at St. Michael's as Sir Frederick's guest :—

> Three things which he told me remain in my memory. 1. He told me that wherever he went, especially in walking about his parish, music was always passing through his mind. 2. He said he never thought of a tune, or of any piece of music, by the treble part alone, all the harmony being equally present to him. 3. He assured me he could enjoy reading Bach or Beethoven in his arm-chair more than he could listening to them at a concert, because when he read the music to himself *there were no false notes.*

Finally, as to the real place which Sir F. Ouseley's name deserves to occupy in the world of music as a composer, the subject must be left for fuller discussion to the two chapters at the end of this book. But meanwhile it may be well to record here Sir John Stainer's view on the question. After paying tribute to Sir Frederick's memory as a man of genius and as a friend, the present Professor of Music at Oxford thus proceeds : (*q*)—

(*q*) *Vide* Sir John Stainer's Address on *The Character and Influence of the late Sir Frederick Ouseley*, pp. 36, 37, in the *Proceedings of the Musical Association* (1890).

In the sphere of historical knowledge of his art, probably no contemporary surpassed him ; but as a composer it is impossible not to feel that he ought to have secured a higher position than he did.

This disappointing fact must be ascribed partly to the neglect of that technical training which even a genius cannot dispense with, partly to what I conceive to be the false historical view which he formed of music, especially of Church music. For this false view Dr. Crotch must be blamed. Ouseley thoroughly imbibed the spirit of Crotch's *Lectures*. In these, Crotch traces the history of music as if analogous to the arts of painting and architecture. Other arts, he argues, have reached a culminating point of excellence, and then have gone into decadence ; therefore the art of music is in a similar condition. As a sequel, students are advised to *imitate* the compositions of the so-called " best period " of style. Crotch was an ardent admirer of Sir Joshua Reynolds's *Discourses*, and his Oxford lectures are simply loaded with quotations from Sir Joshua. If you will take the trouble to read pp. 196 to 202 or 203 of the *Discourses* (1778 ed.), you will find the gist of Crotch's advice to young composers.

But there is this important distinction between Reynolds and Crotch. In Sir Joshua's advice to students to imitate the old masters, you will always find that he guards himself against a reactionary limitation of the scope of art. Not so Crotch in his lectures ; he, an infant prodigy just as remarkable as Ouseley, managed to ruin his career as a musician by his blind imitation of the past ; and I fear it must be said he too truly succeeded in helping to mar the splendid future which Ouseley's early life distinctly promised.

I know no more sad example of the fallacy of the argument by analogy than this creed of Crotch—that music had seen its best days. If you remember that Crotch began to lecture publicly in 1801, or thereabouts, you will at once see what a very false prophet he has proved to be.

Sir John Stainer's conclusion is that a good musical training would have been a greater benefit to Sir Frederick than the prescribed classical course of a university. Undoubtedly, from a musical point of view, this is sound criticism. But whether other parts of Sir Frederick's life-work would have gained thereby, especially that which he did for the Church, is another question.

APPENDIX B.

ON THE OPENING OF A NEW ORGAN.

(A Sermon preached by the Rev. Sir F. A. G. Ouseley, Bart., at All Saints, Worcester, April 12, 1871, and subsequently at several other churches.)

"But now bring me a minstrel. And it came to pass, when the minstrel played, that the hand of the Lord came upon him."—2 KINGS iii. 15.

WHO was this who called for a minstrel? Brethren, it was Elisha the prophet. He needed the aid of music for a particular purpose, and therefore he called for a minstrel. It was no ordinary occasion which led to this event. Great interests were at stake. Three powerful kings had come to consult him, as an accredited prophet of Jehovah. The armies of these three kings were warring against Moab. And the kings of Judah, Israel, and Edom were leading the forces in person. They had got into a wilderness, a desert, where there were no wells, no rivers, and they could find no water to drink. On this, the king of Israel lamented, saying, "Alas! that the Lord hath called these three kings together, to deliver them into the hand of Moab!" But Jehoshaphat, the king of Judah, had more faith in his God, and did not so easily yield to the useless lamentations of despair, he said, therefore, "Is there not here a prophet of the Lord, that we may enquire of the Lord by him?" And "one of the king of Israel's servants answered and said, Here is Elisha the son of Shaphat, which poured water on the hands of Elijah. And Jehoshaphat and the king of Edom went down to him." The next thing we read of is the reception Elisha gave them. He was evidently indisposed to aid them. Jehoram, the king of Israel, was the son of that wicked king Ahab, and that still more wicked Queen Jezebel, who introduced the grossest idolatry into their country, and who had well merited the divine judgment which had been denounced against them by the Prophet Elijah. Nor does Jehoram appear to have been a whit better than his predecessor. No wonder, then, that Elisha felt inclined to refuse a request proffered by such a man. On the other hand, Jehoshaphat, the king of Judah, was comparatively a good king, who served the Lord. And his presence procured that from the prophet which the king of

Israel would otherwise have failed to obtain. Accordingly, "Elisha said unto the king of Israel, What have I to do with thee? get thee to the prophets of thy father, and to the prophets of thy mother. And the king of Israel said, Nay; for the Lord hath called these three kings together, to deliver them to Moab. And Elisha said, As the Lord of hosts liveth, before Whom I stand, surely, were it not that I regard the presence of Jehoshaphat the king of Judah, I would not look toward thee, nor see thee. But now bring me a minstrel. And it came to pass, when the minstrel played, that the hand of the Lord came upon him; and he said, Thus saith the Lord."

Now, with the rest of the narrative which follows I do not propose to deal on the present occasion, but I wish to confine myself to one circumstance alone—and that is, the engagement of a minstrel, an instrumental musician, as an essential preliminary and preparation for the utterance of a divine and prophetical message. In the first place, this is by no means a solitary instance of the connection of prophecy with music. Indeed, there is good reason to believe that the ancient "schools of the prophets," those seminaries or colleges of divine instruction which formed so important an element in the national institutions of the Israelites of old, devoted much attention to the cultivation of music, both vocal and instrumental. It would appear to have been considered a necessary element in the training of a prophet. Would that such were more the case in these days among ourselves! Would that musical knowledge formed a part of the regular education of those who are intended to become ministers of the Church! As an example of this, I would refer you to the wonderful communication made by Samuel to Saul when he anointed him to be king over Israel. You will find it in 1 Sam. x. 5, "It shall come to pass, when thou art come to the city, that thou shalt meet a company of prophets coming down from the high place with a psaltery, and a tabret, and a pipe, and a harp, before them; and they shall prophesy; and the Spirit of the Lord will come upon thee, and thou shalt prophesy with them, and shalt be turned into another man." And all this came to pass literally, in every particular, as we read in the same chapter. It is evident, therefore, from this passage, that the prophets had a band of instrumental music to walk before them, and to excite them to prophecy; and not only so, but that this excitement communicated itself also to Saul, so that he became for the time a prophet likewise; and that this last was so unusual an occurrence as to excite great wonder, is proved by the fact of the exclamation of the people, "Is Saul also among the prophets," being recorded, and also by his change of manner and habits being accepted as a token and evidence of his divine appointment to the kingdom of Israel. I may also refer to another very salient instance of the use and power of music to affect the energies of the mind—it occurs only a very few pages farther on in the same book of Samuel, and forms also a part of the history of King Saul. You will doubtless remember that, on the disobedience and rebellion of Saul, the Prophet Samuel was sent to announce to him that the kingdom should be taken from him and given to another, and then we read of the anointing of David to be Saul's successor. And immediately afterwards, probably as a direct consequence of this, the Spirit of the Lord departed from Saul, and an evil spirit was allowed by God to torment him (or, as the original word rather implies, to terrify him). A kind of melancholy madness appears thenceforth to have taken hold of the afflicted king, and, doubtless, all the then known resources of medicine were invoked to cure or to alleviate the malady. At length the use of music was suggested, as we read in 1 Sam. xvi. 15, 16, 17, "And Saul's servants said unto him, Behold now, an evil spirit from God troubleth thee ; let our lord now command thy servants, which are before thee, to seek out a man, who is a cunning player on an harp : and it shall come to pass, when the evil spirit from God is upon thee, that he shall play with his hand, and thou shalt be well. And Saul said unto his servants, Provide me now a man that can play well, and bring him to me." The result of this was that David, the very man who had been appointed to be Saul's successor, was selected ; and Saul made him his armour-bearer, and took him into his highest favour. And then in ver. 23 we read, "And it came to pass, when the evil spirit from God was upon Saul, that David took an harp, and played with his hand : so Saul was refreshed, and was well, and the evil spirit departed from him." Josephus, the Jewish historian, asserts, further, that David was inspired to compose some of his psalms when he thus played on his harp for Saul's relief—and it is probable that this was a universal tradition among the Jews, very likely founded on fact. And if so, then is it not most probable that, when David struck the chords of his harp, they disposed him and fitted him for the reception of those divine inspirations which have been handed down to the Church in all subsequent ages as a most precious inheritance, and have won for their originator the well-merited title of the "Sweet Psalmist of Israel?" I cannot doubt but that the harp of David acted on the diseased and troubled mind of Saul in a twofold way. Indirectly, by inspiring David to compose his Psalms, and to pray more earnestly to God on Saul's behalf; and directly, by composing the nerves and quieting the fury of the maddened king, in a way which music has been known to do in countless other cases, and in all ages and countries.

If we turn to the records of secular history in ancient days, we find this faith in music as a powerful engine to affect the mind to have been well-nigh universal. Sometimes it was used to excite passion, sometimes to allay it. Seneca tells us that "Pythagoras quieted the anxieties of his mind with the sound of his lyre," and then he adds, "Who does not know that trumpets and clarions are excitements to action, whilst certain vocal strains are blandishments by which the mind is softened?" (Seneca, *ex Pythag. de Ird.* cap. ix.) Asclepiades, the physician, was accustomed to smooth and allay mental passions and diseases by the use of music. Timotheus, by his wonderful performance of music, could so excite Alexander of Macedon, that he madly would seize his arms, burning to fight. In short, music was recognised among the ancient Greeks as a powerful agent for the quieting and curing of lunatics and maniacs of every description. And, from the cases to which I have already referred, it is plain that the Jewish nation was not ignorant of its efficacy. And when the music performed was of a sublime and solemn nature, it naturally provoked and encouraged feelings of religious devotion and ecstasy. An instance of this may be found in the account we have of the dedication of Solomon's temple. With the exception, perhaps, of the delivery of the Law from Mount Sinai, and of the supernatural events which accompanied the death of Christ on the cross, no event recorded in Holy Scripture is so astonishing, so calculated to fill our minds with awe and with reverential fear, as the account, in 2 Chron. v., of the manifestation of God's Presence which was vouchsafed to Solomon on the occasion to which I have referred. "It came even to pass, as the trumpeters and singers were as one, to make one sound to be heard in praising and thanking the Lord; and when they lifted up their voice with the trumpets and the cymbals and the instruments of music, and praised the Lord, saying, For He is good; for His mercy endureth for ever: that then the house was filled with a cloud, even the house of the Lord; so that the priest could not stand to minister by reason of the cloud: for the glory of the Lord had filled the house of God." We see from all these instances, then, that music, not only vocal, but instrumental, was recognised both by heathens and Jews, in ancient days, as of vast power and usefulness as a means of influencing the mind. We see, too, that such an application of it, with reference to religious objects, had direct divine sanction, and is recorded for our instruction in the pages of Holy Writ. When to these considerations we add these further ones : that such music formed a regular and ordained part of the Jewish service,—that it was kept up not only in Solomon's temple, but in the second temple, and in the synagogues,—that our Lord Himself frequented the Services in which it was employed, and Himself took part in them,—that after His last reception of the Passover, and the institution of the Lord's Supper, He and His apostles joined in the regular Hymn, or great Hallelujah, which always concluded the Paschal Feast,—that in St. Paul's Epistles are several allusions to music, and injunctions to sing psalms, to make melody, and so forth,—that it is matter of history that, from the earliest period of the Christian Church, music has ever formed an important and integral part of her Services ; when we duly reflect on all these facts, we cannot for a moment doubt that it is not only lawful, not only expedient, not only scriptural, not only primitive, not only edifying, but that it is also, and especially, our bounden duty not only to sing God's praises, but to do so "with the best member that we have," to do so with all the best appliances of the art of music which we can secure, to do so without grudging either the time or the expenditure of money which it may incidentally involve. It is an offering to God : therefore we should be ready to say, as David did to Araunah, "God forbid that I should offer to the Lord of that which doth cost me nothing."

But here, and in these days, there is no fear of controversy as to the desirability and necessity of vocal music in the Service of the Church. Nor is it my object to discuss that branch of my subject. Indeed, it does not properly belong to it, nor does it in any direct way flow from my text, to which I wish now to return. We read that when Elisha wished to utter his prophecy, and to quiet his spirit from the indignation caused by the sight of the wicked king of Israel, he said, "But now bring me a minstrel. And it came to pass, when the minstrel played, that the hand of the Lord came upon him," and he immediately uttered his prophecy. Nothing was sung—no psalm, no invoking words ; only the minstrel played, and the divine inspiration flowed into the prophet's soul. From which it is plain, I think, that instrumental music, by itself, may be of the greatest efficacy for spiritual purposes. Who can doubt it ? If the sound of a military band can excite the ardour and zeal of the marching army ; if the Neapolitan *tarantella* can suffice to cure the deadly bite of the *tarantula* spider ; if in these mundane affairs instrumental music can work such wonders through the medium of our emotions, who can doubt that it may be equally powerful as an incitement of devotion, or an assistant to the other externals of worship, in riveting the mind of the worshipper on the unseen object of his adoration? Music has not lost its powers ; on the contrary, during the last 400 years it has risen to an unprecedented degree of perfection, both as an art and as a science. If, then, the simple minstrel in the wilderness of Edom could so affect the prophet as to fit him to receive direct communications from on high, surely we may expect corresponding and most blessed results to ourselves through the agency of that noble instrument, the organ, which as far excels the rude harps and lutes of the Israelites as a modern steamship transcends the ship which wrecked St. Paul.

Although the organ was not unknown to the ancient Greeks and Romans, yet it was not introduced into the service of the Church till about A.D. 660, when (according to Bellarmine) Pope Vitalian sanctioned its use in divine Worship. The earliest representation of an ancient Church organ occurs in a valuable MS. known as the Utrecht Psalter, which also contains the earliest known copy of the Athanasian Creed, and is ascribed by some to the sixth century, and by others to the eighth or ninth. The organ was first introduced into England by Aldhelm, Bishop of Sherborne, in the seventh century ; William of Malmesbury describes one given by St. Dunstan to Malmesbury Abbey, in the reign of King Edgar, and the same Saint gave a similar one also to Glastonbury. Œlfeg, Bishop of Winchester, in 951, obtained for his cathedral the largest organ then known, which has been duly celebrated by poets and historians. But it must not be supposed that the organs of that period were at all like those we now possess. They had no separate keys, no stops, no pedals. Only one note could be sounded at a time, nor indeed was more needed, for harmony did not then exist—melody of the crudest kind was alone in use, and this the early organ could play. As music was brought gradually to its present state of perfection, organs were improved or enlarged, till at length they became what they are now.

Of course, I take it for granted that the music played on the organ should be always of a solemn and sublime kind, suitable to the Sanctuary, and to the devout Services therein offered up. When such is the case (which alas ! is not always), the effect of the voluntaries and interludes played on the king of musical instruments will always tend to dispose the mind of the worshipper to fresh acts of devotion and holy fervour. But that is by no means the only, or the most important, part of the functions which the organ is intended to perform. For, after all, its chief use is to accompany the musical parts of the Service—to blend into one harmonious whole the voices of the singers, to enable them to sing many things, to God's glory and praise, which would be out of their power without such aid, and thus to conduce, indirectly, indeed, but no less effectively, to the great ends for which we come together in Church. And what are those ends? First and chiefly, to glorify our God by acts of worship; and secondly, to receive edification and instruction for ourselves. Of all the arts, music is the most adapted for sacred use, for it is the only one which we know will survive the grave. In heaven we are nowhere told that there will be painters, or sculptors, or architects, but we are told much of musicians—ay, and of instrumental musicians too. St. John in his vision saw and heard "harpers harping with their harps: and they sung, as it were, a new song unto the Lord." And when the angel announced to the astonished shepherds the glad tidings of the birth of Christ, then immediately "Heaven's white-robed choristers appeared," and sang their glad anthem, "Glory be to God on High, and on earth peace, goodwill towards men." Such, indeed, would appear to be the constant habit of the blessed spirits on high—they never can, they never will, tire of hymning God's praises, till the empyrean shall ring again with their voices for ever and for evermore. Glorious thought! Oh! that men would so habituate themselves to singing God's praises here below, that hereafter they may find themselves fit to join the angelic choir!

Let the organ be to you a figure of your own spiritual life. It sounds by means of a combination of pipes and mechanism, acted on by wind, and regulated by the intelligent will of the player. He causes the proper pipes to sound, when they are in proper order, and supplied duly with wind. They are silent unless so acted on and so supplied. Nor will any amount of wind-supply produce music without the pipes and the player. Now let us apply this figure. We are all made in God's image, with full capabilities for good. When we duly use our mental and bodily gifts to God's service, and according to His commands, we are truly doing the work we are sent into this world to do, and that work is—our own salvation; and in working it out we are promoting God's glory, which must always be considered the ultimate end and object of every good thing in the universe. Now, what is the power by which we set all our works in motion to this good end? what is the *wind-supply* for our organ pipes? It is *faith* which works by *love*. Without faith it is impossible to please God. Without Christian love—love to God and love to man—our faith is dead and worthless.

9

But can we acquire this loving faith for ourselves? Can we apply it properly to the end in view by ourselves? Can our organ play itself? No ;—and just so we cannot save ourselves without God's direct help. "By grace are ye saved through faith ; and that not of yourselves, it is the gift of God," and therefore we must strive earnestly to "work out our own salvation with fear and trembling, for it is God which worketh in us both to will and to do His good pleasure." When you hear the sounds of this organ, then, dear brethren, think of your own state as before God, and ask whether you have properly responded to His heavenly Touch, to the Master-Hand which ever strives to reduce your discordant parts to perfect harmony ; ask whether your faith is of the right kind, whether it is mere empty wind, producing no music of the soul, a mere inflation of vanity and self-delusion, or whether it duly issues in that heavenly harmony of Christian faith in Christian character which is the distinguishing mark of all true servants of Christ. And, lastly, pray earnestly to God to send His blessed Spirit to guide aright all the imaginings of your hearts, and all the actions of your lives, so that there may be no more discord, no more harsh sounds, jarring the even song of heavenly Service ; but that you may be continually enabled to utter those blessed strains which, though imperfectly begun in this nether world, shall at length burst forth into the perfection of angelic worship in the glorious realms of future and eternal bliss.

[*The following postscript was added when this sermon was preached in the Abbey Church of Tewkesbury on September* 26, 1882 :—]

In this church you have a very remarkable organ, which possesses many points of historical interest. It is one of the very few organs which escaped the wholesale destruction dealt by the Puritans, at the time of the Great Rebellion, against all instruments and music books in Churches. It is, consequently, a curious link between two very divergent epochs in musical history. It is also, I believe, the only known extant specimen of the work of its original builder. It was built in 1637 by one Harris, the grand-father of the celebrated organ builder Renatus Harris, for the chapel of Magdalen College, Oxford. Oliver Cromwell is said to have taken it to Hampton Court, where Milton the poet often played on it to solace the stern Protector. In 1660 it was restored to its original position at Oxford. In 1672 it was repaired by Harris, son of the man who built it. And then, in 1690, it was enlarged and reconstructed by Renatus Harris, the third generation of the Harris family who had to do with it. It was then considered one of the finest instruments in England. In 1737 the organ was removed to this splendid Abbey Church, and after a long period of neglect was renovated and modernised, in 1848, by the well-known builder Henry Willis. It is undoubtedly not only an interesting organ from an historical point of view, but it is also a fine and well-toned instrument, *as far as it goes.* But you will remember that it never was intended for a Church of such large dimensions as this, nor for the accompaniment of such a body of voices as have been brought together here to-day. Indeed, it is in many ways utterly inadequate. It is deficient in variety of effect, in power, and in mechanical contrivance, and not only behind the age in these respects, but miserably unequal to the requirements of this magnificent building. Let me then strongly press upon you the duty of subscribing to its completion and enlargement—for which £500 at least is required. Do not grudge your donations to so good an object ; remember that it is all for the glory of God and the better setting forth of His praises.

THE SURPLICE.

(A Sermon preached at St. Lawrence, Ludlow, August 23, 1874, by the Rev. Sir F. A. G. Ouseley, Bart.)

" But Samuel ministered before the Lord, being a child, girded with a linen ephod."—1 SAM. ii. 18.

IT is probable that nine out of ten persons who read these words look upon them as little more than an amplification of the eleventh verse of this same chapter, and so pass them over without any special consideration. And yet there is very great importance to be attached to the difference between the two verses, as I hope presently to show. In the eleventh verse we read that on Elkanah leaving his son Samuel with Eli the priest, he " went to Ramah to his house. And the child did minister unto the Lord before Eli the priest." Here we have the simple fact related that Eli took charge of the child Samuel, and employed him as an acolyte or server in the service of the tabernacle of the Lord in Shiloh. But the eighteenth verse adds an important item to this information. It tells us that " Samuel ministered before the Lord, being a child, girded with a linen ephod." Now, this garment called an ephod was specially appointed as a holy garb for the priests when they ministered before God, as we may see by a reference to Ex. xxviii. 4 and 6. And we find also, in the second verse of that chapter, that Moses was commanded to make these holy garments for his brother Aaron, "for glory and for beauty," *i.e.* in order to advance God's glory by enhancing the beauty of His worship. The ephod is here described as adorned with embroidery, gold, and precious stones, that being the way it should be made when used by the priests. But we find that it was also used by the Levites, the singers, and other officials of the Jewish Church. And when so used it is probable that it was made simply of white linen. That it was used also by those who were not of the family of Aaron, or of the tribe of Levi, is clear from 2 Chron. v. 12, where we find that, when Solomon dedicated the temple solemnly to God, his enormous band of singers were all arrayed in white linen ; and this is an important instance, because it is not only the first and the grandest sacred musical festival on record, but also the most wonderful instance of God's visible appearance in answer to solemn public invocation. I will read you the whole passage. " It came to pass, when the priests were come out of the holy place : (for all the priests that were present were sanctified, and did not then wait by course : Also the Levites which were the singers, all of them of Asaph, of Heman, of Jeduthun, with their sons and their brethren, being arrayed in WHITE LINEN, having cymbals and psalteries and harps, stood at the east end of the altar, and with them an hundred and twenty priests sounding with trumpets :) It came even to pass, as the trumpeters and singers were as one, to make one sound be heard in praising and thanking the Lord ; and when they lifted up their voice with the trumpets and cymbals and instruments of music, and praised the Lord, saying, For He is good ; for His mercy endureth for ever : that then the house was filled with a cloud, even the house of the Lord ; so that the priests could not stand to minister by reason of the cloud : for the glory of the Lord had filled the house of God." And again, in 2 Sam. vi. 14, where we find that when David brought the Ark home to Jerusalem from Kirjath-Jearim, he "danced before the Lord with all his might ; and David was girded with a linen ephod" ; and the corresponding passage in 1 Chron. xv. 27 informs us that all the party of officials who accompanied him on that occasion were similarly attired. "And David was clothed," we read, "with a robe of fine linen, and all the Levites that bare the Ark, and the singers, and Chenaniah the master of the song with the singers : David also had upon him an ephod of linen." In short, it is perfectly clear that those who in any way ministered before God, in the days of the Jewish dispensation, always did so having on them this holy garment, a linen ephod.

We shall have some more to say on this part of the subject presently, but let us first of all turn our thoughts to the circumstances under which the child Samuel began his career as a minister in God's tabernacle in Shiloh. He was no ordinary child. His birth was foretold by an angel, and heralded by a miracle of mercy to his mother, Hannah. Accordingly, she, in her gratitude for this gift, devoted her son to God's service from his birth, and therefore she at length brought him to Eli the priest, who made him take some part in the service of the tabernacle, although he was too young at first to understand what it was that he was doing. Eli's two sons, Hophni and Phinehas, who were also priests in Shiloh, were very wicked and profane men, who greatly offended all devout persons by their irreverent and blasphemous character. And, in process of time, when Samuel had grown old enough to comprehend the message, God called to him miraculously, and commissioned him to inform Eli of the terrible punishment which the iniquity of his two sons would bring on the nation, on his family, and on himself. And as Samuel grew on, he became famous throughout Israel for his prophetical sayings. "For the Lord revealed Himself to Samuel in Shiloh by the word of the Lord." It is not my object to-day to go into the history of Samuel, for time will not allow of it, but I strongly recommend you to read the first chapter of this First Book of Samuel yourselves, and you will find much to interest and instruct you profitably in it. The point I wish now to impress on you is that the priestly garment called an ephod was that which was also appropriate to a child engaged in God's service, and that it was to a child so clad that the wonderful revelations to which I have alluded were made. And in connection with this point, do not lose sight of that passage which I read to you from the 2nd Book of Chronicles, in which we found that this same white linen ephod was the special garb of all those who formed the *singers* before God in the time of David.

Now, of course, the ephod was peculiar to the Jewish services, but there can be no doubt whatever that, from the very earliest days of Christianity, some corresponding white linen vestment has always been the appropriate dress of God's ministers. This is plain from the paintings on the old Roman catacombs, as well as from many passages in the writings of the earliest Christian divines and fathers of the Church. We are therefore justified, as

I think, in applying to our Christian ephod, *i.e.* the surplice, whatever we can find in Scripture as to the symbolical meaning of that ancient Jewish garment. I have already quoted the passage in Exodus which tells us of the institution of the ephod and other Jewish vestments. God there says to Moses, "Thou shalt make holy garments for Aaron thy brother, for glory and for beauty," which can only mean for *God's* glory, and for the beauty of His sanctuary and service. But there are not wanting other passages which speak of the symbolical meaning of white raiment. For example, in Daniel's wonderful vision of the horns, in Dan. vii., we find white raiment mentioned as the adornment of the King of kings. "I beheld," he says, "till the thrones were cast down, and the Ancient of days did sit, *Whose garment was white as snow*, and the hair of His head like the pure wool: His throne was like the fiery flame, and His wheels as burning fire." And it is certain that this refers to God the Son, for it corresponds to what we read in Rev. i. 13, 14. "And in the midst of the seven candlesticks" was "One like unto the Son of Man, clothed with a garment down to the foot, and girt about the paps with a golden girdle. His head and His hairs were white like wool, as white as snow ; and His eyes were as a flame of fire." Another case, in which a shining white robe was seen round the form of the Son of Man, is that of our Lord's Transfiguration. "After six days Jesus taketh Peter, James, and John his brother, and bringeth them up into an high mountain apart, and was transfigured before them : and His face did shine as the sun, and *His raiment was white as the light*"; or, as St. Mark expresses it, "His *raiment* became shining, exceeding *white* as snow ; so as no fuller on earth can white them." From all which we may infer that, when our Lord appears to us in glory at the end of the world, He will be clothed in this same shining white apparel,—His heavenly attire,—of which the Jewish ephod and the Christian surplice are but faint imitations, or rather representations, "for glory and for beauty." But not only is this white garment a *divine* covering ; it is also the dress of angels and glorified spirits. On the morning of our Lord's Resurrection, "Mary Magdalene and the other Mary came to see the sepulchre. And behold there was a great earthquake : for the Angel of the Lord descended from heaven, and came and rolled back the stone from the door, and sat upon it. His countenance was like lightning, and his *raiment white as snow*." St. Mark thus relates it : "They saw a young man sitting on the right side, clothed in a *long white garment* ; and they were affrighted." And that such a white garment will be worn by the redeemed saints hereafter is clear from several passages in the Apocalypse ; for example, Rev. iii. 4, 5 : "Thou hast a few names even in Sardis which have not defiled their garments ; and they shall walk with me in white : for they are worthy. He that overcometh, the same shall be clothed in white raiment ; and I will not blot out his name out of the Book of Life, but I will confess his name before My Father, and before His angels."

Or again, in chap. iv. 4 : "And round about the throne were four and twenty seats : and upon the seats I saw four and twenty elders sitting, clothed *in white raiment*; and they had on their heads crowns of gold." And again, in chap. vii. 9 : "After this I beheld, and, lo, a great multitude, which no man could number, of all nations, and kindreds, and people, and tongues, stood before the throne, and before the Lamb, *clothed with white robes*, and palms in their hands ; and cried with a loud voice, saying, Salvation to our God Which sitteth upon the throne, and unto the Lamb. And all the angels stood round about the throne, and about the elders and the four beasts, and fell before the throne on their faces, and worshipped God, saying, Amen : Blessing, and glory, and wisdom, and thanksgiving, and honour, and power, and might, be unto our God for ever and ever. Amen. And one of the elders answered, saying unto me, What are these which are *arrayed in white robes*? and whence came they? And I said unto him, Sir, thou knowest. And he said unto me, These are they which came out of great tribulation, and have washed their robes, and *made them white* in the blood of the Lamb. Therefore are they before the throne of God, and serve Him day and night in His temple : and He that sitteth on the throne shall dwell among them. They shall hunger no more, neither thirst any more ; neither shall the sun light on them, nor any heat. For the Lamb which is in the midst of the throne shall feed them, and shall lead them unto living fountains of waters : and God shall wipe away all tears from their eyes."

From all these Scriptures, then, it is perfectly clear that white robes are the universal garb of the glorious denizens of heaven— that they symbolise and represent holiness and purity, and are bright and shining just because they are holy and pure ; they are white and shining "for glory and for beauty." Of such pure heavenly garments our white surplices, and the Jewish ephods of old, are the appointed types and figures "for glory and for beauty." And the reason why I have dilated so largely on this point is because to-day your choir, in this glorious and beautiful church, has been for the first time arrayed suitably in white robes, such as we find so copiously described in Holy Scripture, "for glory and for beauty."

In every Cathedral and Collegiate Church in England it has always been customary so to vest those who minister before God, and this custom is in accordance with primitive Christian practice. Nor is it only in Cathedral and Collegiate Churches that such a practice has been in use ; for wherever regular choirs have been preserved, the white surplice has always been their attire, except in those cases where, following the bad example of modern Roman Catholic Chapels, they have thrust their singers into an organ gallery, and so separated them from the other ministers of God, to the great disparagement, detriment, and impoverishment of the Service. But here I must once more remind you of the *meaning* of white robes. We have clearly seen, from the scriptural teaching already quoted, that this meaning is *holiness, purity, innocence*—and *therefore* "glory and beauty." Now, dear brethren, I think there is a way in which this consideration should convey a useful lesson to every one of us. In the epistle to the angel or bishop of the Church of Sardis, in Rev. iii. 4, 5, these words occur : "Thou hast a few names even in Sardis which have not defiled their garments ; and they shall walk with Me in white : for they are worthy. He that overcometh, the same shall be clothed in white raiment ; and I will not blot out his name out of the Book of Life, but I will confess his name before My Father, and before His angels." When we, as unconscious babes, were presented to God at the holy Font, and washed in the cleansing waters of Baptism, we were freed from the stain of original sin, and clothed with the righteousness of Christ. If it had pleased God to take us out of this world *then*, before we had committed any actual sin, we should have been undoubtedly saved ; for our pure baptismal robe of purity and innocence would have been unsullied, and we should have been permitted to walk with God in white, in the ever-lasting realm of life. But since that time who is there amongst us who has not often, nay, continually, stained and defiled his white garment of innocence and purity ? Who is there amongst us who cannot show many a loathsome stain of sin ? Alas ! there is not one who is clear in this matter—not one who has kept his bright baptismal robe in its first state of splendour. What is to be done then ? Can we in any way get rid of those foul stains ? Is there any means of washing out those hideous blots ? Yes, God be praised ! there *is* a way in which we can apply to them the Blood of the Redeemer, shed to purge away our sins ; and the mode of appli-cation is by the tears of penitence and contrition. These, when applied by the act of faith in Christ crucified, will wash out every stain, and restore our white raiment to its original purity and splendour. If, then, by faith and repentance, we overcome the power of sin, and become converted to God, we shall be allowed, through all eternity, to wear the glorious white attire of saints, and angels, and our Heavenly King Himself; for it is the uniform of heaven—"He that overcometh shall be clothed in white raiment, and I will not blot out his name out of the Book of Life," saith the Lord. But if so, then is the converse also true. He that over-cometh *not*, his name shall be blotted out of the Book of Life,—and we know what *that* will signify.

Lastly, I would say a word to the members of the choir. Do not put on your surplices, dear friends, without a thought of what they signify, without a prayer that your lives and conversation may be consistent with that meaning. If ever you are tempted to think of worldly and secular things during service, let the sight of your white robes remind you of Him Whose ministers you are. If you carefully train yourselves to such a habit as this, you will find it a real blessing. You will look back, when old age creeps on you, and your last hour draws near,—you will look back then with joy and gratitude on that holy vestment which kept you from evil thoughts, and accustomed you betimes to making every word of God's Service your own. As the child Samuel, when girded with his linen ephod, was chosen by God to be His chosen prophet, so may you, when hymning God's praises in His sanctuary, be richly endowed with heavenly virtues and the blessed gifts of the Spirit, so that when, in God's own time, you depart hence, you may find yourself forming one of the white-robed choristers of heaven, happy for ever in the immediate presence of Him Whose ministers of song you now are. Yes, may we all meet hereafter in that blissful abode, with cleansed and shining raiment and joyous voices, there to sing the song of Moses and of the Lamb for ever and ever.

CHAPTER VII

As has been already stated, Sir F. Ouseley was in 1855 appointed Professor of Music in the University of Oxford. The chair, established and endowed in the year 1626 by Dr. William Heather, was by no means an easy one to fill. In the first place, the professorship being too poorly paid to remunerate any work beyond the occasional services of an Oxford resident, it had very naturally come to be regarded as a sinecure perquisite for one or other of the leading musicians of the day. Thus Sir Frederick's appointment as a young amateur encountered at the outset a certain amount of professional disappointment, whilst he himself, from a pecuniary point of view, was rather a loser than a gainer. Fortunately, he was independent of the stipend ; and by his gentle, forbearing nature he managed, as time went on, to appease any ill-feeling which may have arisen. But he had more serious difficulties to contend with than anything of this kind. Music in general had reached a low ebb in the University, and the musical degrees had become honours lightly esteemed. Sir Frederick's position in life, coupled as it was with his really unrivalled attainments, did something in itself to improve this state of things. His very name gave to the study of music in Oxford a prestige and an interest which had not previously existed. Needless to say, throughout the whole term of his professorship he sought to lay deeper founda- tions for future improvement than any which might rest on his own personal gifts. His chief object was to raise the standard of qualification for musical degrees in the university, and in the face of many difficulties he succeeded in his efforts.

In 1857–62 the Musical Faculty at Oxford was entirely reorganised. The appointment to the professorship, hitherto resting on the nomination of the two proctors only, and renewable year by year, was made a life - appointment, and the election to it was vested in a representative body of the university. In the same period, public examinations by three examiners were constituted as a necessary step to musical degrees. Candi- dates had to show a critical and historical knowledge of their art, besides having to submit to the Professor a composition of some dimen- sions and length. In 1870–71 Sir F. Ouseley also managed to get the " Musical Statute " passed. As this statute abolished the *perform- ance* of exercises for the Mus. Bac. degree, its critics very naturally called it the " Unmusical Statute." In 1876 a further reform was intro- duced. Candidates for the Oxford degrees in music were now required to show proof that they

were persons of some general education. They
had, as a preliminary, to pass an "arts" examination in elementary classics and mathematics.
This reform was originated, in the first instance,
at Dublin by Sir Robert Stewart, the Professor
of Music there. Ultimately it was adopted at
Cambridge also, and thus the new rule was
made to apply at all three Universities. The
changes do not appear to have given satisfaction
from every point of view. Sir John Stainer
says :(*a*)—

Though these statutes raised the value of the degrees, from a
general point of view, I am afraid they have had an effect not at
at all contemplated when they were passed. It is quite unreason-
able to expect a professional musician, say forty or fifty years of
age, to go in for "smalls," or to sit at a "local examination."
Hence many experienced and able musicians are now deprived of
an honour which used formerly to be within their reach ; and,
worse still, it has encouraged the mushroom growth of all sorts of
diplomas and hoods, and the importation, on a large scale, of
degrees from Canada and the United States.

This, by the way, touches on another difficulty
which Sir F. Ouseley had to face from time to
time as Professor of Music. On one occasion a
man, who was nothing more nor less than an
impostor, but who succeeded in getting recommendations in high quarters, tried by some clever
scheming to persuade the Oxford professor to
confer on him an Honorary Mus. Doc. degree.
Sir Frederick smelt the rat in time, and boldly
but courteously declined any further communication. He also took a leading part in protesting

(*a*) *Vide* Sir John Stainer's Address on *The Character and Influence of
the late Sir Frederick Ouseley*, p. 33. Cf. *supra*, p. 38 note.

publicly against the mischievous custom, adopted by Trinity College, Toronto, of giving *in absentiâ* degrees in music through an agency set up in England. Any such system must, of course, not merely diminish the value of genuine English musical degrees, but must inevitably open the way to bogus degrees of all kinds. It was therefore natural that the careless action of the Toronto University should be resented, as it was, by all representative English musicians.

The following fuller account of Sir Frederick Ouseley's attitude towards this question of the Toronto *in absentiâ* degrees has been communicated by Mr. T. L. Southgate :—

Shortly before Sir Frederick's death, complaints were arising from musicians about the improper action of the authorities of Trinity College, Toronto, who had opened an agency in this country for bestowing, on easy terms, degrees in music. The Charter of this Canadian institution confined its operations to the old diocese of Toronto, but, in order to make money, it was determined to enlarge its sphere, and grant degrees *in absentiâ* in England. Students who had failed at our Universities, and at the examinations for the diplomas of the Royal College of Organists, readily obtained permission to put Mus. Bac. after their names. As the source of these degrees was not indicated, professional musicians who had not taken genuine degrees in music at our Universities sometimes found themselves suffering in their teaching by this unfair competition. The evil grew so considerably that the Universities were compelled to take notice of this invasion of their rights, and the threatened lowering of the general educational standard ; for, in response to an inquiry from the Secretary of State for the Colonies, the Vice-Chancellor of the Canadian college stated that his institution claimed the power of giving degrees in all the faculties, as was common at our English Universities. During the time the matter was under consideration, Sir Frederick died, but his successor, Sir John Stainer, took the presidency of a large and influential Committee, consisting of members nominated to serve on it by the Universities of Oxford, Cambridge, Dublin, London,

Durham, St. Andrews, and Victoria (Manchester), together with representatives of the great schools of music and other recognised educational bodies, and to which some members of Parliament were added. During the time that the discussion on the policy of these *in absentiâ* degrees went on, one of the Colonial College authorities was imprudent enough to state that the late Oxford Professor welcomed the introduction of these imported degrees, chiefly because candidates were not troubled with an "arts" test. This brought out the publication, in the *Times* and the *Musical Standard*, of the following letter, which bears date, February 3, 1888.

"No one has the slightest right to quote me as looking favourably on Toronto degrees *as they exist*, for I wholly disapprove of them. If Toronto authorities would impose a really trustworthy test of literary attainment, equal to what is required by English Universities, it would be quite another matter. As it is, they are simply *undoing*, so far as they can, what we at home have so laboriously and carefully striven to effect in that direction. Of such doings as this I cannot in any way approve. I also should be better pleased if they would confine their efforts to their own country.   FREDERICK A. G. OUSELEY."

This letter had been fortunately preserved. It was written to a friend who inquired whether the Oxford professor was rightly quoted by Toronto papers as approving their imported degrees. Considering that it was mainly owing to the insistence by Sir Frederick of the necessity for an "arts" testing of the general knowledge of those about to go in for degrees in music that the Hebdomadal Council determined on this addition to the "Music Regulations," it was, indeed, daring to pretend that the lately deceased Professor held a contrary opinion.

It may be stated that, as a result of the labours of the Protesting Committee, and the official action taken by them in Parliament and at the Colonial Office, the Trinity College, Toronto, authorities closed their agency, and undertook to issue no more *in absentiâ* degrees.

Sir Frederick Ouseley, from his innate courtesy and earnest desire not to give offence to anyone, was unwilling to refuse a request or pain a person without due cause; but in connection with the carrying out of his professional duties at Oxford it sometimes happened that he had to say, No! Not a few musicians who desired to append Mus. Doc. to their names, but who shrunk from the test of the examinations, asked him for degrees *honoris causâ*, but their requests were invariably refused. He was professor from 1855 till 1889, and during this time the only Honorary Degrees in Music conferred were those given to Sir George Macfarren, the Cambridge professor ; Sir Herbert Oakeley, the Edinburgh professor ; Sir Arthur Sullivan ; C. Villiers Stanford, who succeeded Professor Macfarren at Cambridge, and Herr Hans Richter, the well-known conductor,—musicians all worthy of this high distinction. The following letter (*vide Musical News*, January 8, 1892), written in reply to a question addressed to Sir Frederick respecting the use of an American title by a Mr. L——, shows how firmly he could say, No ! and further serves to show his opinion of American titles :—

St. Michael's College, Tenbury,
October 28, 1887.

My dear Dr. Vincent,—I was at Hereford till to-day, and consequently did not receive, and could not answer, your letter sooner. I am astounded to see from it that Dr. L—— expects *me* to grant him an Hon. Mus. Doc. degree at Oxford ! He asked for one (for which I think he should be styled impudent), but I told him plainly it was impossible at Oxford. He has once tried it on at *Dublin*, and got a similar reply from Sir Robert Stewart. Of course, the Bishop of London has no power to grant degrees—we all know that—so that the whole affair must be a *sham*. If I were you, I would not admit the degree at all. *Is* there a University of Tennessee ? And if so, can it grant degrees in music ? I doubt the fact. It might give an Hon. D.C.L., but even that is doubtful. Has Mr. L—— shown you his diplomas, or whatever name the enabling document goes by ? I have a mind to write to the Bishop of London. But perhaps that would come better from *you* than *me*.—Believe me yours very truly,

Frederick A. G. Ouseley.

[The italics are Sir Frederick's own.]

In justification of the opinion Sir Frederick expresses in this characteristic letter, it may be mentioned that a considerable correspondence took place with the Bishop of London as to this Mr. L——'s qualifications and title. The Bishop, it seems, had merely testified as to his " respectability " to an institution bearing the title of the " University of the South," which had given Mr. L—— some distinction, and the bishop, in a letter dated January 1, 1892 (published in the *Musical News*), says :—

" Degrees are worth whatever value can be given to them by the

143

authority which confers them. I certainly do not think a degree given after the manner in which degrees are given at the University of the South is worth much. The degrees of Universities are of very different values ; and Dr. L—— has obtained a degree which is of no value at all !"

Mr. T. L. Southgate, the same able writer who has been already frequently quoted, thus notes how great a change Sir Frederick's zeal and influence in the Chair of Music gradually worked, not only in the matters of constitutional reform above mentioned, but also to the general regard in which music is now held at Oxford : (*b*)—

During the thirty-four years that he held this distinguished post, the knowledge and the practice of the art has advanced amazingly. That advance is mainly owing to the precept and the encouragement of the late Professor ; he laboured to raise the qualifications necessary for obtaining a musical degree, and instituted an "arts" examination as a preliminary, and he contrived to revive the degree *honoris causâ*. Undoubtedly he has left music, both as to its public performance and the estimation in which it is now regarded, in a very different condition from that which obtained when he first commenced his official work at the University.

Sir Frederick's chief duties as Professor of Music consisted in lecturing once at least each term, and in conducting personally at Oxford the examination of those seeking any musical degree. His lectures were, as a rule, practically illustrated, either by himself or by one of his Oxford friends, on the organ, piano, or sometimes on a spinet. Occasionally the aid was chartered of a small amateur string band also. One of his chief helpers

(*b*) Havergal's *Memorials*, p. 27 ; and cf. also, for the whole subject of music at Oxford, Mr. Southgate's "Brief History of Degrees in Music," pp. 61 ff. of the *Roll of the Union of Graduates in Music*, etc., for 1895.

in preparing these illustrations for the lectures, and one to whom he was never tired of expressing his obligation, was Mr. (now Sir) Walter Parratt, then organist at Magdalen. When Mr. Parratt left Oxford for Windsor, Dr. J. H. Mee rendered much valuable help of a similar kind. Dr. Corfe, the organist of Christ Church Cathedral, and Choragus of the University, had been another valued friend amongst Oxford musicians. Here are the subjects of some of Sir F. Ouseley's lectures delivered during the last twelve years or so of his professorship : *Pianoforte lecture*, seven pieces—from Handel, Clementi, Scarlatti, Dussek, Mozart, Beethoven, Schumann ; *Church Music, Anthems*—Purcell, Gibbons, Croft, Tye, Hayes, etc. ; *English Ballads*—Lawes, Carey, Shield, Dibdin ; *Glees*, " Sumer is icumen in," Gibbons, Purcell, Arne, etc. ; on *History of the Organ* ; on *Spanish Music* ; on *German and Italian Composers* ; on *French and English Composers* ; *Dance Music, old forms*, Minuet, Gavotte, Galliard, Pavan, Corrente, Hornpipe, Chaconne, Rigadoon, Passepied, Saraband ; on *Melody*, illustrated by the Professor himself "with one finger" ; on *Purcell and his Contemporaries* ; on *Construction of Fugue*, "terribly technical" ; on *History of Fugue*. The Professor kept very strictly to the line of his subjects, and never lost sight of the fact that one of his chief duties was to maintain a distinct school of English music. The following are two samples of a large number of letters written in connection with his lectures to

Mr. Parratt, the accomplished friend on whom he relied for constant assistance :—

ST. MICHAEL'S COLLEGE, TENBURY,
April 29, 1875.

MY DEAR PARRATT,—I have to-day got your letter, which has crossed mine of yesterday to you. Your list of Anthems is quite sufficient without any addition. I think Mendelssohn's "Hear my Prayer" would hardly do for my purpose. It is beautiful, of course, but essentially un-English in style. By the by we ought to have an Anthem by *Hayes*. Suppose we say, "Praise the Lord, O Jerusalem," or "Great is the Lord"? Do as you like about that, and print the words accordingly. I am *sure* it is better to avoid the works of living composers. I can mention this in my lecture, and explain why. Once more thanking you heartily for all the trouble you take for me.—Believe me yours always sincerely,

FREDERICK A. G. OUSELEY.

ST. MICHAEL'S COLLEGE, TENBURY,
March 3, 1877.

MY DEAR PARRATT,—Neither "Summer is a coming in," "The silver Swan," nor "Blow, gentle Gales," are *glees*, strictly speaking : for the first is a canonical part-song, the second a madrigal, and the third an operatic quintett. However, I had thought of introducing them just to show the distinction between them and regular glees. On second thoughts I have determined to *omit* the two former, and to change the third for some more genuine glee of Sir H. Bishop's. Which of his would you recommend? You see, he being a composer of real English part-music, and also my immediate predecessor in the Chair of Music at Oxford, I thought it would be very desirable to seize the opportunity of having something of his. . . . —Yours very sincerely,

FREDERICK A. G. OUSELEY.

As is the case with most University Professors, Sir F. Ouseley suffered in the numbers of his audiences from the competition of other lectures. It was a very natural temptation, therefore, to draw the musical world of Oxford by the actual

performances with which his lectures were illustrated. He was pleased, of course, in this way to
make use of some of the junior *virtuosos* among
the undergraduates. But he was not so well
pleased when a certain ill-prepared lecture of his
was criticised by one of the newspapers as *a nice
Concert, illustrated by a few remarks from the
Professor.* The fact was, that, like many other
men of wide reading who have thoroughly
mastered their subject, he was cramped by the
mass of his knowledge. Perhaps he had not the
faculty, which belongs only to a few, of simplifying
his own great stores of knowledge down to the
level of the popular musical intelligence of the
age. Or, if he had the faculty, he probably had
not the desire to do this. His own high ideal of
music, his own critical and refined taste, would
never allow him to yield to mere fashionable
cravings of the day, which, in his judgment, must
inevitably tend to degrade the divine art. As a
teacher, he would never condescend to the use
of mere *ad captandum* language. Whatever he
said as teacher should be real instruction. Truth
and a high standard were his aims ; and, though
he was a man full of imagination, he often, it
would seem, at the risk of being called dull,
sacrificed effect to the higher interests of his
art.

As to the Professor's examination work, the
number of candidates varied considerably from
year to year ; but towards the end of his life the
standard had been so much raised that evidently

neither examiner nor candidates found their work
child's play.   Here is an extract from a letter of
Sir Frederick to a friend :—

CH. CH., OXFORD, *Jan.* 28, 1886.

. . . I cannot write at much length, as I am quite exhausted
after conducting a two days' examination of twenty men, of whom
only nine were passed.

This process of "*plucking*" was indeed the
part of his work which he least relished.   The
most piteous appeals were made to him, from
time to time, by candidates whose prospects, or
perhaps even livelihood, depended on their securing this or that musical degree.   They may have
been admirable executants, yet quite incapable of
mastering the theory of music.   Many of them
were not resident students in Oxford ; and they
could not understand always that no private kindness of heart could interfere with the strict honour
of an examining Professor, or with that just
jealousy with which he sought to preserve the
higher musical standard that had been fixed by
the authorities.   One man, whose exercise Sir F.
Ouseley had returned as utterly hopeless, wrote
to him to this effect : (*c*)—

SIR,—Your rejection of my exercise confirms the opinion I have
long entertained of your utter incompetence for the office you hold.

Another man who had gained the degree of
Mus. Bac., but had been rejected for the Mus.
Doc. degree, is said to have followed the Pro-
fessor about Oxford, from one place to another,

(c) Havergal's Memorials, p. 11.

148

weeping copiously. Sir Frederick called in on several friends, hoping thus to escape; but on each occasion when he came out he found himself waylaid in the doorstep At last, in desperation, the poor Professor of Music ran in by the Turl Street entrance to call on the Rector of Exeter, who let him out by the other entrance into Broad Street and liberty. Not so painful to Sir Frederick's kind heart was the stern rejection, now and again, of "cribbed" exercises. In such cases his wide store of musical reading, coupled with his wonderful memory, stood him in good stead : (*d*)—

A certain exercise was one day brought before him, as examiner, to pass. It was not bad enough to reject, and he was on the point of passing it, when he recognised it as an indifferent passage in the indifferent oratorio, Russell's *Job*.

Another instance of the same kind was that of a certain candidate who had sent in a very curious and powerful essay. "That evening," said the Professor, in afterwards telling the story, "I happened to be turning over some old, out - of - the - way music, and lighted on the very piece. Needless to say, I spun my friend." Of another extremely persistent but incapable candidate, who tried hard to coax a *testamur* out of the pro- fessor and his co-examiners, and induced them somehow to give him a special and somewhat irregular examination all to himself, Sir Frederick wrote to a friend shortly after the inevitable "plough" :—

(*d*) Havergal's *Memorials*, p. 34.

I never knew any one man give so much trouble to so many people in so short a space of time before ; and, with Mrs. Gamp, I heartily wish he was in Jonadge's belly.

As Professor of Music, Sir F. Ouseley was, of course, constantly consulted on various musical questions. The following letter, besides illustrating the readiness and accuracy of his knowledge, shows also how he kept his eyes open for the collection of his valuable library of music :—

[*Undated.*]

MY DEAR PARRATT,—With regard to the Coronation Anthem for James II., you are quite right, Purcell's composition *was* performed. But I possess the autograph MS. score of one by Dr. Blow, for eight voices and quartet-string, which was *not* allowed to be used, because Blow refused to write Roman Catholic music for James II.'s private Chapel. Purcell, we know, was not so scrupulous. The volume containing my MS. above-named contains also a lot of excellent *Madrigals* (*e*), including Merulo's celebrated one on the words—"Hic, hæc, hoc, hujus, huic," etc. ; also Purcell's Sonatas for strings ; and some very ancient Latin Church Music written in "tablature" for the Lute. I saved it from wrapping up cheese, and bought it for ninepence from a Windsor grocer in 1854. I call that a good bargain. . . . —Believe me always most sincerely yours, FREDERICK A. GORE OUSELEY.

(*e*) Considering how much disputed a point the derivation of the word "*Madrigal*" still is, the following note from Professor Whewell to Sir F. Ouseley may be of interest :—

TRINITY LODGE, CAMBRIDGE,
Nov. 26, 1861.

MY DEAR SIR FREDERICK,—With regard to the etymology of "*Madrigal*," which we were speaking of yester-evening, on looking at the books I do not think there can be any doubt that it is from *Mandra* which in Latin means a sheepfold. From this *Mandriale* may very easily mean a "shepherd's song" ; and is, it seems, found in old Italian. Thence *Madriale* and *Madrigale* are natural changes. *Madriale* is a song sung in or from a Shepherd's Cottage, as *Barcarole* is a song sung in or from a Bark. The authorities in Menage are curious. The other derivation seems to me worth nothing.—Believe me, dear Sir Frederick, very truly yours, W. WHEWELL.

The editor of *Crockford's Clerical Directory* used frequently to consult the Oxford Professor of Music on the delicate subject of musical degrees. Alike from his tact and judgment, and from his experience as a Clergyman in such varied capacities, Sir Frederick was a useful adviser on such matters.   Here is a case in point :—

SIR F. A. G. OUSELEY TO THE EDITOR OF "CROCKFORD."

ST. MICHAEL'S COLLEGE, TENBURY, *Jan.* 9, 1884.

. . . I look on the diploma of the Leipzig *Conservatorium* as an equivalent, so to say, of the diploma which I hold as *Fellow of the College of Organists*, though, of course, the *Conservatorium* is a much greater and better institution, and involves more study and more honour. It is in truth the only good thing of the kind in Germany, and to hold its diploma is a very high musical distinction indeed. But the *Conservatorium* is not a College, nor are its diplomas *Degrees*. Therefore you should not insert them in the usual place where Degrees are inserted. If your system will admit of it, I should advise you to add it, parenthetically, in some other part of Mr. J.'s entry, so as to do him justice without introducing the very dangerous precedent of classing foreign diplomas with ordinary degrees.

All the three sister universities of Cambridge, Edinburgh, and Dublin conferred in turn one of their honorary degrees on Sir F. Ouseley.   On June 13, 1883, in company with Sir John Lubbock, Sir Richard Temple, Matthew Arnold, G. F. Watts, and others, he was introduced as follows for his LL.D. in the Senate-House at Cambridge, by Mr. J. E. Sandys, the Public Orator :—

Virum genere nobili cultuque Academico insignem, inter Oxonienses suos rei musicæ Professorem, eo lætius hodie salutamus quod nuper in nostrâ quoque Academiâ studium illud cum litterarum disciplinâ conjungendum esse jussimus. Hic autem in Ecclesiâ Anglicanâ officiis sacris diu dedicatus, musicæ sacræ excolendæ incubuit, et scholam pueris artibus liberalibus et scientiâ musicâ erudiendis destinatam fundavit fundatamque diu liberaliter sustinuit. Illa vero volumina quæ de harmoniæ legibus aliisque rei musicæ arcanis conscripsit, inter artis tam exquisitæ peritos et lecta et laudata sunt. Talis viri exemplar contemplatus, nemo jam mirabitur quod Elysiorum camporum in eadem regione non modo "Threicius" ille "sacerdos," Orpheus, "obloquitur numeris septem discrimina vocum," sed "inter odoratum lauri nemus" etiam illi versantur

> "Quique sacerdotes casti dum vita manebat, . . .
> Quique sui memores alios fecere merendo."

Triplici igitur laude etiam inter vivos dignus est vir et de studiis musicis et de officiis sacris et de alumnis suis optime meritus, baronettus insignis, FREDERICUS ARTHURUS GORE OUSELEY.

To render such polished Latin as that of Mr. Sandys into appropriate English is a difficult, if not an impossible, task. Here, however, is a translation, which may be taken for what it is worth by any who need it :—

A man remarkable by his noble birth and university culture, Professor of the musical faculty in his own Oxford circle, we the more gladly hail to-day because of late, in our own university also, we have ordered that that study of music should be joined together with the learning of letters. He, moreover, who stands before us, having been for a long while dedicated to the office of Holy Orders in the Church of England, has applied himself with zeal to the cultivation of sacred music ; and, whilst he has founded a school designed for the instruction of boys in the liberal arts and in musical science, has also for a long time liberally maintained it. Those books, indeed, which he has written on the laws of Harmony, and on other secrets of the theory of music, have been both read and favourably received among those who are skilled in so delicate an art. Having looked on the example set by such a man, no one will now wonder that, in the same tract of the Elysian fields, not only does Orpheus, that priest of Thrace (*f*), "make music on his seven-stringed lyre," but "amid a fragrant bay-tree grove" there are also found walking—

> "Priests who, while earthly life remained,
> Preserved that life unsoiled, unstained—
>
> .   .   .   .
>
> With all who grateful memory won
> By services to others done."

Of triple praise, then, even amidst the living is the man worthy who has earned the highest meed alike concerning his musical studies, and his sacred office, and his youthful scholars, a baronet of mark, Frederick Arthur Gore Ouseley.

Meanwhile, amid the more serious avocations of his professorship, Sir F. Ouseley found not a little to interest and amuse him in the general musical life of Oxford. He was one of those men who, being full of humour themselves, seem to breathe humour into all their surroundings, and to extract humour from the most unlikely subjects. At Commemoration time he enjoyed presiding now and again in his official capacity at the new organ, which, by his exertions, had been erected in the Sheldonian Theatre. He prided himself not a little on the skill with which he could keep the noisy undergraduates in a good temper by his dulcet strains, or on occasion drown the uproar. He was delighted, too, with the following requisition, which reached him after one of his organ performances in the Sheldonian :—

SIR,—We blowed for you on Tuesday. Is we to be paid? And is you to pay us?—Yours,   THE BLOWISTS.

Sir Frederick also found constant pleasure in the

(*f*) *Vide* Virgil, *Æn.* vi. 646 ff.; and cf. Conington's Translation.

private society and musical meetings of his many friends in Oxford. On one occasion, however, the music appeared likely to be at a discount. The late Rev. H. Deane (*g*) has thus recorded the event, in which he himself was also a proud partaker :—

Ouseley was stopping at the house of ——. —— thought he ought to have some music, and asked my violoncello and myself. But, unfortunately, no printed or copied piece of music was in the house. Ouseley said to me in his quiet way, "Don't you think we can play Beethoven Op. 17 from memory?" And we did.

Perhaps these reminiscences of the Oxford Professor may fitly be concluded by the following story, furnished by Mrs. Piggott, one of his many friends, as to the use he once made in a country parish of his gorgeous academic Mus. Doc. gown. "As nearly as possible"—Mrs. Piggott says— "these were his words in relating the event" :—

Yes! there was A. B——, a dear good fellow, but very strong against the surplice. Nothing but a black gown should ever be seen in *his* pulpit. I used to go and see him every year, and generally I preached for him ; but he would not give way, so I did as I was told—with a protest. One day at Oxford, just after I was made Mus. Doc., I had a letter asking me to preach a special Sermon for him, and he ended by saying, "But you know, my dear Ouseley, I expect you to bring your academic gown." Well, I reached his house on a Saturday evening, and after dinner I said : "Ah! perhaps, as you asked me to bring my academic gown, you had better see it!" "Oh, there is no occasion," he said ; "you know, I prefer that to anything else." However, I went upstairs, unpacked the brand-new red gown and hood (*h*), and, putting them on, I reappeared and pranced round his study. Need I describe the expression of his face, of speechless horror, as if the "Scarlet Lady" herself were present? At last he found

---

(*g*) Cf. p. 13 *supra*, note.
(*h*) White silk hood lined with crimson.

words : " No, no ; not *that* of course—I meant your academic gown !" " But this *is* it ; I brought it, as you desired ; you know my new degree ; I cannot wear the old gown now ; as an Oxford man I must wear the *right* thing, or none. But if you ask me as a Clergyman to wear my surplice, there is always that alternative." Which, of course, poor man, he had ruefully to accept. And so I went up to his pulpit for the first time (but not for the last) in the much-dreaded surplice.

Sir F. Ouseley's connection with Hereford Cathedral began from his first entry into the diocese. As has been already noticed, he was admitted as Precentor of Hereford on June 5, 1855, within a month of his appointment as the Oxford Professor of Music, and more than a year before the Consecration of St. Michael's Church. In an account of him, written during his lifetime, it is said that the precentorship was bestowed upon him by Bishop Hampden (1)—

Doubtless in appreciation not only of his acknowledged eminence as a musician, but of the disinterested work and mission which he was just bringing into his own diocese. . . . No more fitting appointment could possibly have been made ; but whereas this office had, up to this time, been endowed with a sum of £500 a year for the benefit of the occupants (not one of whom had discharged one particle of its duty for at least a century, or been qualified to discharge it), it was now, under the operation of the Cathedral Act, to present the edifying spectacle of an entirely disendowed office, just when, for the first time, perhaps, from its foundation, it was occupied by a man, not only anxious to do its work efficiently, but in every way qualified for such work,—an accomplished musician, a man of zeal, energy, ability, and who, by his courtesy to all, no less than by his influence and example, would soon have thrown new vigour and devotion into the Choir and Services, and been to a Cathedral, as a Precentor should be, the centre of its life and action.

Situated as he was, it was of course impossible

(1) Quoted in Havergal's *Memorials*, p. 23.

for Sir F. Ouseley to have been quite as much as this to Hereford Cathedral. Yet for the space of thirty-four years he did faithfully serve his office there to the best of his ability. As Precentor he had the nominal supervision and the real final authority over all matters musical in the Cathedral. As a fact, his intervention was only called for from time to time. Yet on occasion he could and did hold his own. For instance, those who knew him well can thoroughly appreciate the gentle persistency, coupled with an almost boyish spirit of mischief, with which he once dealt with his good and honoured friend Dean Dawes. There was to be some function at the Cathedral—probably the reopening Services after its restoration. Sir Frederick was anxious that there should be an early Celebration of the Holy Communion. The Dean had determined that there should only be a late one. The Precentor, however, had the clearest understanding of the exact amount of constitutional authority which he himself possessed. All the musical arrangements of every Service in the Cathedral lay in the hollow of his hand, and his simple ultimatum was this—

Well ! Mr. Dean, if you won't have an early Celebration, you shall not have one note of music.

Among the Precentor's chief duties at Hereford, besides those already alluded to, were the selection of candidates for the various posts in the choir, and a standing engagement to preach in the Cathedral on Christmas Day. It was natural also that Sir Frederick should take the keenest interest in the Cathedral organ. At the time of its enlargement, in 1861–64, he not only gave largely from his own purse, but enlisted a good deal of further support. He also collected then a considerable amount of interesting information as to the various organs which had been erected in the Cathedral during the previous three centuries. He had intended at one time to publish the results of these researches but, for one reason or another, the intention was never fulfilled.

So long as he was non-resident at Hereford, the Precentor could, of course, take no regular part in the practical superintendence of the Cathedral choir. But, needless to say, whenever he was present—and this was more frequent, especially during the last few years of his life, after his appointment to a canonry—his ears were keenly attentive to every chord of music that was either sung or played in his hearing. He is remembered as "listening with his hand to his ear, and giving a start when any wrong note was caught." Nor were his eyes less observant. One of the Cathedral boys did not open his mouth sufficiently for the Precentor's satisfaction. The boy was stopped after the Service, and kindly encouraged to open his mouth wide enough to admit a silver half-crown vertically inserted. It was by little kindnesses of this sort that Sir Frederick gained a real personal influence with the Cathedral boys, as he did with his own boys at

St. Michael's.   Now and again he used to get the Hereford choir-boys into his rooms in the Close for tea, and then improve the occasion by playing to them on the piano, taking for his subject his own initials, F. A. G., and working out therefrom some comic little fugue for their amusement.   In these and like ways he made himself a real power as Precentor; and though it would be unfair to others to attribute to him the chief credit of the splendid style and finish which now marks the Hereford choir as one of the best Cathedral choirs in England, yet it may truly be said that the results to-day are in no small degree due to the former inspiration of his name and presence.

Besides serving his office as Precentor, Sir F. Ouseley also sat for over twenty years as Proctor for the Hereford Chapter in the Canterbury Convocation.   He took no prominent part, indeed, in the debates of the Jerusalem Chamber, though he was, of course, looked up to as a valuable authority on the rare occasions when musical matters came into question.   He was, however a very regular attendant at the sessions in Westminster; and his own former fears (*j*), as to the possibility of a revived Convocation "leading to authorised heresy," were no doubt soon happily dispelled in that secure home of orthodoxy.   One interesting piece of work in connection with Convocation he had the honour of superintending during the last year of his life.   In April 1888, at the suggestion of Archdeacon Hessey, a Com-

(*j*) Cf. p. 73 *supra*.

158

mittee of the Lower House was appointed for the purpose of publishing certain early records of Convocation, dating from 1852 to 1857, the first five years of its revival. Of this interesting period in the history of Convocation there had hitherto been no authorised chronicles kept, except in the most meagre form. The Rev. J. Wayland Joyce, however, one of the Clergy Proctors for the Diocese of Hereford, foreseeing that the period would be one of special interest, had from the outset preserved detailed reports of all the various sessions. They were mainly culled from the newspapers, at a time when newspaper reports were full and Convocation was still a novelty. These records the Committee was instructed to examine and prepare for publication. Sir Frederick Ouseley— chiefly, no doubt, in consequence of his close intimacy with Mr. Joyce, who had died in the previous year—was appointed Chairman of this Committee ; and ultimately, under the hands of Prebendary Ainslie, as editor of the *Chronicle of Convocation*, the book was duly published, under the title of "*Early Records*," and presented to both Houses of the Convocation. Apart from its own intrinsic value, the volume will incidentally serve to hand down Sir F. Ouseley's name in connection with an institution which he himself learned to venerate, not only as being the most ancient constitutional body in the land, but as being also —together with her sister Synod at York—the true Church of England by representation.

It was in January 1886 that, on the death of

his old friend, Dr. John Jebb, Sir F. Ouseley was appointed by Bishop Atlay to a residentiary Canonry at Hereford. To the honour of the Clergy of the diocese, it is said that more than one of them in prominent positions declined the Canonry first, saying that Ouseley was the man most deserving of it. Anyhow, the appointment seems to have given the greatest pleasure to its receiver, chiefly, no doubt, as being a public recognition of the work he had done for the Church at large, and for the diocese of Hereford in particular. As for any pecuniary benefit, he could have reaped little, if any, from this as from his other public offices, much as he needed help at that time for his College. He writes thus, inviting a friend to stay with him in Hereford :—

May 19, 1886.

. . . I shall be in lodgings only, as my own house in the Close is ruinous, and I have to rebuild it, worse luck !

For this expensive business the new Canon borrowed part of the cost from Queen Anne's Bounty, but the balance he provided himself.

Besides being busy at these chief centres of his work,—at home, at Oxford, and in direct connection with Hereford Cathedral,—Sir F. Ouseley was incessantly occupied with other outside engagements, mostly, of course, of a musical character. For twenty-seven years he was President of the popular Herefordshire Philharmonic Society. He took a leading part in the encouragement and improvement of the various country choirs in his own diocese through the two Choral Unions of

Herefordshire and South Shropshire (*k*). And, beyond these limits, he was continually travelling up and down England, either to preach or to deliver lectures on musical subjects, or to give practical and gratis advice as to organs and choirs. How highly his services in this latter way were valued, the following extract, from one of many similar letters addressed to him, will show:—

ST. NEOT'S, HUNTS, *November* 1, 1862.

. . . You ask of people here. Indeed, they have not forgotten you: they consider you had a large share in helping them to possess such a choir as there is here at present.

He once spent a fortnight in thoroughly examining and then reporting on the old organ in the Temple, preparatory to its restoration and enlargement. In this case, however, so valuable was his opinion considered that he was offered, and accepted, a very handsome *honorarium*, to be spent, of course, on his College. Extraordinary appeals were sometimes made to his patience and generosity. On one occasion he was requested to set to music eighty-two lines of poetry of a very second-class order indeed, commemorating the fiftieth anniversary of a country clergyman's incumbency. Looking to his somewhat higher engagements, we find that he was one of the Directors, and afterwards a Vice-President, of the

(*k*) To illustrate the condition, or rather the want of condition, of country choirs in the neighbourhood when St. Michael's was first built, it may be mentioned that in one church, only a few miles off, it used then to be the custom for a barrel-organ to grind out the hymn tunes for the requisite number of verses. *No one sang, but the people read the words silently to themselves.*

11

" Royal Academy of Music," of which institution, established in 1822, his father, Sir Gore Ouseley, had been one of the chief founders (*l*). He served also on the Committee of the well-known " Musical Union," founded by Professor John Ella. The *matinées* given by this " Union " are said to have been the predecessors of the modern " Monday Popular Concerts " ; and Ouseley was one of the only people whose advice the autocratic Professor Ella would ever listen to in the matter of programmes and performers (*m*).

This general account of what may be called Sir F. Ouseley's outside work may fitly conclude with some more detailed notice of the various papers he read from time to time on musical subjects in London and at various Church Congresses. An admirable digest of these papers was prepared at the time of Sir Frederick's death by Mr. T. L. Southgate, than whom no abler or more sympathetic critic has done him justice. The following Appendix contains Mr. Southgate's analysis of four Church Congress papers read by Sir F. Ouseley, between the years 1863 and 1874, and also of four lectures delivered by him in London, between the years 1876 and 1886, to the members of the " Musical Association."

(*l*) Cf. p. 3 *supra*.   (*m*) Cf. Havergal's *Memorials*, p. 52.

APPENDIX C.

MR. SOUTHGATE'S ANALYSIS OF FOUR PAPERS READ BY SIR F. OUSELEY AT VARIOUS CHURCH CONGRESSES.

SIR FREDERICK OUSELEY was pre-eminently a church musician ; the cultivation of church music and improvement of our service music was a subject in which he took more than a deep interest ; it was the *métier* of his life. It was quite natural, therefore, that, owing to the exalted place he held in the musical hierarchy, as well as from his clerical position, he should have been frequently asked to lecture on this subject at the various meetings of the Church Congress. It seems to have been felt on all sides that he could speak with special authority on the question of music in our churches. Ouseley was not only a thorough musician, able to boast of considerable experience in the practice of the art, but he was also a clergyman warmly attached to the Church, impressed with her beautiful liturgy, and cognisant of the great value of music as an aid to devotion. He felt that ofttimes the intellect could be reached, and the heart touched, by sweet and solemn music, better than by other means. So the "music question" at the various Congresses was one in which he took very great interest, and to which he frequently contributed a paper, illustrating it with a carefully-prepared performance of church music, the cost of which, with his accustomed liberality, he himself defrayed.

I.

At Manchester, in the year 1863, he read a paper of an historical character : in this he traced the growth of church music from the ordinary reading voice, not musical, through the employment of the monotone and the choral recitative, as used in the *preces*, versicles, responses, etc., to the measurable Psalm-chant, thence to the service and the anthem. The programme of the illustrations will best indicate the contents of the lecture itself :—

Gloria to Benedictus in G minor	*Farrant.*
Gloria to Jubilate in A	*Croft.*
"Hosanna to the Son"	*Gibbons.*
"Thou knowest, Lord "	*Purcell.*
"God is gone up "	*Croft.*
Hymn 193 (H. A. & M.) to the Old 113th.	

II.

In 1867, at Wolverhampton, Sir Frederick Ouseley read a paper on the "Musical Training of the Clergy," from which a sentence or two may be extracted : "I should very much like to see much more encouragement given to the study and practice of music among undergraduates. Unmusical authorities in the universities *naturally* disapprove of, and therefore discourage, the cultivation of music. They regard it simply as a form of idleness, and as an obstacle to classical and mathematical studies. And it must be admitted that it may easily become so, if abused. But, under proper restrictions and regulations, the study and practice of music afford advantages which more than outweigh the dangers and drawbacks to which they are subject."

III.

In 1872, at Leeds, Ouseley was again the chief speaker, taking for illustration—

Some Psalms, chanted.	
The Service : Gloria Patri from the Jubilate . .	*Croft.*
The Anthem : "Call to remembrance" . . .	*Farrant.*
"Hosanna"	*O. Gibbons.*
"Teach me, O Lord"	*Rogers.*
"O God, Thou art my God"	*Purcell.*
"Wherewithal shall a young man" . . .	*Boyce.*
"Praise the Lord"	*Goss.*

In a short section on "Hymns" he instanced as inappropriate *La Suissesse au bord du lac,* sung to an English hymn in a crowded church in London, asking, "How can such tunes,—in 6-8 time, in tripping measure, in secular style, with associations of secular and even amorous and questionable words,—how can such tunes conduce to devotion ? How can they enhance the perfection of sacred art ? How can they fail to degrade that which they seek to exalt ? How can they result in aught but the disgust and discouragement of all musical churchmen, the misleading of the unlearned, the abasement of sacred song, the falsification of public taste, and (last, but not least) the dishonour of God and His worship?" In referring to the great improvement that has taken place in rural choirs, he said : "I think it may be asserted, without fear of contradiction, that the zeal and energy of the clergy in promoting the development of choral resources in their churches is, after all, the *mainspring* of all the great musical church revival to which I refer."

APPENDIX C

IV.

At the Brighton meeting, in October 1874, Sir Frederick Ouseley read a paper on "The Management and Training of Parochial Choirs, and the Organisation of Diocesan Choral Festivals." In this he remarked : "It is difficult in these days to realise fully the ordinary state of our country choirs a century ago. And yet, unless we do so, we shall be unable duly to appreciate the vast improvement which has taken place in them in our own days. Forty years ago this process was already going on, and people then drew very favourable comparisons between the church music of that date and the church music of half a century sooner. By recalling our early recollections, then, and regarding them as an advance upon the ruder and more imperfect attempts in our grandfathers' days, we shall be able, perhaps, to conjure up a tone-picture of the fearful chaos of hideous sounds which was accepted in those days as sufficiently tuneful for the service of the sanctuary." He then drew a picture of the improved state of things, with the larger use of organs or harmoniums, the institution of the chancel choir, as against that of the west gallery, and the formation of diocesan choral festivals, as to which he recommends a different arrangement in successive years. One year, small country gatherings ; the next year, district choral meetings ; and the third year, one large central festival in the cathedral church.

This was the last occasion on which Ouseley spoke in a Church Congress on the interesting subject of church music, and its action on the religious life and thought. He always regarded music as a most valuable element of the religious culture of the day, and was ever an advocate of its extensive employment in our services ; he was constantly urging improvement of the practice and systems of the present, encouraging efforts thereto, and pointing towards an advance in the future. There can be no doubt that the earnestness and skill with which Sir Frederick Ouseley dealt with this subject met with the appreciation of thoughtful audiences gathered together from all parts of England ; and it is equally certain that the good seed he sowed, and the practical advice he gave,'must have met with its due reward. Many clergymen must have carried away from these meetings suggestions and hints of how to employ music in our services that have borne good fruit in many a town and quiet country church in our land.

165

LIFE OF SIR F. A. G. OUSELEY

MR. SOUTHGATE'S ANALYSIS OF FOUR PAPERS READ BY SIR F. OUSELEY BEFORE THE MEMBERS OF "THE MUSICAL ASSOCIATION."

In 1874 was founded in London "The Musical Association," a society having for its aim the investigation and discussion of subjects connected with the art, science, and history of music. The members consist of practical and theoretical musicians, as well as those whose researches have been directed to the science of acoustics, the history of the art, the construction of instruments, or other kindred subjects. Meetings are held monthly, at which papers are read, with any necessary performances or illustrative experiments, and a discussion follows. Most of our representative musicians and acousticians belong to the association, and the annual volume of *Proceedings* that are published show how valuable and useful is the work done by the society. Its founders felt that it was necessary to have as President some prominent man who represented all branches of the art, whose sympathies were wide, whose knowledge was exact, and whose general culture and qualifications undoubtedly fitted him to preside over the meetings of a learned society of this nature. Sir Frederick Ouseley was unanimously elected to the post of President, and right well he performed his duties. Distance from London prevented him from attending all the meetings of the association, but when he was in town he was usually to be found there, and he did good service in occasionally reading papers. These were replete with original research, information, thought, and practical suggestions of much value ; the intimation that the President was going to speak always drew together a large assembly of the members and their friends. Of the papers he furnished, the following were the most important :—

"Considerations on the History of Ecclesiastical Music of Western Europe," read January 3, 1876.

"On the early Italian and Spanish Treatises on Counterpoint and Harmony," read March 3, 1879.

"On some Italian and Spanish Treatises on Music of the Seventeenth Century," read February 6, 1882.

"On the position of Organs in Churches," read February 1, 1886.

I.—*January* 3, 1876.

In the first of these papers Ouseley traced the connection between Christian Church music and that of the ancients, pagan, and Israelite. He examined the theory of Padre Martini, the illustrious author of the great Italian *History of Music*, and showed that his contention as to the Ambrosian chants being traditionally derived from the very notes composed and sung to the Psalms by David and others was impossible. Sir Frederick maintained that the ancient Hebrew music must have been essentially Oriental in its character, and that Eastern music, like the customs of these people, is not likely to have altered. The scale system— *i.e.* the division of the octave into particular notes—of both the brothers Isaac and Ishmael must have been identical. Now, the Arab and Egyptian music is altogether different in its melodic intervals to that of our modern Western music : our untrained ears cannot appreciate their thirds and quarter tones, any more than these Eastern people can understand our music. The melodies, therefore, sung by the Jews of old could not have borne the slightest resemblance to the intervals of the chants sung by the ancient Western Church, founded as these were on the Greek system of tones and semitones. Sir Frederick showed that the Ambrosian and Gregorian melodies were distinctly pagan in their origin, and could lay no claim to divine inspiration, as is often claimed for them. Incidentally he uttered a warning against the exclusive use of so-called " Gregorian music," pointing out what a retrograde course this was, and remarked how difficult it was, on account of the uncertainty in deciphering the early music notation, to determine just what the old "tones" were. Dealing with the obscure question as to the rise of harmony, and the way in which it was engrafted on the traditional plain song of the Church, Sir Frederick quoted extensively from writers on this subject, and inclined to the belief that harmony was invented by nations of Northern Europe, the English taking the lead in this respect. In a masterly way he traced the history of the old art of descant, showing how it became modified, improved, and ultimately developed into independent part writing, until florid counterpoint and the polyphonic style of modern music was reached. A brief sketch of the features of the various great schools of ecclesiastical music followed, and he warned the young composers present against the modern tendency to secularise church music, and advised a deeper study of counterpoint ; as he truly said : " No one would compose worse secular music for having undergone this training, while all who wished to write music for divine service would unquestionably feel the benefit of such a course." The lecturer next dealt with the use of various musical instruments in church. He expressed himself in favour of the employment of instruments, in addition to the service of the organ, proving his position by an exhaustive examination of instances related in the Old and New Testaments. Sir Frederick showed that the use of the organ exclusively was comparatively modern, that village orchestras lingered in many country places until our generation. He concluded by expressing the hope that orchestras would be again employed in assisting in frequent performances of oratorios in churches, and be available for the more complete accompaniment of the canticles and great hymns of the Church. The paper was followed by an animated discussion, in which Sir John Stainer, J. Hullah, W. Chappell, C. E. Stephens, W. H. Cummings, W. Parratt, and Rev. C. Mackeson, took part.

II.—*March* 3, 1879.

In introducing the second paper cited, Ouseley said: "The object of the paper I am about to read is to introduce to your notice some of the principal Italian and Spanish Treatises on Music of the fifteenth and sixteenth centuries. It is a subject which has never been much attended to in this country, probably on account of the excessive rarity of the works in question; but which possesses a great deal of interest, when viewed in connection with the history of musical art." In order to illustrate the subject, Sir Frederick had upon the table several of these rare ancient treatises, thoughtfully brought from his splendid library, and these were examined by the members present with much interest. Before noticing the early Italian and Spanish treatises, Sir Frederick gave a rapid sketch of the progress of musical art from the time of Boethius (*ob.* 526), whose great work was the chief text-book on music for some 800 years, and only became superseded by the writings of Guido, Franco, John Cotton, and Tinctoris. Dealing with the invention of measured music, and the discovery of harmony, Sir Frederick was not content with merely citing the names of the early writers, most of whose manuscripts have been printed by the Abbe Gerbertus and De Coussemaker, but he showed how ample was his knowledge of these works, and how completely he had grasped the main facts of musical history, by tracing the gradual emergence of the art from a melodic simplicity and mediæval confusion into a state of intelligible and scientific order. The first book he dwelt upon was that by the celebrated Franchinus Gaffurius (born 1451), an Italian priest who seems to have been a genius, so varied were his powers and wide-ranging his writings. Sir Frederick described his several books on music, his lengthy controversy with Aron, Spataro, and Vulso (chiefly on trivial questions of intervals and ratios), and explained his contrapuntal rules. Next was noticed Ramis de Pareja, a Spanish theorist (1440), the first to advocate something very like equal temperament. Then came Stefano Vanneus, an Augustinian monk, born at Ancona in 1493; his treatise on counterpoint explains the principle and practice of plain-song, solmization, mensurable music, and notation. Vanneus was the first who advocated the sharpening of the leading note of the scale, and in this valuable treatise are to be found the germs of our modern tonality. Passing rapidly in review the writings of some sixteenth-century Italian and Spanish theorists, Sir Frederick gave a succinct account of the important works by Zarlino, the *Maestro di Cappella* at St. Mark's, Venice, in 1565; he was a man of great ability, and enjoyed considerable fame as a composer, in addition to his theoretical writings. Sir Frederick then noticed the rare works by the learned Spanish Abbott Salinas, and by Cerone, an Italian priest, both of whom flourished in the middle of the sixteenth century. A brief account of the admirable book, *Practica di Musica*, by Zacconi, published in 1592, was the last of the works brought under review: the lecturer concluded with an eloquent peroration, expressing admiration for the splendid music that was produced in the days of Palestrina, and by the worthies of our Elizabethan school, when the art was fenced about with the rigid and cramping rules laid down by the theorists up to the close of the sixteenth century. He showed how paralysing the supremacy of the ecclesiastical plain-song must have been to the originators of new melodies and harmonies, and how wonderful it was that such beautiful and imposing music could have been produced by the men who lived in such times. A long and most interesting discussion ensued, Sir John Stainer (the chairman), Mr. W. Chappell, Rev. T. Helmore, Dr. J. F. Bridge, Mr. W. H. Cummings, Mr. G. A. Osborne, Dr. W. Pole, Mr. C. E. Stephens, and Mr. A. D. Coleridge, taking part in it. Ample testimony was borne to the great value of the paper as an historical *résumé* of the speculative theories and formulation of the rules which had governed the art from its dawn in Europe down to the sixteenth century. The research displayed in this learned paper well exhibited the singular linguistic powers Sir Frederick possessed. He had mastered all the Latin, Italian, Spanish, and French works that had been cited.

LIFE OF SIR F. A. G. OUSELEY

III.—February 6, 1882.

Sir Frederick Ouseley read a paper "On some Italian and
Spanish Treatises on Music of the Seventeenth Century," a com-
plement of the preceding discourse. He introduced the subject
proper by a brief sketch of the progress of harmony from the time
of Palestrina, when discords of suspension and passing notes were
alone permitted, fundamental discords being as yet unrecognised.
Modulation from key to key, as we now understand it, did not
exist, and there was no tonality beyond that of the old ecclesiastical scales. To Monteverde is ascribed the origin of modern
tonality, the employment of dissonant chords without preparation,
and from that came the free use of chromatic harmonies. The
history of the gradual transformation of music, from its severe
scholastic form to the comparative freedom which obtained at the
end of the seventeenth century, was told by Sir Frederick in his
clear and felicitous style, the salient features being tersely pointed
out. The first books he dealt with were the works of Giovanno
Maria Artusi, besides his writings on the art of counterpoint ; this
Bologna Canon fiercely attacked Monteverde and other innovators,
characterising unprepared dominant sevenths and ninths as un-
warrantable infringements of the ancient rules. Then came the
curious treatise by Giovanni d'Avella, a Franciscan monk, who
mixed up harmony with the music of the spheres and judicial
astrology. The works of Doni, the inventor of the "Lyra
Barberini," next passed under review, and Sir Frederick pointed
out how useless was the vast amount of erudition he exhibited in
an attempt to prove that the ancient Greek music was far superior
to that of our own time, considering that no one could tell
accurately what the Greek music was like, and so no comparison
can be instituted. Passing over the mathematical *Sistema Musico*
of Rossi, the productions of Angelo Beradi were next noticed.
This writer was one of the first to treat on double counterpoint,
the art of conducting a fugue by means of a *tonal* answer to the
subject, an invention which substituted free fugues for canonical
ones. Turning to the Spanish authors, Sir Frederick cited *El
Porque della Música* (1672), by Lorente, the Commissary to the
Inquisition at Toledo ; and Pablo Nassarre's famous work on
music, *Escuela Música segun la Practica Moderna* (Zaragosa, 1723);
this work, by the organist of the great Franciscan monastery at
Saragossa, is an admirable and well-arranged compendium on
music, accounting for every practical rule on philosophical principles, and dealing with all the cardinal features of the art. The

170

book, on account of some of the speculations indulged in, came under the condemnation of the Inquisition, and it is very rare. Copies of all the books alluded to were placed upon the lecture-table for the examination of the members present, and much gratification was expressed at the opportunity Sir Frederick had afforded of looking at these treasures he had brought up from Tenbury. In the discussion that followed, Sir George Macfarren, the Music Professor at Cambridge, and Principal of the Royal Academy of Music, made a lengthy speech, in which, *inter alia*, he stated that the chord of the dominant seventh ascribed to Monteverde was to be found in a composition by a native of Lorraine, Jean Mouton, who lived about a hundred years before Monteverde. Other speakers were Sir John Stainer, Dr. J. C. Bridge, Dr. W. Pole, Mr. C. E. Stephens, and Mr. W. Chappell. Mr. Cummings, the chairman, concluded by expressing the thanks of the meeting to Sir Frederick for the splendid paper he had read, and for the pleasure he had afforded the book-lovers by the production of these valuable old Spanish and Italian works on harmony, etc. Sir Frederick Ouseley's thoroughness and vast learning may be gauged from the reply he gave to Sir John Stainer, that he had read through every one of the books he had laid upon the table.

IV.—*February* 1, 1886.

Sir Frederick read a valuable paper "On the Position of Organs in Churches"; Sir John Stainer being in the chair. The question is one of exceptional interest to all who have to do with church architecture, or church music; on account of the many extraneous considerations which must necessarily enter into the subject, the problem is not an easy one to solve. It is evident that no one great general law can be laid down which shall apply equally to every case. The paper was an especially good one, and it well illustrated Ouseley's accumulated experience and thought in dealing with so complicated a matter as the proper place for an organ in a church. He treated his subject (1) historically; (2) from a consideration of continental practice; and (3) with special reference to English places of worship at the present time. In the first division, Sir Frederick quoted from Dr. Rimbault's books, the *Syntagma* of Prætorius, the *Harmonicorum Liber* of Messennus, the organ treatise of Dom Bèdos, Dugdale, and the splendid work on old organ cases lately published by Mr. A. G. Hill. He showed how the ancient portative organ, which was small and could readily be moved to any position, gradually grew into the large and com-

171

plete organ of later times, for which a distinct and fixed position had to be found. This position followed no set rule, but varied in the different cathedrals, particulars of which, gathered from old records, books, and drawings, were described. Owing to the sacrilegious violence of Cromwell's soldiery, almost every old organ was destroyed, Chester being the only cathedral where the small primitive organ escaped ; here it stood on the left (north) side of the choir. The lecturer said that prior to the Reformation there is no authenticated instance of an organ either on the rood loft or at the west end of a church. Sir Frederick related his experience of the effects produced by different organs in notable churches abroad, detailing what a variety of positions were adopted, and pointing out that in some cases, two, three, and even four separate organs were employed for worship purposes, whereas one suffices for our English service music. In approaching the consideration of our own modern requirements he remarked : " It is evident that there are several, various, and often conflicting interests to be consulted in the selection of a proper site for a church organ. There are first the interests of the clergy, who regard the matter, perhaps, from an ecclesiological point of view. Then there are the interests of the singers in the choir, who will view the question on its vocal side. Next we have the interest of the organist, who regards the position of the organ from a comparatively instru- mental aspect. After him comes the architect, who chiefly looks at the appearance of the case, and too frequently hates the organ altogether, and would fain conceal as much of it as possible. Lastly, there is the organ builder, who knows how much better his instrument will sound with free space around it than when boxed up in a small chamber, and who feels that his reputation is more or less dependent on the decision as to locality to which those who have the management of the affair shall finally come. Here is, then, a fruitful source of quarrels and differences, of contentions and recriminations, of jealousies and revilings, of grumbling and discontent." Sir Frederick protested that he must not be expected to lay down some general or universally applicable rule for finding the best place for an organ. As he truly said, what was suitable for a large cathedral would be unsuitable for a small country church. In cathedrals he inclined to think that the best place *musically* was over the choir screen, though *architecturally* that position rendered it impossible to gain an uninterrupted view of the interior of the cathedral from west to east. He continued : " Speaking as a musician, and a lover of cathedral services, I am inclined to advocate in all such cases the retention of the organ on the rood screen ; the bad effect to the eye can often be mitigated by dividing the organ, so as to keep all the middle part at a low elevation, putting the tall pipes and all that tends to obstruct the view on either side, as has been done at Westminster Abbey and Rochester Cathedral." The other alternative was to place it over the choir stalls on one side, but this has its disadvantages, so far as antiphonal singing is concerned. As the lecturer said, a better plan is to divide the organ into two portions ; thanks to the excellent mechanical actions of to-day, such an instrument can be readily brought under control. Sir Frederick concluded by advocating a small but good and well-planned organ placed in the choir of small churches for choir accompaniment only ; but, "in a large church where there was no choir, but the whole congregation were in the habit of singing hymns at the top of their voices, what would be imperatively needed would be a large and powerful organ in a west-end gallery to dominate and lead the singers, and to drown their shouts if the cacophony became intolerable." The paper provoked a long and interesting discussion, in which the chairman, Mr. J. Higgs, Dr. Pole, Mr. T. L. Southgate, Professor W. H. Monk, and Mr. Herbert took part.

CHAPTER VIII

AT the time of Sir F. Ouseley's death one of the
newspapers (*a*) described him as "pompous in
appearance." Such an epithet was almost the
very last he deserved. What chiefly impressed
most people in his appearance, speech, and
manners was the mixture in them of great
refinement and courtesy with the most perfect
simplicity. A peculiar dignity seemed to be combined in his person with an utter absence of all
pretentiousness. In a like way his occasional
shabbiness of dress, his old coat, frayed shirt-
cuffs, and the well-worn soft hat, often more green
than black, sitting, as it usually did, on the back of
his neck, contrasted curiously with a magnificent
sapphire ring, an heirloom of his family, which he
was accustomed to wear. Another newspaper (*b*),
at the time of his death, criticised the supposed
luxurious *entourage* of St. Michael's College. The
fact was that no establishment of its size could
well have been managed more economically. The
" liveried footmen " referred to were general ser-

(*a*) The *Hawk*, April 9, 1889.   (*b*) *Truth*.

SIR FREDERICK OUSELEY

AT THE AGE OF ABOUT 60.

Photographed by T. Jones, Ludlow.

vants in a school of some twenty-five boys, with two or three resident masters, besides continued relays of musical visitors. Sir Frederick never cared to spend on himself. From the day when St. Michael's was first founded, his one object always seemed to be to enrich the college and church at his own expense. He indulged in neither horse, carriage, nor coachman, his usual equipage being nothing more ambitious than a farmer's gig, hired in his own parish. Indeed, he has been known, on occasion, to travel from his College to Woofferton Station, a distance of four miles or more, in a donkey-cart, driven by a young boy.

As to his own personal appearance, he was of medium height, and inclining to stoutness as he grew older. His head was of an extremely beautiful shape, though curiously flat at the top, and could not be overlooked as "a clever head." His hands, too, were beautifully formed, strong, and very sensitive. His hair, brown in youth, darker as he grew to manhood, and then in his later years gradually whitening and thinning to baldness, grew in those crisp, small curls which are generally supposed to betoken great energy of mind. As some one (c) has quaintly conjectured, the strength which a vigorous man's hair imbibes from him makes it necessary to do something, and "curling is all that hair can do." His forehead, high and fully - developed, had that appearance, which some foreheads do have, of being packed with brains. His eyes were brown,

(c) F. R. Stockton, *A Borrowed Month*, p. 24.

large, and prominent, the iris prominent in particular—a sign, this is said to be, of capacity for
language.   In middle life he had very thick and
strongly-marked eyebrows.   His ears were small
and flat to the head.   He had a peculiarly flexible
mouth, the expressions of which served as a constant tell-tale of his feelings.   The face, taken as a
whole, might have been that of a Spaniard.   It
was not English at all.   And whilst the features
could certainly never have been called handsome,
some people might have deemed them actually
ugly.   But it was with his face as with the faces
of most other clever men,—when he spoke, or
when his feelings were moved, it lighted up at
once with the greatest animation.   This, indeed,
was his normal expression; for, though sometimes suffering from low spirits, one of his chief
characteristics seemed to be an abounding happy
life and energy.   Wherever he went he seemed
to carry sunshine with him, and to fill his surroundings with vitality.

Four portraits, at least, are known to have been
painted, representing Sir F. Ouseley at different
periods of his life.   One hangs in the private
dining-room of the Warden's house at St. Michael's.
It represents Frederick Ouseley as a child of seven
or eight years old.   No artist's name is decipherable, but the picture is a charming one.   Another
portrait was the work of Mr. James Joyce (*d*), a
notable antiquary, but no mean draftsman either,
who was afterwards Vicar of Strathfieldsaye.

(*d*) Cousin to the Vicar of Dorking of the same name.   Cf. p. 26 *supra.*

This picture was painted at Dorking early in 1841, when Frederick Ouseley was between fifteen and sixteen years old. Unfortunately, its present whereabouts does not seem to be known. Another portrait of Sir Frederick, at the age of thirty-one, hangs now in the hall of St. Michael's College. It is a full-length picture, and shows him in his Mus. Doc. robes, as the newly-appointed Oxford professor. It was presented by the Warden and Fellows of Radley College early in 1857. The artist was Mr. W. H. Florio Hutchinson, once a pupil of Fuseli in London, then a resident in India, afterwards drawing-master at Radley College. The picture is not a happy one. It not only lacks animation, but gives a melancholy look to its subject, which he certainly did not wear in his later life. The fourth portrait was painted, after Sir F. Ouseley's death, by Mr. Arthur Foster (*e*), partly from memory and partly from a good photograph. Considering the disadvantages under which he laboured, this young artist has produced a work of considerable merit. His picture also represents the Professor in Mus. Doc. robes, but at the age of about sixty. It was the gift of a small Committee of Sir Frederick's personal friends in Oxford to the collection of musicians' portraits at that University (*f*). There also exists a life-

(*e*) Son of the Mr. John Foster mentioned above. Cf. p. 77 *supra*.

(*f*) This fine collection was originally hung in the old "Schola Musicæ" (now thrown into the Bodleian Library), but has since been transferred to a room in the New Examination Schools. The collection is a fairly complete one of musicians famous in the old days at Oxford, but it lacks any good portraits of Dr. Crotch and Sir Henry Bishop.

sized bust of Sir Frederick, modelled in clay by
one of his Herefordshire friends, Mr. H. J. Bailey,
of Rowden Abbey, near Bromyard. The bust has
never yet been cut in marble; but it is a pleasing
likeness, and a good reproduction of it might well
grace some day the hall or the library of St.
Michael's College.

Like many of the world's best benefactors, Sir
Frederick Ouseley was full of humour. Nothing
pleased him more than a good story, whether he
was the teller or only the hearer. A capital
raconteur himself, he always wanted to hear "the
last" from his friends. He delighted to exchange
commodities; and a large collection still exists,
contained in two or three good-sized volumes, of
odd letters, queer stories, malaprops, and funny
translations, which he had gathered from various
sources. Many of these are, of course, musical
oddities; but the collection is by no means confined to music. A friend recalls how very intimate his knowledge was of *Pickwick*. He could
repeat whole pages of that immortal work by heart.
He himself used to say, with regard to his lack of
poetical taste: "I never care for poetry, unless
there's a story in it; and then I think it's better
told in prose." Certainly the following poem, the
only one extant of Sir Frederick's composition,
has a story in it, and might not have lost much if
it had been thrown into prose instead of into
poetical form. Evidently the rhyming exigencies
at the end of the fourth stanza were of a severe
order. The poem is dated January 17, 1840, and

must then have been written when he was more than fourteen years old :—

FABLE OF THE THREE DOGS—WITH A MORAL APPLICATION.

By F. A. G. Ouseley.

As I was sitting once alone,
  Where I am wont to sit,
I saw a dog which gnawed a bone,
  And ate it, bit by bit.

But soon I saw another dog,
  With countenance and gait
So sour, that it my blood did clog,
  And turned my trembling pate.

The surly to the good dog came,
  And took away his meat :
They both did fight till both were lame,
  And each forsook his seat.

At last a third to them did come,
  And with an effort small
Did take away their every crumb
  (And he was very tall).

Thus oft with us men it doth be,
  Says I, as I did go :
In waging useless wars, you see,
  We know not what we do.

For while we, for ambition's sake,
  Have more than we can keep,
Another takes what we would take,
  And thus we lose a heap.

Although never anything of a sportsman, Sir Frederick was exceedingly fond of games, engaging in them with all the eagerness of a child.

Croquet and bowls were his favourite pastimes out of doors. He was an extremely fine and rapid player at backgammon, and was fond of cribbage. His whist was not so good. At card tricks, puzzles, and various feats of sleight-of-hand he was a thorough adept. To several of his correspondents he used to write in ciphers, one of these being his own invention (g).

To entertain boys, he would take infinite pains to construct a Hampton Court maze, a most laborious pen and ink proceeding, where he delighted in throwing every difficulty in the way of your finding your way in with a pin.

At one time, also, he is said to have been no mean performer with the billiard cue, though that game was a luxury in which he seldom indulged in his maturer years. He was not a smoker. Indeed, throughout his life he seems always to have had a strong antipathy to tobacco. Although a spare consumer of wine, as well as a most temperate eater, he was too old-fashioned in his views to sympathise much with the Total Abstinence movement. When invited by a friend to take part in some " Rechabite " demonstration, he enquired whether it would be necessary for the participators to *"dwell in tents"*?

As he entered into all games with a child's eagerness to win, so he was not infrequently seized with a child's impatience when he was kept waiting, or when things went wrong. It is said that once at croquet, after making an unsuccessful

(g) From a correspondent to the *Globe* newspaper, quoted in Havergal's *Memorials*, p. 38.

stroke, he was obliged to ring the door bell, and ask the servant to fetch his mallet, which had "gone over the wall." There is a tradition that, on another occasion, the Warden of St. Michael's, finding himself in some way fastened into his study by the catching of the door-latch, could not wait one moment until the door might be opened from the outside, but, rushing at it full tilt, kicked a panel right through, and so escaped. It would give an absolutely false impression of him to suggest by these reminiscences that he was ever violent or ill-tempered. But little details like the above will illustrate, better than any description in words could do, the childlike impetuosity of his character. His faults were those of a child, as were all the many graces with which he was endowed—the quick recovery, the loving heart, the simple, guileless spirit. One who knew him well (*h*), and is himself a shrewd observer of men and things, has noted the following points with regard to his friend's personality and characteristics :—

Though his ear was so remarkable, his eyes seemed to lack the power of appreciating artistic or other beauty to any great extent. Did you ever notice this? Beyond scenery and buildings, I hardly ever heard him remark upon the beauty of anything as presented to the eye. What admirably formed hands he had !—you must often have noticed them. And how supple they were ! He could work all the joints of his fingers at will, and I believe those of his toes too ! With regard to the excellence of his handwriting, he took rather a pride in it ; he always made his own pens, and never much liked

---

(*h*) The Rev. Marmaduke C. F. Morris, formerly Headmaster of St. Michael's, and now (1895) Rector of Nunburnholme, York. (See Havergal's *Memorials*, p. 60.)

other people using them, and if by any chance they did so without wiping the pen, he was always "down upon them" for it. His numerous correspondents could not but notice his uniformly exquisite writing. The original copy which I have of a song he wrote for me some years ago, "O where," is quite a model of penmanship. Sir Frederick's love of indoor games was another of his characteristics ; even those of the simplest kind he entered into with all the zest and freshness of a boy, and he never seemed to grow weary of them. If, however, he was defeated through what he thought was his own stupidity, he would sometimes fly into a sort of passion, which, I need hardly add, like a passing cloud, was over directly, and his wonted sunshine appeared again.

The impatience (i) already alluded to was a characteristic which ran through all parts of Sir F. Ouseley's life. He was, for instance, the most polite of men, but no code of manners was strong enough to make him sit still for long together, if, as was usually the case with him, he wished to be on the move. Mr. H. J. Bailey records his own painful experiences in the process of modelling this restless musician's head. To begin with, a quarter of an hour at the most—and this only twice or thrice—was all the time which could be spared. And then, in Mr. Bailey's own words, this was what the modeller had to put up with :—

I looked across the room to get the exact curve of his lips—he was yawning, with his mouth wide open. Soon after I looked up to catch the expression of his eyes—all I could see was the back of his head ; he had jumped up, turned right round, and was gazing at the books in his shelves.

Again, no one could have had a more hospitable heart than the first Warden of St. Michael's. He thoroughly enjoyed bidding his guests welcome.

(i) Cf. p. 31 *supra*, note.

He took almost a childlike pleasure in showing off his College and its treasures. Most neat and methodical in all his ways, he cherished the typical bachelor care of his drawing-room and best bed-room. But when it came to the final ordeal of pairing off his guests in due order at a dinner-party, his patience invariably gave way, and it became a proverbial word of command on the part of the host at St. Michael's, as he himself marched off with the *prima donna* of the evening, " Now, ladies and gentlemen, sort yourselves." But his patience was still more sorely tried, and with better reason, when a certain visitor stayed on and on at St. Michael's, until he seemed likely to become " chronic." Poor Sir Frederick, being the soul of hospitality, was at his wits' end to know what to do. At last the happy idea struck him that, being himself Founder as well as Warden of a collegiate institution, he might venture to add to its rules. So he gravely informed his guest that it was one of their regulations that all visitors, after a certain time, should *pay* so much *per diem* for board and lodging. This notification soon had its desired effect.

Sir Frederick's impatience made him a bad ruler when difficulties arose. To begin with, he was a poor judge of men. Or rather, he was too easily pleased with the first looks and words of those he had to do with. Then, when his eyes were opened, he had not the strength and the steadi-ness of will, or perhaps it may have been only that he had not the hardness of heart, to face the consequences of his mistake, and to make the best of it. With him men were too often either gold or dross. He could not deal with alloy. But this must only be taken as applying to cases in which he had to act as ruler and disciplinarian. So far as his own personal relations to men were concerned, in matters independent of discipline, few have ever possessed a larger share than he did of the spirit of charity and forgiveness. As one of his friends said, at the time of Sir Frederick's death : (*j*)—

It seemed an instinct in him to discern what was good in others rather than their defects, to rejoice in their well-being, to be ready to make allowance for their faults, and to be kind in his correction of them ; and, not only to promote peace amongst others, but to follow out the precept of being "*at peace with all men.*" I myself knew an instance in which, through years of ill-will and misconstrued motives on the part of another, he had won his way, by sheer force of desire to do kind acts in requital for unkindness, until the person who had thought hardly of him became his warm friend. There were times in his life when—as happens to any man who has to deal with many person, or who is raised above the ordinary level—his character and aims were misunderstood and misrepresented ; and he was harshly judged and hardly dealt with. And, although his sensitive, gentle, spirit suffered acutely from such treatment, he never nursed sentiments of malice or revenge, but set to work with Christian purpose to forgive, and, as far as possible, to forget, and to take every opportunity of showing that he did so.

Indeed, this spirit of forgiveness was one of Sir Frederick's strongest and happiest characteristics. It enabled him in an extraordinary way to reconcile to himself men who had formerly been violently opposed to him. Quite one of the most

(*j*) Sermon preached by Rev. Preb. T. A. Ayscough, late Vicar of Tenbury, April 14, 1889. (Quoted in Havergal's *Memorials*, p. 49.)

feeling references to his worth and friendship, published at the time of Sir Frederick's death, was written by a musician with whom he had once had very disagreeable dealings, but whose goodwill, nevertheless, and whose admiration he had succeeded in retaining. It would be hard to say on which of the two men the published eulogy reflected the most credit, whether on him who had died or on him who survived.

If any illustration were wanting of Sir Frederick's munificence, beyond the very existence of St. Michael's itself, it might be furnished by the following event. The late Bishop Gray of Cape Town, in the midst of the Colenso troubles, came to England to plead for the church in South Africa. He stayed for a night at St. Michael's. His host told him with the deepest sympathy that his own liabilities in connection with the College left him powerless to help with money. Next morning, as the bishop was going, he said, "I cannot refuse you a trifle. If you like to sell that stone for your Mission, do so." It was in a jewel box, and the Bishop did not open it till he got to London. A well-known jeweller, to whom he then took it, said, "I suppose you really are a Bishop: why, this is a Persian stone of the rarest value, the whereabouts of which no one has known for years." The stone, of course, had belonged to Sir Frederick's father; and when Bishop Gray had given satisfaction of his own personal identity, he was astounded by the sum of money which the jewel realised.

Here is another instance of Sir Frederick's kindness of heart, related by one who feels no longer bound by a promise not to mention the tale. A little concert was given in a village to raise funds for the Church organ. There took part in it some of the village musicians, the governess at the house of the squire playing the accompaniments, while the Vicar arranged the entertainment. Unfortunately, a popular song was sung, the property of one of the sharks who made it a practice to pounce down upon those who had unwittingly performed the piece, and, under threats of legal proceedings, compel them to pay penalties. The shark heard of the performance. Forthwith the Vicar, singer, accompanist, and every one who took any part in the concert—for such was the law at that time—were served with notices to pay full penalties, under threat of legal proceedings. The accumulated amount came to upwards of £30, a sum impossible for those poor people to pay. The Vicar had known the Professor when he was at Oxford, and wrote asking whether this preposterous demand was legal? Unhappily it was, and there was nothing to do but to pay it, or endeavour to get the gross amount reduced. Much correspondence ensued, and in the result Sir Frederick paid the money, and rescued the unfortunate and poor people from their trouble. In connection with this, he never ceased to advocate an alteration in the law over the performance of copyright music.

Sir Frederick's hospitality was proverbial, not

merely in the way of being, as he was, a genial host at his own table, but as being delighted to show his Church and College to visitors of all kinds. Whether they were members of some club or association, or only one or two private individuals, he was always ready, when he had the time to spare, to show them round the buildings. He would sit down at the organ and play, in his clear, vigorous style, one of Handel's songs or choruses ("Fixt in His Everlasting Seat" and "Arm, arm, ye brave!" were two of his favourites), or one of his own extempore fugues.

Besides this kindness of heart, a genuine modesty was a leading feature in Sir F. Ouseley's character. Herein, without doubt, lay one chief secret of that intense personal affection with which he was regarded by the wide circle of his friends. He never seemed to consider any person, or any subject, to be beneath his notice. He had a way of talking with ordinary people as if they were all on the same level of intellect and learning with himself. However it may have been in his writings, he certainly never in ordinary society (*k*) "posed as the learned Dr. Ouseley." A girl was once singing, or going to sing, at a country house where Sir Frederick was a guest. Someone suggested that she would be shy of performing before the Oxford Professor of Music. He sprang up at once, with real concern in his face: "Oh! no one could be afraid of me: but, look, I will hide behind this

(*k*) See Mr. W. A. Barrett's criticism. Cf. p. 197 *infra*.

pillar." The story is exactly typical of all his dealings with feeble or incompetent musicians, many of whom, no doubt, tried him sorely at times. Now and again he may have mimicked a few pretentious performers in the privacy of his own sanctum, especially if their vainglory consisted in singing flat or playing wrong notes. But to the ordinary amateur he was never anything but kindness and sympathy personified. To young musicians especially, who were seeking to make a start in the profession, he was the most generous and helpful of friends. In all such cases he was ever ready to do what he could, by advice, by recommendations, not seldom by substantial assistance. A large part of his life, indeed, seemed to be spent in promoting the advancement of others at the expense of his own.

He was quick also to discern early promise of genius. Sir John Stainer gives the following happy description of their first meetings : (*l*)—

It was soon after Ouseley's appointment as Professor that he came to examine the chorister boys of St. Paul's, of whom I was one. I shall never forget the nervousness with which I approached this musical and clerical dignitary when summoned to meet him in the drawing-room of our master, the Rev. J. H. Coward. But I played a prelude and fugue by Bach, from the "forty-eight," by memory, and, at its conclusion, Sir Frederick gave me a few words of good advice and much kind encouragement. How little could he have dreamt that he was patting his successor on the head !

The next interview I had with him was full of moment to me : it constituted a turning-point in my life. I was then between sixteen and seventeen years of age, and was playing the afternoon

---

(*l*) *The Character and Influence of the late Sir Frederick Ouseley*, an Address delivered on December 2, 1889, before the "Musical Association," and published by Novello, Ewer, & Co. Cf. p. 38 *supra*.

Service at St. Paul's, both Goss and Cooper being absent for a few days. During the Service Ouseley came quickly into the organ loft, and, after greeting me, watched me closely as I accompanied the music from the old "scores." On the same evening I had a letter from him to say that the object of his visit to St. Paul's had been to find an organist for St. Michael's College, and he offered me the post. I must apologise for thus introducing myself into this paper, but it explains why and how I came to know so much about the character and abilities of my patron and friend.

Twenty years ago the number of photographs a man possessed was no bad test of the number of his friends. There still remains at St. Michael's College an old writing-cabinet of Sir Frederick's. Its drawers are crammed with an enormous collection of photographs of friends in all stations of life. The number of weddings, too, at which he officiated was very large, as was the number of his god-children, in whose welfare, nevertheless, through life he seldom failed to take an individual interest.

It should be mentioned also that Sir Frederick was always most good-natured about playing at private houses; although once his indignation almost got the better of his amusement when a lady in London society asked him to one of her "At Homes," telling him it would be so nice if he would play to them, as it would "set all the people off talking." (Why, by the way, should musicians be the only artists to whom this familiar insult has been so often addressed?) "I came to enjoy your society," he answered very brusquely; "not to play upon your piano." On another occasion he was good-naturedly playing his best on an extremely bad pianoforte in a country house.

Someone began to chatter: he jumped from the music-stool like a flash of lightning, saying, "And I forget the rest!"

Sir Frederick, however, was well able to take care of himself in matters of this kind. If he would never consider any person beneath his notice, on the other hand he was in no awe of any human being, and he was not afraid to speak his mind to those who considered him beneath their notice. A certain peer, who had been one of his chums at Oxford, was vulgar enough once, in after years, when he happened to be in the company of some grand people, to ignore Sir F. Ouseley. Then, on a later occasion, meeting Ouseley at a railway station, he came up and began to patronise him. All the answer he got for his trouble was this: "My lord, if it was not convenient to you to notice an old friend when you were with highly superior persons, I find it distasteful to be accosted by you now." Sir Frederick then bowed and walked away.

How he valued his true friends, and sought to "grapple them to his soul with hooks of steel," is well shown in the following letter :—

St. Michael's College, Nov. 22, 1884.

My dear Parratt,—How are you and all yours? Since you left Oxford we seem to have "lost touch" of one another somehow. I mean, that we meet seldom, and correspond but little. And I don't like it to be so; for I am a staunch friend, and never like to lose sight of those whose friendship I value, as I do yours. It is going on for two years since you were here. Can't you come and see me? And if so, when?—Believe me always sincerely yours,

Frederick A. G. Ouseley.

To pass once again to some of Sir Frederick's more special musical faculties, instances have already been given of his wonderful acuteness of ear. His musical memory was little less marvellous. The present Warden of St. Michael's, the Rev. J. Hampton, contributed the following reminiscences, illustrative of each of these gifts, to Mr. Havergal's *Memorials* (p. 11) :—

At Cambridge, in the year 1861, I heard Beethoven's Septett for the first time, and on my return mentioned the fact to Sir Frederick, who immediately went to the piano and commenced the work, pointing out each instrument that had any prominent part. He played on for twenty minutes, and then only stopped from fatigue (*m*). I told him that I wondered that I had never heard him play it before. He said that he had never done so—had not seen it in print, and only heard it once in his life, ten years before, at Rome.

When living in London it was his delight to visit the organ lofts of St. Paul's and Westminster Abbey. After an absence of several months in Spain, Italy, Germany, Switzerland, and Paris, where he tried every organ of any size, he returned to England, and soon visited his friend, Sir J. Goss, at St. Paul's. Sir John asked him to sound C, which he did ; then Sir John put down B, which was in perfect tune ; whereupon Sir Frederick immediately smiled and said, "You have had all the pipes cut down since I was last here." Sir John assured me that the pitch of the organ *had* been raised a semitone.

Another instance of Sir Frederick's wonderful musical memory has been recorded by Mr. T. L. Southgate : (*n*)—

We were discussing the question of dancing as a part of Church public worship, and I read him a letter received from a friend in

(*m*) In the *Life of Sir George J. Elvey* the writer, speaking of those who used to meet sometimes in his drawing-room at Windsor, says : "Sir Frederick Ouseley used to rest in that room after playing extempore fugues on the chapel organ, or Handel's chorus, 'Fixt in His Everlasting Seat,' over which he would get so excited that he has been known to break off before the end from sheer exhaustion and inability to execute the music at the pace he had worked up to."

(*n*) *Musical Standard*, December 28, 1889.

Abyssinia, who told me that there they still "danced before the Lord," as it is recorded David did. "Oh!" said Ouseley, with a smile, "I have seen that much nearer home. In 1851 I went to Spain for a tour, and on a special high day I saw a solemn *fandango* danced in front of the high altar at Seville; and this was the music it was danced to." He then went to the piano and played the movement, a delicate little piece, quite Spanish in tone, with the exception of a peculiar use of the chord of the Italian sixth. I asked him whether that was correct, and expressed astonishment that he should have remembered this piece, heard but once some thirty-six years ago. "Quite right," he replied; "I thought that chord would startle you." And then he continued: "If I thoroughly give my mind to receive a piece of music, I generally succeed in mastering, and never afterwards forget it."

The Archdeacon of Ludlow, the Ven. H. F. Bather, gives the following record of a similar kind :—

In the year 1886, or thereabouts, when Sir Frederick Ouseley was spending a day with me at Meole Brace, the conversation turned on the subject of musical memory. I said: "You have a good musical memory, Sir Frederick, have you not?" "Yes," he said, "I have; and I will give you an amusing instance of it. I was staying once at a *pension* in Switzerland, with a German lady, among others, in the house, who was a good pianist. She had with her in MS. an unpublished pianoforte piece by Schubert, of some length, which she played to me once or twice. When about to leave, I asked her if I might copy it; but she replied that she was under a promise not to part with it to anyone. Well! I said, at least you will give me the pleasure of hearing it once again. So she played it. Now, I said, taking her place at the piano, have the kindness to tell me if this is correct—and, to her surprise, and not a little to her discomfiture, I played it through! The feat is the more remarkable inasmuch as Schubert's pianoforte music is exceptionally difficult to remember."

This story recalls another which has nothing, indeed, to do with musical memory, but which, in common with other instances already recorded, illustrates well the mischievous politeness with which Sir Frederick loved sometimes to "score off" his opponents. He was travelling one day by rail. In the railway carriage were two English ladies (?) who, presuming that their ability to speak German was a very rare accomplishment, kept up a running fire of criticism in the German tongue upon the personal appearance of their fellow-traveller. Among other derogatory epithets, Sir Frederick's quick ear caught that of *Frosch* (frog). Anyone who remembers his wide, open eyes, and his springy postures, can quite appreciate the ladies' meaning, if not their good taste. But the tables were turned with a vengeance when the ladies got out a few stations on, and Sir Frederick asked, in his choicest German, if he could do anything to assist them with their luggage.

One more instance may be given of his musical memory. Sir Frederick once took Mr. Southgate up to the organ-loft in Hereford Cathedral, and said: " Now, what shall I play you? see if I can remember anything you would like?" On that, a number of pieces were asked for ; excerpts from the oratorios, the works of Bach, Handel, Haydn, Mozart, Beethoven, Mendelssohn, Schumann, and other writers,—music of the most varied kind, and very very rarely was he at fault in any piece that he had heard. If memory failed for a moment, Ouseley's fingers never did ; he went on so closely imitating the style of the piece he was playing, that only those who knew the music could detect where the master left off and the player supplied the gap.

13

Mr. Southgate relates also that on one occasion he was playing, as a pianoforte duet with Sir Frederick, Spohr's quartet in G minor, Sir Frederick taking the *primo*. It was an old copy, and the last leaf of the *finale* on the treble side was missing. It made no difference to him,—he went on to the end, duly playing his part, and then remarked :—

Dear me ! I haven't seen that quartet for twenty years. I almost think I had better get a new and perfect copy.

His associate thought that after this extraordinary effort of memory there was little need of this.

Another of Sir Frederick's notable characteristics was his extraordinary power of abstraction from the things of sense when absorbed in musical thought (*o*). He seemed sometimes to imagine that he was actually producing musical sounds, when in reality he was only thinking in music. Once, for instance, in the course of some orchestral practice, he was called to order by the conductor for not playing his part on the violoncello. "Oh! yes," he said; "I am playing"; whereas someone sitting close to him noticed that he was only moving his bow backwards and forwards, without making any sound at all, being

(*o*) It is said that the poet Wordsworth used sometimes to fall into a kind of rapt mood, in which he seemed to be scarcely conscious of what was going on around him. He himself speaks somewhere in this connection of "these vanishings and fallings away." At such times he has been known to go up to a five-barred gate and shake it with both hands, to make sure that he was in a material world of things sensible. Evidently, in other things besides music and poetry, there would seem to be some close relation between genius and this power of mental abstraction.

rapt in thought over some abstract harmonies
far away from his own instrument. He never
became a very proficient player on the 'cello.
Nevertheless, he thoroughly enjoyed performing
on it; and once, when the most excruciating
sounds were proceeding from a certain amateur
stringed quartet, or trio, in which he was not the
least offender, he was heard to reply to the protest
of some bystander, " I don't care : I know how it
ought to sound." It should be added that this
took place at a private gathering in a private
house. Otherwise it would be difficult to reconcile the "don't care" with a rule once laid down
by Sir Frederick Ouseley himself : " I look upon
a wrong note in any public performance as a
positive *crime*." Another instance of this power
of musical abstraction is recorded by the Bishop
of Wakefield :—

I stayed twice with Sir Frederick at St. Michael's, and have
listened to his improvising on the piano in his study. He had a
set of pedals attached to his piano, the incessant rattle of which
destroyed all my enjoyment of the music, though I imagine it was
unheard by the player.

Perhaps this may be the best place for inserting
the following notice (*p*) of Sir Frederick, written
at the time of his death by his valued friend, the
late W. A. Barrett of St. Paul's Cathedral. It is
quite one of the truest and happiest appreciations
that have been written of the subject of this
memoir. It has also the recommendation that it
came from the pen of a critic as clever and

(*p*) See Havergal's *Memorials*, pp. 63, 64.

experienced as he was in full sympathy with his friend :—

The majority of musicians who only knew Sir Frederick Ouseley through the medium of his compositions had no means of forming a true estimate of his genius. His versatility was extraordinary, and his modesty was only equalled by the extent of his powers. He could perform well on many instruments, and knew the peculiarity of those he played upon so as to get unusual and even humorous effects from them. Often when he has concluded a difficult solo, or at the end of a graceful trio or a classical sonata, the buoyancy of his spirits was elevated to such a degree that they could only be reduced to their level by a little exhibition of pleasantry. Thus, keeping the violoncello in hand when he had finished his part and the music was ended, he would startle his hearers with the performance of an eccentric fantasia, such as "The pigs' march," accompanied by extraordinary grimaces, probably wrung from his musical sensibility by the hideous sequence of sounds such as the animals might be supposed to utter under the influence of compulsory rhythmical progress.

He would sing Spanish songs in various Castilian dialects, after the manner of the native singers, in a more or less tuneless style. He would sometimes accompany himself in one key and sing in another. This was for him not a difficult feat, so much as one of great self-denial. His ear was so sensitive and acute that it was a great trial to him to have to endure anything sung or played out of tune. Many other like things he would do in music, thus showing that the most highly cultivated minds are as keenly appreciative of the ludicrous as well as of the serious side of art. He could tell stories with the greatest relish and graphic power, and, unlike most storytellers, he was not impatient of rivalry. He loved to hear his own anecdotes "capped," as he loved to "cap" other people's stories. He collected droll and amusing replies to musical questions, which had occurred within his own experience or those of his friends, and these sort of commonplace books he delighted to exhibit to all who could relish and enjoy their peculiarities.

As a musician he shone best in private life and among sympathetic friends. It is a singular fact that when he took pen in hand to write, he was a totally different being to what he was seated at his own pianoforte pouring out his mind. No one than he was better acquainted with the intricacies of musical composition. He knew every knot and subtlety of contrapuntal art, and could deal with them in a more ready way than any of his contemporaries. He was pedantic often in his writings, but he was not so in himself. He possessed great facility in composition, and, having the power of dealing with its intricacies, sometimes thought that the proper and direct way of acquiring ease in writing was gained through self-restrictions. Thus he was wont to affirm that all composers ought to write one or more canons in various styles before breakfast, because this form of artifice gave him no trouble. It would seem as though, when he prepared himself to write his thoughts, he posed as "the learned Doctor Ouseley." Consequently, those who knew his great musical powers did not find them always represented in his compositions. His great imagination, represented in his earliest years by the composition, among other things, of a cantata descriptive of his sufferings during the progress of a fever, is only to be traced in his later instrumental works, rarely in his vocal compositions. It found full expression, however, in his extempore playing. In this, competent judges have expressed their opinion that he was unrivalled by any musician of the present century. None like him were able to treat a theme with all the resources of the art of form, or to invest it with an interest such as is found chiefly in the master works of the acknowledged best composers. Unlike many extempore players, who have a convenient stock of passages which they employ to disentangle themselves from occasional embarrassments, his ideas were always fresh, appropriate, and so well ordered that he seemed to be playing an already written piece from memory, rather than an impromptu effusion growing under his hand. Had the instrument for registering performances been perfected, and a record kept of Sir Frederick Ouseley's extempore effusions, sonatas, airs with variations, fugues, and fancies of all sorts, those of his fellow musicians who knew him only by his name, and his printed compositions, would have been enabled to form as high an estimate of his musical genius as that which is held as a cherished memory by his personal friends, and by none more earnestly than by

WM. ALEX. BARRETT, M.D.

Nov. 5, 1889.

It is easy to understand how many laughable stories, chiefly of a musical caste, a man of Sir F. Ouseley's sense of humour would be likely to gather round him. As has been said already, he himself took the keenest delight in either telling or hearing such things. Nor was he the least

197

ashamed, as some tellers of good stories are, of re-petition. Here are a few examples which will no doubt be familiar to some of his surviving friends.

Once a week there used to be instrumental practices in which most of the staff at St. Michael's were expected to take part. These practices were prolonged to a somewhat late hour, and the double-bass player, preferring his own fireside, became rather remiss in his attendance. Accordingly, he was asked one day why he had not been at a certain practice. His answer was: "Please, Sir Frederick, I am very sorry, but I have *mislaid* my double-bass." This same musician, like many other men besides musicians, never would admit himself to be in the wrong. He was found fault with after a Choral Service for singing out of tune. His reply came promptly: "No! it was the organ, Sir Frederick, that played out of tune." But the stories which used to tickle Sir Frederick most of all were those connected with the grand-iloquent language of this same worthy official, who would never use a short word where he could find a long one. Most of these once oft-quoted ex-pressions are now, it is feared, lost to fame, but here is one which may be preserved for posterity. There was to be a burial in the churchyard, and some discussion arose as to what depth the grave was to be dug. The matter was summed up by the announcement: "The parties desire profundity."

As has been already shown, Sir Frederick Ouseley, when he first came into the neighbourhood of Tenbury, was received with a certain amount of suspicion, on account of his real, or supposed, views. One lady in the neighbourhood had made it her business to warn his future parishioners against the dangerous tendencies of his teaching. Walking one day in St. Michael's parish soon after Sir Frederick came there, this lady met a little girl, and accosted her as follows : "Oh! my poor, pretty child! they will be sure to make a nun of you." When, as he so frequently managed to do, Sir Frederick had made a friend of his enemy, he took her to task for what she had said. But she stoutly maintained her position, resting her theological opinions on this statement : "I must know, for I am great-niece to Hervey's *Meditations !*"

The same lady, on another occasion, had the pleasure of hearing Sir Frederick play the overture to *Esther* on the organ, and thanked him for "that beautiful chorus of Handel's." "Well! it is an overture," said Sir Frederick ; "not exactly a chorus." "Indeed, I think I ought to know," was the answer, "considering my great-aunt once heard Handel play on the organ!"

This lady's husband was as fond of music as she was. Being himself remarkable for his stoutness and weight, he appears to have had a preference for music of the light and airy order. He had once heard Sir Frederick performing some piece of this kind which had touched his fancy, and which he wished to hear again. The only clue he could supply was that the words went something like this, "Whisky, whisky, whisky, whisky." It turned out to be Lord Mornington's glee—

Here in cool grot and mossy cell
We rural fays and fairies dwell . . .
We frisk it, frisk it, frisk it, frisk it.

Many of Sir Frederick's musical experiences in country houses afforded him intense amusement, mingled at times, it would seem, with not a little pain. At one house, where he was visiting, he was entertained after dinner with a performance of the "Hallelujah Chorus," played on three flutes. Another musical performance, in the neighbourhood of St. Michael's (which, if Sir Frederick did not witness himself, he could scarcely have failed to hear of), was that of a certain unaccompanied vocal trio, which was started in the following manner. Three ladies, who for purposes of description may be called A, B, and C, stood by the piano. Whilst B and C closed their ears, A sounded her note on the instrument, and then, softly humming it, and closing her ears, went and sat down at the farther end of the room. B and C, each in turn, and taking the same precautions, followed suit. Then, at a given signal, all three voices sounded forth their notes alone, and, the fingers being now removed, the trio was safely launched on its way. But perhaps the most unique of all Sir F. Ouseley's visiting experiences was one which he often delighted to relate to his friends. A certain eccentric clergyman, who had a great passion for musical boxes, and possessed a large assortment of them, invited Sir Frederick to give a lecture on music in the schoolroom of his parish. On the arrival of the Oxford professor at the vicarage, five or six of these instruments, all playing different tunes, were set going, as a kind of musical *salvo*. Several of the boxes were large; one was very powerful. The lecture could scarcely be called a success, being very learned, not to say dry, and the audience consisting of a few pious old women, who came in and knelt down in prayer, but could not understand a single word of the lecture. At the end of the proceedings another surprise was in store for the distinguished visitor. In the words of the local press, "the Rev. Baronet was greeted with a musical ovation." The shutters of the schoolroom all closed simultaneously; and on the opposite wall at the end of the room a chromotrope cast its reflections with marvellous gyrations and ever-changing colours, a fresh musical box meanwhile playing loudly the "Hallelujah Chorus." But this was not all. On the lecturer's return to the vicarage, the musical-box reception was resumed. One box was playing in the hall as they entered; one played throughout dinner in the dining-room; one played after dinner in the drawing-room. At last came bedtime. The unhappy Professor longed for peace. But lo! another box was awaiting him at his bedside. On and on it played. At last, in a kind of awful nightmare, the listener, half-awake and half-asleep, heard the tune run down with a feeble gasp at an unresolved discord.   When the maid came in in the morning she wound up the box, by her master's orders, and Sir Frederick awoke to the resolution of the chord.   After breakfast the visitor, needless to say, was eager to catch his train.   But a further ordeal had to be faced.   Time was arranged for a visit to the church, where the organ, containing three barrels of twelve tunes each, proceeded to wind out its whole series of thirty-six.   The railway station was only just reached in time, and the host's last words to his departing guest, as the train moved off, were these :—

Thank you, indeed, Sir Frederick, and the *next* time you come to us we must manage to give you an even better reception.

Now and again Sir Frederick also suffered considerably from amateur essays in composition, and from the early efforts of juvenile extempore players.   But he was always kindly and good-humoured about these trials.   Here is an extract from one of his letters to a sympathetic friend :—

A chant sent to me yesterday by a " musical " lady—

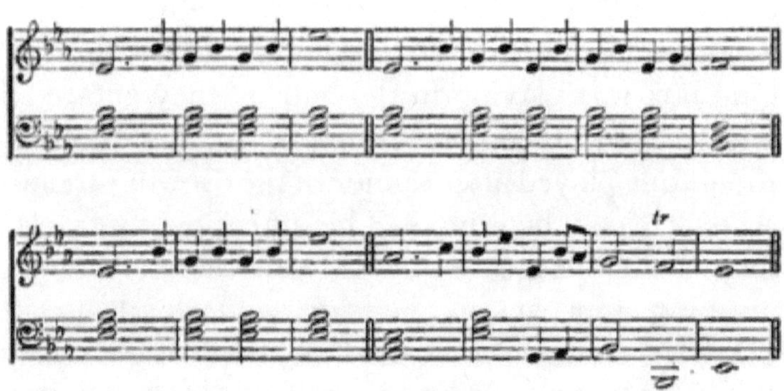

Sweet?—she says she got it done in her parish Church last Sunday ! ! !

And here is another extract from a letter, in which the sufferer describes himself as left to the tender mercies of a youthful organist—

not altogether the best performer in Europe. But he does his best, and we get along somehow. He is given to play extempore preludes to anthems, in which occur such pleasant things as that which he gave us last Sunday—

atque alia similia. Imagine my feelings, and pity me!

As may be surmised from all that has gone before, Sir F. Ouseley was intensely conservative in his musical views. This may account for the peculiar antipathy he cherished towards hymns. or perhaps it would be fairer to say, towards the modern taste in hymns (*q*). His friend, Mr. A. H. G. Morris, sends the following reminiscence on this subject :—

He used to affect that he never cared about hymn-tunes ; but I could hardly believe that in his innermost soul he did not appreciate them. I have frequently heard him say in old days that he almost disliked them. However, he rather contradicted himself at times by saying that he admired the breadth there was in the old-fashioned tunes. And if he admired one of that class more than another, it was the old 113th—" From highest heaven the Eternal Son "—I mean the music set to those words ; because he selected the hymns to be used, and we so frequently had that particular one on Sunday evenings.

(*q*) His real views on this subject may be found briefly formulated in Mr. Southgate's analysis of a paper read by Sir F. Ouseley at the Leeds Church Congress in 1872. Cf. p. 164 *supra*; and cf. also p. 115 *supra*, on *Hymns Ancient and Modern.*

If Sir Frederick held strong views on popular hymnody, he held views not less strong on the use of Gregorian chants. Personally he disliked them intensely, though it is more than probable that on a question of this kind, which seems to draw such an exact line of cleavage between one half of church musicians and the other, he would find it hard to make good his absolute condemnation of their use. One of his objections to "Gregorians" was that he considered them "unsuitable to the English language"; and he held strongly that, if sung at all, they should be sung only by men's voices.

It may be worth while to add here a few more of Sir Frederick's *obiter dicta*. They are thrown together at random, and must be taken for what they are worth. They may serve at least to bring back something of the speaker's voice, expression, and views to some of his surviving friends. He frequently prophesied that the use of instruments would come into vogue again in village Churches. For the last ten years or so of his life he always had a small string band to assist in the accompaniment of his own Michaelmas Services. With regard to the vexed question of the position of the organ in Churches he used to say : "Whatever you do, don't have it pent up in a chamber." When he heard two bells ringing at a village Church, he said :—

Ah ! your bells are not quite half a note apart ; but that is better than our two at St. Michael's, which are not quite three-quarters of a tone. Bells, when there are only two of them, should be a whole tone apart.

A friend once asked him what note a railway engine, with steam blowing off through the safety-valve, was sounding. " All sorts of notes," he said, " but chiefly B and D." He used to notice that, whether by rule or only by coincidence in his own experience, "gardeners have high voices." Though he never followed up any other branch of art than his own, he quite appreciated the breadth of the term " art," and was quick to discern the connecting links between its various branches. " Drawing and music go together," was another of his sayings. Of a certain organist whom he had been hearing he once said : " His accompaniment is as good as a commentary on the Psalms." Speaking at one of his annual Michaelmas gatherings, and returning thanks, no doubt, to the toast of " The College," Sir Frederick, expressing his difficulties as chief engine-driver, said : " A college is like a machine, worked in various wheels and pinions." As to new Oxford, Sir Frederick did not altogether appreciate it. " In my young days," he would say, " the High Street exhibited little more than dons and undergraduates ; now it swarms with nursemaids and perambulators." He used also sometimes laughingly to say, when asked why he did not marry: " I prefer my piano to any other wife, because I can always, when desirable, shut her up."

In politics, as in music, he was a rigid, not to say a bigoted, Conservative. He would entertain no compromise with " Liberal " opinions. He joined the Primrose League when it was first started, and went so far on one occasion as to preside at one of its meetings in his own parish. He used to relate with "gusto" how he once had the happiness of telling Mr. Gladstone of his faults. Mr. Gladstone was in Oxford, and paid him a canvassing call. The Professor of Music, who had the clearest conception of his own views, alike in matters of Church and State, was at no loss of what to say; and he said it. To him, as to many Oxford men of his day, the development of Mr. Gladstone's views seemed little short of disloyalty to the Church, on the part of *Alma Mater's* most gifted son. Such a *volte-face* Sir Frederick could not forgive. It roused in him feelings of the deepest and most real grief, mingled with no little anger. With Dissenters, however, of the religious kind, he always endeavoured to be on peaceful and friendly terms; and staunch as he was to his own faith, he quite admitted that their opposition might in some ways be helpful to the Church. An argument was one day going on in his presence on this question. One of the company was contending that Dissent in a parish might sometimes have a healthy influence. There was some laughing on the part of the others present. Sir Frederick's face grew grave; then he looked up and said quietly, "He is quite right."

His Arms were "Arg: a chevron sa. between 3 holly leaves pr: a chief of the 2nd with the insignia of Baronetage thereon, as usual." He was fond of telling the legend of his family crest, a wolf's head, with a bloody human hand in its mouth, the motto being *Mors lupi agnis vita*. The legend was something of this kind, according to an ancient tradition in the Ouseley family : (*r*)—

A gallant warrior of that name had married a most beautiful young lady named Agnes, about the period that King Edward I., after his return from the Holy Land, marched through Shropshire to attack the Prince of Wales. Ouseley, being a man of some rank in that country, considered it his duty to go a day's journey to meet the King and invite him to his house, although he left his bride, even for a short time, with reluctance. Agnes on the following day proceeded a short distance to meet the King and her husband ; but just as, accompanied by her maidens, she approached the royal party, a huge black wolf rushed out of a holly thicket and bit off her hand. So intent was the ferocious beast upon his prey that the enraged husband was enabled to seize him, to strangle him in the presence of the King, and to tear his head from his body. Before this adventure, the Arms of the family of Ouseley were "Or, a chevron in chief, sable." But upon this occasion the King granted the augmentation "of three holly leaves, vert.," and added the crest of a black wolf's head erased, with a right hand in its mouth, couped at the wrist, gules, on a ducal coronet with the motto, *Mors lupi, agnis vita* ; and it is said that there existed in a Church in Shropshire a monument containing the figures of this warrior and his lady, in which the latter was represented without the right hand.

The College crest (*s*), like the small statue over the front door of the Warden's house, represents the contest of St. Michael and the dragon.

Here, for want of any better place for their insertion, may be mentioned (if they are rightly remembered) two samples of Sir Frederick's

(*r*) Reynolds's *Memoir of Sir Gore Ouseley*, pp. vi. and vii.
(*s*) This crest also may be seen on the cover of this book.

conversational recipes. One was the distinction once given by a promising candidate in a musical examination : "Melody is playing in one key; harmony is playing in all the keys together." The other was the famous peroration of a certain speech said to have been delivered by an Oxford alderman :—

And, in conclusion, when I see before me the spontaneous dome of the Radcliffe Library, the basilisk of Blenheim, and the merryanderings of the river Cherwell, I feel gratified, nay ! more, I feel proud, to think that I have discharged my civic duties without partiality, on the one hand, and without impartiality, on the other.

This chapter has been mainly filled with illustrations of the secular, and more especially the humorous side, of Sir F. Ouseley's life. But it would be an utterly mistaken view to give of him that such was the only, or even the chief, side of his character. From the crown of his head to the soles of his feet he was a thoroughly religious man ; and though, like many of the best Englishmen, he was reserved, and did not wear his heart on his sleeve, yet without any doubt religion was to him the mainspring of his work, as it was the one grand object worth living for. Thus although, as has been shown, he was fully alive at times to mundane interests and pleasures, one often felt on meeting him that his usual thoughts must have been of unseen things, that they were continually ranging above the ordinary round of life. Always in walking he looked up, not down, as so many thinkers do. The fact was that, more than most men, he had a vivid realisation of the presence around us of unseen beings; and what some people call superstition was in him a very real belief in the agency and ministrations of powers beyond our ken. It was one of the sayings of his friend Liddon:

I do not, of course, hold it as a matter of faith on the same level with the Articles of the Apostles' Creed—but yet I do hold it as a certain truth in my own mind—that about us and around us the air is full of angels, though we see them not.

A large part of Sir Frederick Ouseley's life-work undoubtedly rested on that belief. And it seems only in accordance with this that his Church and College should have been dedicated, as they were, to St. Michael and All Angels. Certainly, one effect of the dedication itself must always be to draw the thoughts of others also to the invisible.

One other subject may be mentioned here, akin to the one just noticed: and yet care should be taken that the two subjects are not confused. Sir Frederick was what is popularly called a "believer in ghosts." He did not, of course, regard the question of spiritual apparitions as either of equal certainty or as of equal importance with that of angelic ministrations. But he did undoubtedly always refuse to regard the question of ghostly appearances from the merely sceptical point of view. He was once asked, when telling some ghost stories, if he felt any fear at the sight of a ghost. His answer was:

I know that spirits are always near me; and why should I be afraid if I were allowed to see one?

14

Indeed, he claimed for his family that one or other of them was warned by a "rorast" (if this be the correct Scotch term) when any member of the family was about to die. He used to tell a tale of how a cousin of his saw her sister one night appear to her with all her hair cut off. The sister was on her way to India, and by the next mail news came that she had died of fever on the very night of the appearance, and that her hair had been cut off previously by the doctor's orders. Mr. T. L. Southgate recalls the fact that Sir Frederick never affected to explain these phenomena, but in conversation on the subject would remind his hearers of the witch of Endor episode, and other supernatural appearances in the Bible. These, he would point out, could not be explained by the logic of *natural* laws. Dean Kitchin, whilst evidently no believer himself in ghosts, bears witness no less strongly to the views of his old friend on the subject :—

Ouseley was a man who *could not help* coming in contact with ghosts ! His very eyes told you so.

The following is one of the Ouseley ghost stories. Its veracity cannot be vouched for in every particular ; for, like many similar tales, it has grown larger in the telling. At a certain house, with which Sir F. Ouseley was once connected, an apparition was often seen. All kinds of weird things were also continually happening there at night. Bells rang ; windows and doors, which had been duly shut and locked at evening, were found open on the following morning. In the vulgar version of the story, the ghost took the form of an old man with a brown coat; and, so strong was the local belief in the ghostly character of the apparition, that at last no one would live in the house, and eventually it was pulled down. But before this happened, Sir Frederick's experiences were as follow. Having retired one night as usual, he remembered that he had left a book he wanted in the drawing - room. With the intention of fetching it, he opened the door of his bedroom, which led into a long old - fashioned corridor. There, at the end of the passage, he saw to his astonishment a bright unearthly light; and in the middle of the light he saw distinctly the figure of a man, clothed in a dressing-gown, with a flowing "wateau" back, such as was commonly worn a century before. The expression of the man's face was fearful,—suggestive of all manner of sin and wickedness; and, feeling instinctively convinced that what he saw was an evil spirit, Sir Frederick made the sign of the cross, and by the name of the Blessed Trinity adjured the spectre to depart. On coming down to breakfast the next morning, Sir Frederick said nothing of what he had seen. Determined, however, to find out if there were any story connected with the house which might account for the vision, he went to the village close by and applied to the old clerk, in the hope of obtaining some information. From him he learned that, a hundred years before, the house had been occupied by a certain bad squire, who murdered his wife and afterwards put an end to himself. This story was corroborated on examining the parish registers ; for these contained the statement that the Lord of the Manor, of that date, having murdered his wife, and having then committed suicide, his body was refused Christian burial, and was buried at the cross roads. Sir Frederick still mentioned nothing of this to any of the inmates of the house. Exactly a year afterwards, however, an Oxford friend of his, of a somewhat reckless and rowdy character, was invited to stay in the same house for a week or two. He came and was quartered in a bed-room near the end of the house, to enter which you had to go down three steps at the end of the corridor already mentioned. On the morning following his arrival the visitor came downstairs looking wretchedly ill and haggard. He announced that he had received bad news, which necessitated his immediate return to London. Indeed, he had ordered a fly to catch the first train. The news was such that he begged his hosts to ask him no further questions about it. A few weeks later Sir Frederick happened to meet his friend in the street in London, and the friend then said :—

I can tell you now what I could not tell you before about the reason of my departure the other day from ——. In the middle of the night I was awakened by the sound of a terrible struggle in the passage outside my room. I sat up in bed and listened. There were the most frightful mutterings and fearful oaths, interspersed with the words—"Too late ! Too late !" All the while I felt certain that the utterances were those of a lost soul. Presently the noise of the struggling ceased, and was followed by the sound of steps labouring along towards my door, evidently the steps of someone dragging a heavy weight along the floor. A moment more, and my door was burst open with a tremendous crash, and the footsteps came down into my room, followed by the heavy weight, bump, bump, bump! down the three steps outside. I *saw* nothing, but was in a state of helpless terror all the rest of the night.

Whatever may be thought of the credibility of this story, so wholesome and permanent an effect had the event upon Sir Frederick's friend, that, from having been a thoroughly fast and careless man, he became, it is said, from that time forward completely changed, and was afterwards known as one of the most earnest and hard working of London clergy. The strangest part of the story (if it be true) remains still to be told. It is said that the occupier of the house, in consequence of these ghostly apparitions, determined to leave it altogether. For this purpose he went, in company with Sir Frederick Ouseley, to the owner's house in London. As the owner happened to be engaged at the moment of their arrival, they were shown into the dining - room. Immediately on entering the room, Sir Frederick, pointing to an old por- trait which hung over the mantelpiece, exclaimed : " *There, ——, that's the very man I saw !* " The picture was that of a man with an evil counten- ance, and wearing the style of dress such as was worn a hundred years before. When the landlord came in, his visitors took the opportunity of ques- tioning him about the portrait. He was very unwilling to tell them much, as the portrait represented a very disreputable ancestor of his, from whom he had inherited the property. This ancestor had committed suicide, if not murder also, a century before. They could not ascertain many particulars, but all that the landlord said coincided exactly with what Sir Frederick had before discovered in connection with the old " Manor House."

CHAPTER IX

Two things seem to have troubled Sir F. Ouseley, and to have caused him a great deal of real unhappiness, during the closing years of his life. One was his anxiety as to the financial future of his College; the other was his own position in the musical world.

To a large extent the maintenance of St. Michael's depended on rents from land; and when the agricultural depression began, Sir Frederick found himself no exception to the rule of hard-hit landlords. As has been implied already, he never succeeded in making his school self-supporting; and, indeed, in this respect its peculiar constitution, and its distance from any large centres of population, would have handicapped many a better manager than he himself was. Moreover, he would never do anything, if it could be avoided, which might tend to lower the standard of that splendid musical Service which was the chief result, as it had been the chief object, of his foundation. Thus the reduction in his income in the last few years of his life became a serious trouble to him; and when he began to feel that his own tenure of life was uncertain, this anxiety was, of course, intensified. More than once he received timely and generous assistance from his good friend and neighbour, the Hon. Miss Rushout of Burford, who had always taken the deepest interest in the Church and College. Eventually, but after Sir Frederick's death, this lady, in 1890, left a large legacy for the benefit of St. Michael's, supplementary to the Founder's own benefactions; and thus the future maintenance of the College on its original lines has been assured.

The other trouble of his closing years evidently touched Sir Frederick's heart even more deeply than any pecuniary anxieties. This was the neglect with which he felt himself to be treated by the musical world generally. Rightly or wrongly, he believed that in certain influential quarters there was some professional jealousy at work against him. His own rank, private fortune, and position had of course rendered him independent of music as a profession; and his feeling was that on this account he had not been given fair play in the musical world. If he was wrong in his surmise, as it is quite possible he may have been, it must be remembered, on his behalf, that he was in one sense a lonely man, and therefore peculiarly at the mercy of any such morbid impression. He was a bachelor, and in his later years had no near relatives living. Moreover, although he had hosts of friends, yet it would be only to a very few, if any, of them that he would care to pour out his whole heart on a delicate subject of this kind. Thus what seemed to him a neglect of set purpose may have been nothing more than that dropping out of particular notice which comes to many men as they advance in years, and as the best work of their life is becoming a thing of the past. He may have exaggerated little things into great, and brooded over them unnecessarily. On the other hand, it is quite certain that any such spirit of brooding over grievances was no ordinary feature in his character. Naturally he was not in the least either a jealous or a grasping man. He was modest, generous, and open-handed to a fault. He would do anything, and did do much, to help on young beginners in the musical profession, more especially those of them who might be endowed with only small means. It was said of him after his death that he had been (a)

The personal friend of every minor canon, lay clerk, and chorister in England, and certainly those of their connection never had such a friend as they possessed in Sir Frederick Ouseley.

And this, indeed, seems to have been one of the sorest points with him in the matter alluded to. He was always proud to identify himself with the musical profession. " Music to the glory of God " had been, as it were, the very motto of his life. And therefore, when he felt that he was not being allowed his fair place in the particular profession he had adopted, and for which he had done so much, he felt hurt,—as if his own brothers had

(a) Havergal's *Memorials*, p. 44.

turned their backs on him. It was certainly not a case of mere disappointment at ill-success, either in the matter of fame or from a pecuniary point of view, ready as he always was to make a few pounds by his pen for his beloved St. Michael's. That it was really a case of deep personal feeling, the following letter will show, written to one of his most valued friends, and one who now holds a distinguished place in the musical world :—

ST. MICHAEL'S COLLEGE, TENBURY,
July 25, 1883.

MY DEAR ———.—I am very glad you like the Sonata in its printed form, and that you will play it. You are, I fear, the only man who ever plays my compositions for the Organ. I look through the list of things played at various recitals, and recorded in the *Musical Standard*, and elsewhere, and hardly once a year do I see anything of mine recorded. This is very discouraging to me, and I feel it much. ——— bought the copyright of this last Sonata of me for three guineas only, and made a favour of that! I cannot but fear there is some professional jealousy at work against me. Perhaps after I am dead it will be different. I don't think I shall compose any more organ-music ever again. Excuse my grumbling! You must admit I have some cause. . . . I am suffering from whooping-cough, *not* a pleasant thing at my time of life! . . . —Yours very sincerely,

FREDERICK A. G. OUSELEY.

Nevertheless, there were proofs given before Sir F. Ouseley's death, as well as after, that his musical abilities as a composer, as well as otherwise, were appreciated at no mean order in musical circles generally. Here is an instance, recorded by the then secretary of the Bach Choir :—

In the year 1882 the committee of the Bach Choir, under the advice of the musical director, Mr. Otto Goldschmidt, decided to include in one of that season's concerts at St. James's Hall three representative English anthems by composers of the 17th, 18th, and 19th centuries. The anthems selected were, "Sing joyfully" (W. Byrd) ; "I will sing of Thy power" (Dr. Greene) ; and "Great is the Lord" (Sir F. Ouseley). As the secretary of the Bach Choir, I had the pleasure of communicating this decision to my friend Sir Frederick, and of receiving from him a reply, couched in terms which showed how highly he appreciated this recognition of his position as a composer for the Church.   A. H. D. PRENDERGAST.

This, too, may be the best place for noticing how generous a response was made at the time of Sir Frederick Ouseley's death to the appeal for an endowment fund for his College, as being the best memorial to his honour. Some £3000 was raised, largely in the musical world,—upwards of £500 being subscribed by his friends in Oxford.

It has been assumed in the previous pages that Sir F. Ouseley was an unambitious man ; and in the ordinary meaning of the term it would not be hard to prove that he was such. Yet he would seem to have had one ambition, or rather, it may only have been, one ideal of ambition, in the thought of the Deanery of Westminster. It is not likely that he ever seriously anticipated such a preferment for himself, although it is said that a Westminster Canonry had at one time been promised to him by Mr. Disraeli. But Sir Frederick certainly regarded the Deanery of Westminster as one of the most enviable posts which a man of his own calling and attainments could have reached. In truth, he was a man who would have lent a charm and an interest to any position, however high, that he might have been called to fill ; and he was one out of whom a great position might have drawn a good deal which his natural modesty kept in the background. Larger congregations, closer contact with the keen intellect of London life, and the historic enthusiasm derivable from the Abbey itself, would no doubt have developed in him much of that power in preaching, and otherwise, which in his humble sphere of life never reached its full force. That he was not, however, in any general sense of the term an ambitious, much less a disappointed, man, was proved by the genuine, almost childlike, pleasure with which he regarded his appointment to the Hereford Canonry three years before his death. To most of his friends that honour seemed to be a very modest recognition of his powers and of his work for the Church. But to him it was an honour to be proud of, and it certainly added no little happiness to his last years.

An event of wider interest to the Church at large than any promotion falling to his own lot also gave him intense pleasure towards the close of his life. In 1887 Truro Cathedral, so far as it was then finished, was consecrated by Archbishop Benson. The foundation-stones had been laid in 1877, with grand masonic honours, by the Prince of Wales, as Duke of Cornwall. Ten years later, on November 3, 1887, the Prince was present also at the consecration; and Sir Frederick Ouseley, who, by the way, was himself a Freemason of considerable standing, attended the ceremony. He was invited as one of the chief guests on the occasion, and his own anthem, "Great is the Lord," was performed in the afternoon. A few days afterwards he was graphically describing to a sick friend in his own neighbourhood the splendid function ; he was saying that the processional Psalm, " Lift up your heads, O ye gates," was one of the most impressive things he had ever witnessed ; and he was expressing his great thankfulness that such a thing was possible in our days. Then all at once his feelings overpowered his self‐control, and, in a way very uncommon with him, he sank his head in his hands and burst into tears. The incident betokens how intense were his love and loyalty for God's glory in the Church of Christ. To that end he had used his "one talent" for upwards of thirty years ; and the consecration of a new Cathedral for a new (or rather, for a revived) Diocese appealed to his heart in a way few men could have felt as he did.

It is a matter of regret that so few letters of any general interest are forthcoming as having been written by Sir Frederick in the latter years of his life. Here, however, are three extracts out of a small bundle which has come to hand. They are samples of the short notes he was accustomed to write to numbers of his friends. Moreover, as the receiver (*b*) of these particular notes says of them, "they have a touch of the true nature of the writer about them." There

(*b*) The Rev. V. K. Cooper, Precentor of Durham, and formerly Headmaster of St. Michael's College.

are the happy little jokes of which he was so fond, and there is the sad touch in the last letter as to "setting his house in order"—a presentiment, it would seem, of the end :—

May 1886.

. . . Did I tell you of the splendid version, given at the Newnham College for Ladies, of Καλῶς ἔχει τὸ γέγονος—"The baby is doing well." Coming, as it did, from ladies, it is, methinks, a perfect specimen.

---

9 CASTLE STREET, HEREFORD,
August 10, 1886.

I MEANT to have written to you before this to thank you for your most amusing letter. I only wish I had anything half so good to give you in return. "*Ventum erat ad limen*" (Virgil), "The wind was at the door"; and "*Nulla dies adeo est Australibus humida nimbis*," etc. (Ovid), "Not a day passes in Australia, but what there is a shower," are not bad. I am very glad you enjoyed your visit here. *I* did! I expect S. and some other friends here to dine on the 12th, which is my birthday. Think of me then, fast developing into the "lean and slippered pantaloon," and wish me well through it!

ST. MICHAEL'S COLLEGE, TENBURY.
December 18, 1888.

. . . I have not been at all well since May. My *heart* is all wrong, and I cannot walk without horrid agony there very often. I fear this is incurable, as it is hereditary. It is a warning to "put my house in order."

There are other evidences besides the one just quoted which show that Sir Frederick, for some months before his death, quite understood that his end was likely to come suddenly. He had reached the critical age of sixty‑three; and the doctors had warned him that, with his hereditary weakness of heart, he must beware of any excitement or violent exertion. All his life hitherto he had been a good walker. But now he would frequently have to apologise to one or another of his friends when asking them to stop till he should recover breath. " I suppose I must have a weak heart," he said to one of them, after halting a good many times on the hill which goes up from Tenbury to St. Michael's ; and then he added with a smile, "but I trust it is not a bad one." During the last year or so of his life he would talk not infrequently on the subject of sudden death. He once asked a friend if he thought it was wrong to wish to die suddenly. The friend reminded him that Bishop Samuel Wilberforce had desired to die such a death, and that the Bishop used to point out in this connection that the petition in the Litany : " From sudden death, good Lord, deliver us," really meant nothing more than "from unprepared death." Very naturally also Sir Frederick, like most other hard-working men, had a strong desire, if so God might will it for him, to " die in harness." A prolonged old age would, indeed, have been likely to prove no happy experience for him. He was unmarried ; all his near relatives, and many of his oldest and most valued friends, were now dead (c). And, although his College was still

(c) His two sisters had died in 1861 and 1862. " The death of Wayland Joyce [1887] certainly left the blank in Sir Frederick's life which *his* death has in my life—and in the life of how many more ! " N. M. L. in Havergal's *Memorials*, p. 44.

the first thought in his life, yet he felt keenly enough some of his losses in the ranks of those who had been as brothers to himself.

His last sermon at St. Michael's was preached on the second Sunday in Lent, March 17, 1889, on 2 Sam. xii. 7, " Thou art the man." Soon after he went to Hereford, and stayed at his residence in the Cathedral Close. Apparently he was just then in better health and spirits, and was looking forward to spending Easter at home. Only three days before his death he wrote the following interesting letter to Mr. Ebenezer Prout, author of the well-known work on " Harmony," who had been staying with him at St. Michael's for a week during the preceding Christmas :—

THE CLOSE, HEREFORD, *April* 3, 1889.

MY DEAR SIR,—In the first place, I must apologise to you for the delay which has occurred in my reply to yours of March 13th. The fact is, I have been very busy, and much "worritted," as folks say, by some bothers connected with . . . , involving a large amount of correspondence, and I have also been far from well, and utterly unable to fix my attention on matters of musical theory, etc. Now I am better and stronger, and I therefore take up my pen once more to make an attempt to reply to what you say as to the results of your study of Helmholtz. No doubt he is right, and you are right, in saying that we cannot regard such remote harmonies as the 17th and 19th quite as we do the 3rd, 5th, and 7th. But still, for all that, *they exist*. Although we may be unable to detect them by our unaided ears, when sounding as part of a complete compound sound or tone, yet they do sound, and do exercise their respective influences upon the *quality* of the tone. We are therefore quite justified in taking them as the explanation furnished by nature of those chords which we use in our musical compositions. Moreover, I am not *sure*, after all, that they are altogether inaudible. I fancy I have detected them in the sound of a 32-*foot reed pipe* : but in this I may be mistaken too.

In any case, however, we *select* for use any overtones we need ;

and these two (the 17th and 19th) we need very much. The minor 3rd and major 3rd, of course, must collide harshly when both heard at once. But when we silence one of them we can use the other. For that reason I always advocate the plan of making all Tierces in organ specifications to *draw separately*, and not be included in the ranks of the mixture stops. They can thus be shut off when playing in the minor key. And yet, when properly voiced and duly subordinated, they do not practically sound so badly as one might expect, *except in the extreme bass*. That is my experience as an organ-fancier.

There is a wonderful faculty in the human ear of, as it were, regarding an approximately correct interval as though it were absolutely correct. Were it not for that faculty, we could not tolerate equal temperament. Now, it seems to me that the small comma 96 : 95, by which the true minor third 19 : 16 differs from the minor third which exists between a major 3rd and a perfect 5th, viz. 6 : 5, is ignored by the ear, and that thus the true minor 3rd appears *as concordant as though its ratio were simpler*.

With regard to the *minor ninth*, no such explanation is needed, as it is heard to be *a discord*, and about as discordant as its *high numbers* would warrant us in expecting it to be, but not more so.

The *major* ninth is a *square*, 3×3, and being the fifth of the fifth, the dominant of the dominant, does not sound by any means so discordant as the true harmonic 7th. The ear in the case of the latter has to accommodate itself to the comma 64 : 63, which is a much larger interval than the 96 : 95 of the minor third. And that power of accommodation is the only æsthetic consideration for which I see any need in this matter of harmony.

On looking over what I have written, I fear you will think it beside the question, or little better than twaddle. But I have a great difficulty in expressing myself clearly ; and I know that, whatever my words may seem, my meaning is *not* altogether twaddle. I shall be glad to hear from you on the subject. I remain here for a week more, and then go back to Tenbury. You may be interested to hear that last night I composed a strict canon, 12 in 6, before going to bed. I have not been doing anything in the composing way of late, and I wanted to get my hand in, a bit! I do not want to lose the power *yet*. Believe me very sincerely yours,   FREDERICK A. G. OUSELEY.

On Saturday, April 6, Sir Frederick attended the Cathedral Service in Hereford, at 10 A.M., and

15

read the Lessons. He seems to have spent the rest of the morning at home. At this time he had been a good deal worried about certain arrangements at St. Michael's. After luncheon he called out to his housekeeper:

I am just going to write a letter to Mr. Hampton, who is coming over on Monday: see that it is posted. Then I shall go over to the club or library, and come back in time for service.

As he went out of the Close into Broad Street one of the choir-boys was running in, and took off his cap to the Precentor. Sir Frederick's greeting in return was characteristic of all his dealings with choristers and choirmen. Always ready with a kind word for them, he never forgot, and would never let them forget, the object of their profession.   To him the daily offering of worship in the Church was a real sacrifice to the glory of God. "Well, little man," he said, "and what is to be the Anthem this evening?" Before that Anthem was sung God had called His servant away. The Precentor's seat that evening was vacant. When Evensong was ended there followed the usual Saturday choir practice in the Cathedral. In the middle of this practice a note was handed to the Sub-Chanter, the Rev. J. R. G. Taylor, who, having opened and hastily read it, said to those present, "Sir Frederick is dead!" Then he added solemnly, "And may the Lord have mercy on his soul!" There was a hushed "Amen" uttered by several voices. With such awful suddenness had the news come upon them that several of the men as well as most of the boys quite broke down. Instinctively the Hereford choir felt that in the death of their Precentor the whole Church of England had lost a leader who had been more to choirs, and had done more for them, than any other musician or clergyman of his generation.

From the accounts subsequently published in the newspapers it appeared that, on passing out of the Close, and after looking in for a moment at the City and County Club, Sir Frederick had met Prebendary E. B. Hawkshaw in Broad Street. Whilst the two friends were talking together the former was suddenly seized with a severe spasm of the heart. They were standing close to the Birmingham, Dudley, and District Bank; and with the aid of Mr. Kenrick, the bank manager, who happened to be standing in the street, Sir Frederick was taken at once into a private room belonging to the bank. There his medical adviser, Mr. Turner, was quickly with him, and restoratives were given in the form of ether and brandy. His servant also was fetched from the Close, and Sir Frederick said to him, " I am so glad you have come to take me home." It is clear from what followed that, directly his pain was relieved, the sufferer thought the crisis was passed. He must have known that he had been near death. Indeed, he said as much to those who stood round him. But he does not seem to have realised that even then he had but a few short moments to live. He went on to speak

quite naturally about his immediate engagements
for the rest of the day (*d*)—

He began to chat in his usual affable manner. He said several
times, "I thought I was going to die." He talked for about ten
minutes after the restoratives had been administered, and the
doctor said, "You are better now," and he replied, "Yes! I am
very much better; I shall be all right in a few minutes." He
mentioned that he was to have dined at the Deanery that evening,
but Doctor Turner said that it would not be possible for him to do
so. He was immediately seized with an epileptic fit, and Mr.
Turner promptly shook him, cut open his collar and shirt band, and
asked Mr. Kenrick to turn him over on his face. Mr. Kenrick had
him in his arms, and had half turned him over when he suddenly
ceased to breathe. Mr. Turner states that Sir Frederick had
suffered from a weak heart for a long time, and recently he had
been subject to spasms of the heart. The attack on Saturday
afternoon was undoubtedly the severest he had had, but the immediate cause of death was the epileptic fit.

When the tidings of their Founder's sudden call
reached the College and parish of St. Michael's on
that Saturday evening, the news at first could
scarcely be believed. The St. Michael's boys
were away for the holidays, but were due back for
Easter. Probably never, until the news of Sir
Frederick's death reached them, had any of his
fellow-workers, scholars, or parishioners, realised
how closely his life and work and personality had
become entwined in their own affections.

Until the following Wednesday his body lay at
his residence in the Close. On that day, after a
short, impressive Service in the Cathedral, it was
taken by train to Tenbury, and thence conveyed
to St. Michael's, lying for one night in the College
library, covered with wreaths and crosses of

(*d*) *Tenbury Advertiser*, April 16, 1889.

flowers. On the following afternoon, at three o'clock,—Thursday, April 11, 1889,—all that was mortal of Frederick Ouseley was laid to rest in the acre which he himself had once given to God —the Founder's grave lying most fittingly beneath the east window of the chancel. Needless to say, everything was done which love, care, and reverence could do to make his burial worthy of the man. Moss, violets, and primroses, gathered by the children of the parish school, lined his grave. Numbers of friends from all parts of England had come to pay their last tribute. Even with the short notice that was only possible, no fewer than twenty-one of those who in former days had been scholars under Sir Frederick's care had gathered round his grave. The choir was one befitting the occasion. Besides the St. Michael's staff there were present all the clerical and lay members of the Hereford Cathedral choir, the Precentor and four choristers from Worcester Cathedral, and many other musicians and clergy. Still more significant was the large attendance of his own poorer parishioners, showing by their hushed demeanour how truly they had loved their gentle pastor. Bishop Atlay read the opening sentences of the Burial Office, and the Lessons ; the Rev. J. Hampton conducting all the musical parts of the Service. Psalm xxxix. was chanted to Purcell's chant in G minor ; and, after the Lesson, was sung "Jerusalem on high," the beautiful chorale at the beginning of Sir Frederick Ouseley's *Hagar*. At the grave the Bishop said the

words of committal with the concluding prayers.
Then was sung, unaccompanied, as perhaps it
had never been sung before, the hymn, "They
come, God's messengers of love," to the very
tune Sir Frederick had composed for the dedication festival of St. Michael's more than thirty
years before.

On the two Sundays following Sir Frederick
Ouseley's death there were, as might have been
expected, numerous sermon references to his
memory.   Not only in Hereford, and in the
neighbourhood of St. Michael's, but in Oxford
and in London, and, indeed, throughout the whole
country, his name was mentioned with loving
words in many a Church and Cathedral.   Canon
Ince, the Oxford Regius Professor of Divinity,
preaching in Christ Church Cathedral, on the
Palm Sunday morning (April 14), drew a touching comparison between the names of Keble
and Ouseley, the Church poet and the Church
musician,—each a son of Oxford, each in his own
generation one of her Professors :(e)—

I am unwilling to leave the pulpit this morning without some
words of reference to a loss just sustained, which must awaken
peculiar memories and profound regrets in Oxford, and more
especially in Christ Church. Death, startling in its suddenness,
has removed from earth Sir Frederick Ouseley, our eminent and
highly-valued Professor of Music. A born musician, if any man
ever was, . . . he has devoted the whole of his life to the cultivation of his noble gift, especially in the service of religion. . . .

By a singular coincidence the poem for Palm Sunday in the
Christian Year has a stanza which, containing a confession of the
poet's own incapacity for music, points to the fitting attitude of

---

(e) Canon Ince's sermon, quoted in Havergal's *Memorials*, pp. 48, 49.

those who, whilst they admire, cannot yet appreciate fully the services of music as the handmaid of religion—

> "Lord, by every minstrel tongue
>   Be Thy praise so duly sung,
>   That Thine angels' harps may ne'er
>   Fail to find fit echoing here :
>   We the while, of meaner birth,
>   Who in that divinest spell
>   Dare not hope to join on earth,
>   Give us grace to listen well" (*f*).

Some of us, who are neither musicians like Ouseley nor poets like Keble, while we lay our tribute of feeble words on the fresh grave of the great master of music whose loss we deplore, may perhaps be allowed to adopt for ourselves words of the same master of song, occurring in yet another of his poems :—

> "In vain, with dull and tuneless ear,
>   I linger by soft Music's cell,
>   And in my heart of heart's would hear
>   What to her own she deigns to tell.
>
>   .   .   .   .   .   .
>
> But patience! there may come a time
>   When these dull ears shall scan aright
>   Strains, that outring Earth's drowsy chime,
>   As Heaven outshines the taper's light" (*g*).

Though our "psalms and hymns and spiritual songs" may be as inartistic as were the Hosannas which, as on this day, the children raised in the Temple of Jerusalem to the King of Israel on the eve of His Passion, we may comfort ourselves with the poet's thought—

> "Childlike though the voices be,
>   And untunable the parts,
>   Thou wilt own the minstrelsy,
>   If it flow from childlike hearts" (*h*).

But, indeed, "childlike minstrelsy" is a phrase which might be taken as no unfitting description of

(*f*) *Christian Year*, fourth stanza for Palm Sunday.

(*g*) *Christian Year*, for fourth Sunday in Advent.

(*h*) *Christian Year*, last stanza for Palm Sunday.

Sir Frederick Ouseley's whole life and character, viewed apart from his own special musical gifts. There was in him a strain of music capable of touching men's hearts with a finer tone than that of either human voice or instruments of wind and string. All his life long he gave forth the music of a childlike heart; and it drew to him not friends only, but foes as well sometimes, with a wonderful power. Every good man's life must have its own secret. Sir Frederick Ouseley's chief influence lay in the simple, guileless, affectionateness of his nature. And what was once said of James Fraser, the second Bishop of Manchester, may be said with equal truth of this other workman for the Church of Christ—"*He kept his child's heart to the end.*"

On Sir Frederick Ouseley's grave is a Memorial recumbent Cross, subscribed for by fifty of his friends. It was designed by Mr. Aston Webb, and consists of a block of polished red granite, on which lies a cross of white marble supported at the ends by four small pillars cut out of the granite. The inscription runs as follows :—

IN LOVING MEMORY OF THE

REV. SIR FREDERICK ARTHUR GORE OUSELEY,
BARONET:

Born the 12th day of August 1825 ; *died the 6th day of April* 1889 :

Vicar of this Parish :

Founder of the Church and College of St. Michael and All Angels :

This stone is laid on his grave by a number of his friends.

On the upper ledge on either side of the stone are inscribed the following verses from Holy Scripture :—"*He shall give His Angels charge over thee, to keep thee in all thy ways,*" and "*The redeemed of the Lord shall return, and come with singing unto Zion.*"

Close to Sir Frederick's accustomed stall in St. Michael's Church has been placed a brass Cross, with this inscription :—

IN GRATEFUL AND PERPETUAL REMEMBRANCE OF

FREDERICK ARTHUR GORE OUSELEY, BARONET,

First Vicar of this Parish :

Born August 12th, 1825 ; *died April 6th,* 1889 :

From his Parishioners.

CHAPTER X

IT is no doubt a difficult matter for those who have shared the rich inheritance of modern English music to realise the full value of the work achieved by Sir Frederick Ouseley. He was essentially a great Church musician; and in the music of the Church so great a change has come over our Cathedrals and parish Churches within the present century that, to fully estimate the services which this noble and resolute man rendered to English Church music, it is very necessary to have a clear idea of its state at the time when he first devoted himself to raising its condition. The very success of his labours tends to obscure them; for the more earnest and the more devotional the Church music of to-day is, the more difficult it becomes to understand the barrenness and poverty which marked it only half a century ago. Sir Frederick Ouseley's greatness lies in part in the noble unselfishness with which he devoted himself to a great purpose.

In the early part of the century, though there were many composers who showed that English instinct was still alive,—men, indeed, who in many forms of music had earned for themselves a just

reputation,—there was, nevertheless, no great cause
for national pride in the aspect of English Church
music. It had lost much of its earlier strictness,
and had become loose and irregular. With the
earlier writers, there was always a sense of that
due discipline which permitted as much freedom
as possible without infringement of any necessary
laws of art. But at this time there was no clear
government, and Church music, following the
caprice of the composer, had become erratic.
The tendencies of the age, which were entirely
romantic, no doubt led writers to indulge in
personal emotion and wayward flights which
represented the fitful moods which might pass
over them. Music thus had less relation to its
due province than to the disorderly emotions of
the writer. The older music created by the
English mind at its sanest moment was purely
ideal. There was real relationship between the
earnestness of belief and the simplicity of its
expression, or again, between the architecture of
the Cathedral and the dignity and purity of its
music. The art was passing, as were literature
and thought, through a transition period in the
earlier part of the present century, and licence
prevailed instead of law, just as, in the absence of
authority, individual impulse improvised its rules.
The result was that Church Services were lacking
in purpose, in austerity, and even in devotion.
But there was another evil no less grave. Musical
education was inefficient and little cared for.
Music had fallen almost into disrepute as a study

in our seats of learning. The conservatism of
the Universities regarded it as frivolous, as a thing
quite aside from culture. And thus, instead of
there being a tendency to develop the musical
talent of the day, and to make it effective, there
was a force quite in the other direction. Those
who had the musical instinct had few means of
competent instruction, and were left to their own
resources, as if pursuing a harmless, unimportant
fad. No general culture was expected of those
who were bold enough to seek a Degree. And
thus, just at the time when English music was most
in need of organised and scientific direction, it
had to stumble along as best it might, with little
academic training of any value, and without the
stimulus of an honourable recognition.

It is necessary to bear these two facts in mind
in estimating the value of Sir Frederick Ouseley's
services to English music. There was at once
general weakness and inaptitude in Services of
the Church, coupled with very poor manner of
rendering them, and there was no sound School of
musical training. Music was poor, the choirs were
untrained, and the Universities were indifferent.
It was the task of many men to produce a revolution in these vital defects. But Sir Frederick
Ouseley, it may justly be claimed, was in the fore-
front of the fight, and devoted himself with as
much resolution as those around him, and with
much more fixed purpose than most of them. His
position, added to his abilities, fitted him well for
the task, and he may be taken as a worthy repre-

sentative of the great movement that sprang up in his time and established afresh the ancient traditions of choral music in the Church of England.

Sir Frederick, of course, had the incomparable advantage of natural genius. The interesting and somewhat pathetic account of his eldest sister proves, if proof were needed, his extraordinary aptitude for music. The sense of pitch seemed to be almost innate. There is no need to dwell overlong on the effect of a certain piece of music on his infant ears, for it becomes the critic to look with suspicion upon the recollections of over-anxious relatives, but there is no question that at a very early age he had a distinct notion of harmony, and even composed a little piece at about three years of age. He was constantly surprising those around him with his quick ear, and his readiness to name notes struck casually upon the piano. These accomplishments may not, it is true, be so rare now as they seemed to be in those days, but they are important to notice as being the evidences of a mind naturally apt, though untrained, and as giving proof of an acute ear at an extraordinarily early age. The mathematical sense thus early made itself felt. It was a sense that grew with years, and may be said to have predominated the genius of the musician. It is, in fact, the keynote of Sir Frederick Ouseley's success as a theorist, just as it marks his limitations as an original writer. For it is noticeable that, during all these early days of boyhood, the stories that are told bear witness to the acuteness of his faculties rather than to the sensitiveness of his imagination. The first point of definite interest in his youthful days is an effort at composition made when he was a little over six and a half years of age. The small work which is here reproduced is descriptive of his sensations on recovery from an illness at that time, and is certainly remarkable for its ideas and for sense of humour and of contrast.

Iller than ever.
Blisters.
rall.
rall.
A little better.

YOUTHFUL COMPOSITIONS

In even his earliest compositions he began to show the influence of Mozart in a remarkable manner, and this influence, indeed, may be traced in almost all his instrumental works to the end of his life.

EXAMPLE II.

From this time he seems to have been fairly prolific in similar efforts. and to have given pleasure to many distinguished musicians. The Duchess of Hamilton (at that time well known for her skill

242

in music) describes herself as affected to tears by a little collection of his pianoforte pieces. But whilst his biographers have contented themselves with repeating innumerable stories, all bearing upon the boy's special aptitude and gift for music, the most surprising fact of all lies really in the absence of any attempt to train the faculty. It was easy for the youth to delight a drawing-room, and to bring tears to the eyes of a duchess, but it did not seem easy to give him such training as might make a great musician of him. He was always the infant prodigy. No one thought seriously of the art as such, or considered the responsibility which devolved upon them to train so promising a mind to the full fruition of its talents. The young composer had to struggle along as best he might. The chances are that it never entered the minds of any one that the godson of the Duke of York and the Duke of Wellington, the heir of a Baronet and the holder of an honoured name, should devote himself to a profession which at that time was not in the highest repute. It is difficult, indeed, to conjecture what Ouseley might have been had he only received a thorough and adequate early training and been encouraged to develop his art. To-day these early years present the spectacle of a youth wasting his hours in using as an amusement what should have been reverenced as a gift. There is no question that this want of thought upon the part of those responsible had a considerable and most unfortunate effect upon his artistic career. It was impossible for him to be at this period much more than an enthusiastic amateur. Not accustoming himself to the regular and serious expression of his thought, he did not acquire, as it were, a sufficiently early mastery over the vocabulary of his art. True, he always was a master of form, deeply learned in all the various modes adopted by the great composers, and an adept in all the machinery of correct writing. But for original work of a high character there is needed more than this. There is needed a form native to the genius of the individual, which can only be secured by a constant habit of shaping the ideas which occur into their true and most expressive form. If this be neglected, a scientific knowledge of an art invariably tends to prevent originality, by emphasising unduly methods which can only truly live when animated by the force and power of those who used them first. There seems little doubt that Sir Frederick Ouseley had an original genius of a much more romantic order than most of his works might lead one to suppose. But it cannot be said that his early training was such as to give him full command of it. Indeed, early and late he seems to have been left very much to his own resources.

CHAPTER XI

So it remained, as far as there is evidence to show, until he moved to Oxford to go through the usual course of a University education. Here he seems to have worked with more or less system in his musical studies, and it was at this time that he came so strongly under the influence of the older writers of English Church Music. Some early Church works, written probably about this time, show very clearly the style which he had adopted, and which in later years he brought to a great state of perfection. But as yet he was giving no serious thought to Music ; he did not yet see, or at anyrate did not appear to realise, that here lay his particular talent, that to Music should be dedicated all the energy of his life. As an undergraduate he was very popular, and his powers of improvisation were even then well known. Many anecdotes which have been recorded in earlier chapters give us considerable insight into his life at this period. After leaving

245

Oxford, his next thought was to prepare for Holy Orders, and in 1849 he was ordained Deacon, beginning his ministry in troublous times. It was only during his stay abroad (during a holiday rendered absolutely necessary after his hard work at St. Barnabas, Pimlico) that he realised strongly the duty of devoting so great a gift to the service of God. And as the idea of the foundation of a school began to shape itself, his course became more and more clear. He was to give all his energy and ability to raising the Choral Service of the Church of England to its former dignity, thus rendering it a fit and worthy offering. And to this aim he devoted himself with single-hearted purpose during the remainder of his life. His whole plan of carrying out such an idea was indeed characteristic of his gentle earnestness. In the endowment of St. Michael's College, Tenbury,—that group of buildings rising at the end of the Old Wood Common, accessible at the time it was built only by a drive of thirty miles across country from Worcester,—one can see how quietly and unobtrusively he began the great task he had set himself. The very atmosphere of St. Michael's breathes the modesty and unselfishness of its Founder. To carry out his purpose, he began to devote himself seriously to the composition of Church Music, upon the lines he had already adopted in his earlier writing. From this time he began to pour forth a perfect stream of Anthems and Services, and it is upon these that his great reputation as a composer chiefly rests. Many are of a most elaborate nature, containing magnificent instances of contra-puntal writing which are only to be compared with the finest examples of the Madrigalian Period. As an example out of many, one might instance his Service in F for eight-part chorus, solo voices and accompaniments for Orchestra and Organ, a work which, while it has all the austerity and dignity which characterise the writings of the Tallis School, has all the melodiousness of the somewhat later School to which Blow, Purcell, and others may be said to belong. The *Te Deum* and *Benedictus* of this Service were performed at the opening Service of the Worcester Festival of 1887 with grand effect. It has been said that Ouseley erred in looking too constantly to the past for his models in composition ; and while one may admit the truth of this statement so far as his instrumental works are concerned, it is certainly doubtful whether he was not in the right in basing his style in Church Music upon the splendid models of the earlier writers. No man had a higher ideal in Music for the Church than he had, and where it is so obviously a question of the particular standpoint that is taken, it must ever be impossible to say a decisive word. He was always a hater of sentimentalism in Music, and sought for a style which should at once be lofty, devotional, passionless, and ethereal. In his view, Music, when designed for the Church, was to some extent fettered. In the Church Music was but the handmaid of religion, and no longer an art which soared free, breathing alike the joys and sorrows of men, but an art which sought to shadow forth that heavenly calm which exists beyond the fever and fret of human life. It has been sought to show that Ouseley's attitude towards Church Music is almost wholly traceable to the influence of Dr. Crotch's Oxford Lectures, and to the very conservative views put forward in them, and it is no doubt true that Ouseley was to some extent influenced by him in many forms of composition. But this theory is unsatisfactory when it is brought to bear upon Ouseley's views of Church Music. Sir Frederick's ideas were too deeply rooted, and his views too characteristic of the unostentatious piety of the man, to be the mere outcome of the passing influence of a few Oxford Lectures. It is a style which was almost, one might say, a part of his creed; it is a style which alike pervades the simplicity of "How goodly are Thy Tents" and the grandeur of "Great is the Lord"—two thoroughly representative Anthems (a). He had a great power of writing music suited to large masses of voices, and knew well how to obtain fine, broad, choral effects. Indeed, some of his Anthems were especially written for Diocesan Festivals, and other occasional Festivals, and are splendidly laid out for such purposes. A fine example of such

---

(a) In connection with "How goodly are Thy Tents," it may be mentioned in passing that this exquisite little Anthem, which Goss considered one of the gems of English music, was composed whilst Sir Frederick was in Italy. He conceived the idea of it on first seeing Milan Cathedral in moonlight. *Vide* Note in Mr. Bumpus's bibliography, p. 258 *infra*.

an Anthem is his " It came even to pass," written for the reopening of Lichfield Cathedral ; and no one who has heard this Anthem adequately performed by a large body of voices could ever forget its magnificent effect. When one compares such music with much of the flimsy Church writing of to-day, one cannot help thinking of a similar comparison which might be drawn between the dignity and nobility of the older Hymns (of which "O God, our help in ages past," is a striking example) and the feebleness and mawkishness which characterise many of our modern Hymns. Indeed, the spirit of the old *Chorale* is thoroughly present in the Hymn tunes he has left us,—in the beautiful tunes to " They come, God's messengers of love," and " The radiant morn hath passed away." It is no exaggeration to say of these tunes that they are amongst the finest in *Hymns Ancient and Modern*.

It is of interest to refer to his Hymn tunes, for they afford another example of the beautiful way in which he handled anything in the nature of Church Music. From the most elaborate Anthem to the simplest Hymn tune there was always the same reverential touch ; indeed, there was nothing for the service of the Church which was too slight to demand his utmost care. Another striking feature in his choral writing, and one which is unhappily almost entirely lost sight of by Church writers nowadays, is the great beauty of his inner part writing. No doubt this is due in great part to his unusual facility in contrapuntal

methods, but over and above this he had undoubtedly a great feeling for true melody in all his
parts. Though all his works afford countless
examples which would thoroughly establish the
truth of this statement, one cannot help citing,
as an illustration of peculiar beauty, his Anthem
for six voices, "They that wait upon the Lord."
No one can fail to see the purity of his writing
in this, which may certainly take rank amongst
the finest examples of part writing that we have.
He could seldom allow himself to depart from the
strict style in Church compositions ; and though he
wrote Anthems in the somewhat freer vein of S. S.
Wesley or Goss, it was many years before he
would allow them to be published. It was only
after considerable pressure from his friend Mr.
Hampton, and other enthusiastic admirers, that
he consented to include "And there was a pure
River" in the second volume of his "Collections
of Anthems for Certain Seasons and Festivals."
Those who know very little of Sir Frederick's
works are apt to dwell too strongly upon the
scholarly side of his writing, but to those who
knew the man and his works, what great possibilities of style are suggested by this Anthem—
had he cared to deviate from the particular ideas
of Church Music which he had formed !

He wrote two Oratorios, *The Martyrdom of
Saint Polycarp* (an exercise for his Doctor's
Degree) and *Hagar*, produced at the Hereford
Festival of 1873. That these works are not
popular is probably due to the fact that they

are not modern in their tendencies. Both contain too frequent instances of fine fugal writing to be ever popular with Choral Societies ; nevertheless, they are excellent examples of good, sound music of a thoroughly English character.

In his organ works, as in other music written for the Church, his influence was strongly for good. At a time when the works of Wély, Batiste, and other French writers had gained undue hold upon English organists, he was bringing out his many Preludes and Fugues for the organ,—works which are not only of the greatest utility as Church Voluntaries, but are also of the greatest possible value to every organist who has any love for the truest forms of organ music. In his Sonatas for the same instrument, one notices very strongly that flavour of Mozart which runs through so many of his instrumental works in a greater or less degree. They have lately found a place in most programmes of good organ music, as, indeed, have many of his Preludes and Fugues.

In many other ways he rendered the Church vast services, in editing the " Collection of Cathedral Services by English Masters of the Seventeenth and Eighteenth Centuries," few of which had been printed before, and by his edition of the Sacred Compositions of Orlando Gibbons, a task which was not accomplished without extraordinary difficulties.

Ouseley had a marvellous gift for extempore playing, and when in the vein would produce examples of every known art-form, from the Sonata to the Fugue. Indeed, when seated at the piano or organ he was at his best. Nothing was wanting to him, and he may truly be described as one of the finest extempore players who ever lived. At such times he showed a perfect wealth of ideas, through which his individuality was very clearly discernible. The form he was then using, though easily traceable, was never stiff and rigid. It seemed always to adapt itself readily to the general drift of his thought. There was a complete absence of that formality which characterises his written instrumental works, though in his later years—no doubt owing to his secluded life and long absence from the great world of musical thought—his playing was not always free from a certain conventionality in phrases, though this was more noticeable, perhaps, in his codas. As an extempore player, Ouseley was chiefly known by his improvisation of Fugues, but, as it has already been pointed out, he showed a full and complete mastery over almost every other form. On one occasion, when Sir Robert Stewart was staying at St. Michael's College, Sir Frederick was asked to extemporise a Sonata. He quickly consented, but asked for a subject. This Sir Robert Stewart gave him, and after a few minutes' thought he began his first movement. It was noticeable that in this and the succeeding movements there was very little, if any, allusion made to the subject itself. Nor did it appear until the last movement, when, however, he gave it out as a subject from which was developed a most elaborate Fugue, whose counter-subject had already appeared in the first movement in a more or less emphasised form. The whole Sonata was considered by Sir Robert Stewart and the present Warden, Mr. Hampton,— men of exceptional musical judgment,—most masterly, and worthy even of Beethoven. The incident is remarkable, as proving his wonderful quickness in seeing almost at a glance how far it was possible to develop any subject that was given him. He was frequently called upon to extemporise, and in the case of Fugues generally preferred, where it was possible, to have a subject proposed to him. If thoroughly suited to good contrapuntal treatment, he would start at once upon the theme, developing it to its utmost limit by every known device. The man who proposed a subject to Ouseley might well marvel at the profusion of ideas called forth by his theme ; and to him it was often a striking instance of the glorious power of art, to weave, from material not always of the best, a rare fabric of marvellously complicated texture. But it frequently happened that the subjects suggested to him were not entirely suited, and he was quick to point out how, by the modification of perhaps one note, the theme could be made fit for his purpose. It is clear from this that he was able to anticipate almost entirely the treatment most suitable to his subject, and this fact very strongly emphasises the mathematical side of his genius to which I have already alluded. In his extempore playing, as in his written works, he leaned to the style of Mozart, though in this form of composition, as was natural, his ideas received very much freer treatment. Still, the Mozart influence even here was very strongly evident. In the Sonata form, too, he was never known to avail himself of the Scherzo form, preferring the Old World Minuet, which he treated in a particularly graceful manner. Indeed, he loved all the old forms, and used all alike with the most perfect freedom. He was very fond of extemporising upon his own organ at St. Michael's College, or again at Hereford Cathedral, and frequently recalled the practice of Bach, in treating a subject in several forms previous to its final elaboration as a fugue in which the deepest science and the most vivid imagination alike played a part. In these days fugal extemporisation bids fair to become an extinct art, and it is doubtful if we shall ever come upon his equal again.

In this rapid and necessarily unsatisfactory survey of the musical side of Sir Frederick Ouseley's life-work and influence, I have endeavoured to point out how that he was first and foremost a great Church Musician, how that in almost all his works, in his Services, in his Anthems, in his Organ Works, and even in his Hymn Tunes, he had but one object—to render beautiful and noble the service of that Church which he so dearly loved. And truly, looking back upon the many years during which it was my great privilege to know him, from my early school days to his death, I cannot help tracing this object in all he did that was best, in all those works which are, and will ever remain, the memorial of a life lovingly and faithfully devoted—

Ad Majorem Dei Gloriam.

G. R. S.

APPENDIX D.

CATALOGUE OF THE COMPOSITIONS OF THE REV. SIR F. A. G. OUSELEY, BART., Mus.D.Oxon., COMPILED BY MR. JOHN S. BUMPUS IN 1892, AND REVISED IN 1896.

N.B.—In his original prefatory note Mr. Bumpus says :—

" I have used my best endeavours to make the list as complete as possible up to the time of going to press ; but there are, doubtless, very many compositions existing only in manuscript in various private hands, besides those I have mentioned. For Sir Frederick Ouseley had such facility in writing, that anybody who asked him for a particular composition was sure to receive it, and scarcely ever was a copy of it made. The first copy in his own handwriting—and a beautiful handwriting it was—was always fair, and ready for the printer.

" I beg to acknowledge, with feelings of the deepest gratitude, the very courteous and ready assistance of the Rev. John Hampton (Sir F. Ouseley's successor in the wardenship of St. Michael's College, Tenbury) in response to several of my inquiries."

I.

SACRED.

N.B.—Compositions under this section are all published by Novello & Co., and in folio size, unless otherwise stated.

SERVICES.

*In A (à 4 v) Te Deum, Jubilate, Kyrie, Credo, Sanctus, Gloria in Excelsis, Cantate, and Deus Misereatur—*dedicated to the Dean and Canons of Christ Church, Oxford* (a).

N.B.—Services and Anthems marked * were published by Rev. Sir F. Ouseley in the collected edition of his Cathedral Music (folio, Novello, 1853). All others have been printed since, and, with the exceptions named, by Novello, Ewer, & Co. Anthems designated † were published by Sir F. Ouseley in his *Collection of Anthems for Certain Seasons and Festivals*, Vol. I., folio (Cocks & Co.), 1861 : Vol. II. (Novello), 1866.

(a) This beautiful and effective Service in A, together with that in G, was included, some time before its publication, in Ouseley's volume of 1853,

APPENDIX D

In B flat (à 4 v) Magnificat and Nunc Dimittis.

*In B minor (à v 4) Te Deum, Benedictus, Kyrie, Credo, Sanctus, Gloria in Excelsis, Magnificat, and Nunc Dimittis.

In C (for double choir) Venite, Te Deum, Benedictus, Benedicite, Jubilate ; Kyrie, Credo, Sanctus, Gloria ; Magnificat and Nunc Dimittis, Cantate and Deus Misereatur—*composed for the reopening of Hereford Cathedral after restoration, June* 30, 1863 (*unpublished*) (*b*).

In C (à 4 v) Office of the Holy Communion—Kyrie, Credo, Sanctus, and Gloria in Excelsis (8vo).

In D (à 4 v) Chant Service for the Te Deum (8vo).

In D (à 4 v) Gloria in Excelsis (to match and complete Dr. Rogers' Service in D) (8vo and folio).

*In E (à 4 v) Te Deum, Jubilate, Kyrie, Credo, Sanctus, Gloria in Excelsis, Magnificat, and Nunc Dimittis.

*In E flat (à 4 v) Te Deum, Jubilate, Kyrie, Credo, Sanctus, Gloria in Excelsis (this movement is for men's voices), Magnificat, and Nunc Dimittis.

In E flat (for men's voices) Magnificat and Nunc Dimittis —lithographed only. *Sung at St. Paul's Cathedral.*

In F (à 8 v, with orchestra) Te Deum, Benedictus, Kyrie, Credo, Sanctus, Gloria in Excelsis, Magnificat, and Nunc Dimittis.

In F (à 4 v) Te Deum—*composed for the Ely Diocesan Church Music Society* (8vo).

*In G (à 4 v) Te Deum, Jubilate, Sanctus (*c*), Kyrie, Credo, Magnificat, and Nunc Dimittis.

ANTHEMS IN THE SHORT FULL STYLE.

Blessed be the Lord God of Israel (à 4 v)—for Epiphany (8vo).

Except the Lord build the house (à 4 v)—for a wedding.

†From the rising of the sun (à 4 v)—for Epiphany (8vo and folio).

Happy is the man (à 8 v).

Hear my cry, O God (à 4 v)—*dedicated to Dr. C. W. Corfe.*

I will love Thee, O Lord (à 4 v).

---

in a collection of Cathedral Services appearing in periodical numbers under the editorship of Dr. William Marshall, who was organist of Christ Church Cathedral, Oxford, from 1826 to 1846.   Dr. Rimbault was engaged upon a similar task about the same period.

(*b*) The *Cantate* and *Deus* have been lithographed for the special use of the choir of King's College, Cambridge.

(*c*) This Sanctus was intended for use as an Introit.   It has the words "of the Majesty" interpolated.

†Is it nothing to you? (à 4 v)—for Good Friday.

Judge me, O God (à 4 v)—for Passion Sunday (8vo).

Lord, be merciful to us sinners (à 4 v)—published by Morley & Co., 269 Regent Street (8vo).

Lord, I call upon Thee (à 4 v) (8vo and folio).

Love not the world (à 4 v)—*inscribed to the Rev. T. C. Heartley, M.A.*

†My song shall be alway (à 4 v).

O Lord, Thou art my God (à 4 v) (8vo and folio).

O Saviour of the world (double choir)—for Good Friday.

Rend your hearts (à 4 v)

Righteous art Thou, O Lord (à 4 v).

*Haste Thee, O God (à 4 v).

*How goodly are Thy tents (à 4 v) (8vo and folio) (*d*)

*I will give thanks (double choir)

*O God, wherefore art Thou absent (double choir)

*O praise the Lord all ye heathen (à 6 v)

> Dedicated to the Rev. Hy. Fyffe, M.A.

*How long wilt Thou forget me (à 4 v)

*I know that the Lord is great (à 4 v) (8vo and folio)

*O Almighty and Most Merciful God (à 4 v)

*O how plentiful (à 4 v)

*O love the Lord (à 4 v)

*Thy mercy, O Lord (à 4 v)

> Dedicated to A. T. Crispin, Esq.

*Blessed is the man (à 4 v)

*Be merciful unto me (à 4 v)

*O Lord, we beseech Thee (à 4 v)

*Save me, O God (à 4 v)

*To the Lord our God (à 4 v)

*Unto thee, O Lord (à 4 v)

> Composed at Rome in 1851, and inscribed to E. J. Ottley, Esq.

(*d*) The circumstances attending the composition of the anthem, "How goodly are Thy tents," are exceedingly interesting. A considerable portion of the year 1851 was spent by Sir Frederick Ouseley in continental travel, one of the many places he visited being Milan. In the course of a solitary midnight walk through that city he came suddenly upon the huge marble cathedral, bathed in moonlight. The sight produced a profound impression on Sir Frederick, as, indeed, such an one always must on any thoughtful mind. The words instantly occurred to him, and he there and then conceived the idea of setting them to music. It is hardly necessary to observe that the anthem is one of the most expressive and beautiful of Ouseley's shorter compositions.

APPENDIX D

All the kings of the earth (à 4 v)
Behold, how good and joyful (à 4 v)
Blessed is he whose unrighteousness (à 4 v)
In God's word will I rejoice (à 4 v)
Like as the hart (à 6 v)
O praise our God, ye people (à 5 v)
The salvation of the righteous (à 4 v)
Whom have I in heaven but Thee? (à 4 v)

} Dedicated to the Rev. Thomas Helmore, M.A.

LONGER ANTHEMS.

†And there was a pure river of Water of Life—*composed for the baptism of the daughter of the Rev. Hy. Fyffe* (verse à 5 v).

And there was war in Heaven (for the Feast of St. Michael and All Angels) (full à 4 v)—published in Fowle's *Short Anthems for the Church Seasons* (4to, 1873).   (Printed for the editor.)

Ascribe ye greatness (Festival Anthem).

†Awake, thou that sleepest (double choir)—for Easter.

Behold now, praise the Lord (double choir)—*composed for the great Choral Festival in Peterborough Cathedral, June 1863 ; dedicated to the Rev. Chas. Daymond, Minor Canon of the Cathedral, and the Rev. E. B. Whyley, Headmaster of the King's School, Peterborough.*

Blessed be Thou (double choir)—*written for the reopening of Hereford Cathedral, June 30, 1863.*

†Christ is risen from the dead (verse)—for Easter.

Give thanks, O Israel (full with verse à 4 v)—lithographed only.

Great is the Lord (full with verse double choir) (8vo and folio).

Hear, O Lord, and have mercy (full à 4 v) (8vo and folio).

Help us, O God (full à 8 v).

I waited patiently (tenor solo)—*dedicated to Rev. J. Hampton, M.A.*

I will give thanks (double choir).

*I will magnify Thee (full à 5 and 8 v)—*dedicated to Rev. Sir W. H. Cope, Bart., Minor Canon of St. Peter's, Westminster, 1853 (c).*

(c) The Rev. Sir W. H. Cope, Bart., of Bramshill, Hants, died Jan. 7, 1892.   While Minor Canon of Westminster he edited a useful collection entitled *Anthems by Eminent Composers of the English Church* (8vo, Olivier, Pall Mall, 1849). It contained many of the masterpieces of Tallis, Farrant, Gibbons, Byrde, Batten, Childe, Rogers, Aldrich, Blow, Locke, Creyghton, Goldwin, Kelway, and W. King.   He also published an original Communion Service in F (8vo, Novello).

259

†I saw the souls of them that were beheaded (full with verse à 4 v)—for St. James' Day.

In Jewry is God known (full with verse à 5 v)—lithographed only.

In the sight of the unwise (trio for S. S. S., from the oratorio, *St. Polycarp*) (8vo).

It came even to pass (full with verse à 4 v)—*written for the reopening of Lichfield Cathedral, Oct.* 22, 1861, *and sung by* 980 *voices* (folio and 8vo).

It is a good thing to give thanks—*Festival Anthem, scored for orchestra; produced at the great Choral Festival in Salisbury Cathedral, June* 6, 1889).

Let all the world in every corner sing (full with verse à 4 v)—lithographed only.

O praise the Lord with me (full with verse à 4 v) (8vo and folio).

O sing unto God (double choir).

One thing have I desired of the Lord (full with verse à 4 v)—*composed for the Choral Festival held in Tewkesbury Abbey, Sept.* 1884—lithographed only.

Plead Thou my cause (full à 4 v)—published by Metzler & Co., Great Marlborough Street (8vo).

Rejoice with Jerusalem—unpublished.

Sing, O Daughter of Sion (full à 4 and 5 v).

Sing unto the Lord—Festival Anthem, composed for the Annual Festival of the Norfolk and Suffolk Church Choral Association, 1865.

†The Lord is King (à 6 v)—for Ascension Day.

The Lord is my Shepherd (full à 4 v)—*dedicated to the Rev. J. Wayland Joyce.*

The Lord shall roar out of Zion (à 4 v).

†They that wait upon the Lord (à 6 v).

Thou art my portion (treble solo).

†Thus saith the Lord (double choir)—for Epiphany.

†Unto Thee will I cry (verse à 4 v)—for Lent, *dedicated to Captain E. J. Ottley.*

†Who shall ascend (verse à 2 v)—for St. Bartholomew's Day.

†Why standest thou so far off (verse à 2 v)—for Advent, *dedicated to Francis Deffell, Esq.*

The following were elaborately scored for a full band and organ by Sir F. A. Gore Ouseley :—

And there was a pure River.
Ascribe ye greatness.

Awake, thou that sleepest.
Blessed be Thou.
Christ is risen.
Give thanks, O Israel.
Great is the Lord.
I waited patiently.
In Jewry is God known.
It came even to pass.
O sing unto God.
Sing, O Daughter of Sion.
Sing unto the Lord.
The Lord shall roar out of Zion.

*The two following, the property of the Rev. J. Hampton, are in
MS. at St. Michael's College, Tenbury :—*

O send out Thy light (tenor solo and verse à 3 v).
O ye that love the Lord (full à 4 v).

CHANTS.

Twenty-nine Single and six Double Chants, printed in *Anglican
Psalter Chants*, edited by Dr. E. G. Monk and Rev. Sir F. Ouseley
(4to, 1876, Novello) (*f*).

Thirteen Single and Six Double Chants, as sung at St. Michael's
College, Tenbury—lithographed for use there only.

Two Double Chants in G and B flat, composed for and printed
in *The London Chant Book* (oblong 4to, 1886). Seven Single
Chants, in the same collection.

Double Chant in E flat, published in Bemrose's *Choir Chant
Book* (1882).

HYMN TUNES.

In " Hymns Ancient and Modern,"

edited by Dr. W. H. Monk (enlarged edition, 1889).

No. 19. "The radiant morn hath passed away" (St. Gabriel).
No. 28. (Tune 1). "Sweet Saviour, bless us ere we go" (Christ
Church).

(*f*) Those printed in other Chant Books are, as a rule, taken from the
above.

No. 84. "Once more the solemn season" (Hereford).
No. 118. "Throned upon the awful tree" (Gethsemane).
No. 424. "They come, God's messengers of love" (Woolmers).
No. 443. "For man the Saviour shed" (Aberystwyth).
No. 476. "Behold the sun" (Brightness).
No. 503. "Forty days Thy seer of old" (Confidence).
No. 509. (Tune 2). "Be near us, Holy Saviour" (Sharon).
No. 517. "When all Thy mercies" (Contemplation).
No. 544. "Praise the Lord, His glories show" (St. Ethelbert).
No. 547. "Children of the Heavenly King" (Bewdley).

In "*The Hymnary*," edited by Joseph Barnby

(Novello, 1872).

No. 43. "Go to dark Gethsemane."
No. 78. "Father, by Thy love and power."
No. 82. "O Lord, the heaven Thy power displays."
No. 177. "O love, how deep."
No. 185. "O Lord of health and life" (Langley).
No. 337. "Be present, Holy Trinity."

In "*Church Hymns*" (*S.P.C.K.*), edited by

Sir Arthur Sullivan, Mus.D. (1874).

No. 16. "The radiant morn" (St. Gabriel).
No. 185. "O God, the Son Eternal" (Tenbury, No. 2).

In "*The Dublin Church Hymnal*," edited by

Sir R. P. Stewart, Mus.D. (1883).

No. 169. "Go to dark Gethsemane."
No. 192. "Glory to God on high" (St. Augustine).

In Rev. *Peter Maurice's* "*Choral Harmony*" (1854).

No. 184. "Weep no more, Zion" (Langley).
No. 265. "The God of harvest praise."
No. 267. "To God Hosannas sing" (Peterstowe).
No. 285. "Hosanna be our cheerful song" (Tenbury, No. 1).

APPENDIX D

In "The National Book of Hymn Tunes, Kyries, and
Chants" (4to, 1884).

No. 38. "Exultation."
No. 72. "Faith."

In "The Anglican Hymn Book," edited by
Dr. E. G. Monk (Novello, 1871).

No. 19. "Saviour, breathe an evening blessing."
No. 238. "O Death, thou art no more."
No. 291. "Far from the world, O Lord" (Lovehill).
No. 341. "Ye servants of the Lord."
No. 346. "If thou wouldest life attain."
No. 362. "The God of harvest praise" (St. Augustine).
No. 389. "Walking on the winged wind."

In "The Children's Hymn Book" (Rivingtons).

No. 255. "All things bright and beautiful."
No. 124. "Easter flowers are blooming" (In Excelsis Gloria).
No. 186. "Shepherd, good and gracious" (Star of the East).

In "The Holy Year" (musical edition by W. H.
Monk, 1868).

No. 122. "When the Architect Almighty" (Shekinah).
No. 120. "O Lord, Who in Thy love divine" (Ordination).

In "The Home Hymn Book" (Novello, 1887).

No. 253. "When sinks the sun" (Thornton).

In "The Hymnal of the Episcopal Church of America,"
edited by W. B. Gilbert, Mus.B., Oxon.

No. 91. "Pain and toil are over now" (Pruen).

In Rev. R. R. Chope's "Hymn and Tune Book" (1863).

No. 60. "Great mover of all hearts" (St. Cyril).

263

In Dean Alford's " Year of Praise" (1867).

No. 229. "Ten thousand times ten thousand" (Eastham).

This tune is also set to the hymn, "The ocean hath no danger," in *The Church of England Hymnal* (*g*). In the same book there is the tune, "Exultation," set to the hymn, "There is no night in Heaven."

In " The Song of Praise," edited by Geo. Prior.

No. 505. "Angels Holy" (St. Winifred).

In Dr. Steggall's " Hymns for the Church of England."

No. 76. "You, that like heedless strangers."
No. 151. "O God, the Son Eternal."

In the Appendix to "Hymns Ancient and Modern" (1868).

No. 278. "Hail, gladdening Light."

"Now, brothers, to the holy ground"—Funeral Hymn: *In Memoriam*, Bishop Selwyn, Princess Alice, and Archdeacon Moore (Novello).
Arrangement of the tune "Hanover" for chorus, orchestra, and organ (8vo—Goodwin, 71 Great Queen Street).
"Royalty"—a Hymn for Coronation Day (June 28) (8vo, Novello).
"Holy Lord, Thy tender mercies."—Home Mission Hymn (8vo).

CHRISTMAS CAROLS.

"Angels singing, church bells ringing" (à 4 v) (Novello).
"Come, tune your heart" (Stainer and Bramley's Collection, No. v.).
"In Bethlehem, that noble place" (No. xxxii., Stainer and Bramley).
"Listen, lordlings, unto me" (No. xviii., Stainer and Bramley).

(*g*) Musical edition by Dr. A. H. Mann, organist of King's College, Cambridge, 1894.

APPENDIX D

CANTATA.

"The Lord is the true God" (exercise for his degree of Bachelor in Music, Oxford, 1850—unpublished).

ORATORIOS.

The Martyrdom of St. Polycarp (exercise for his degree of Doctor in Music, 1855—Novello & Co.).

Hagar (produced at the Hereford Festival, 1873—Novello & Co.).

ORGAN MUSIC (all published by Novello) (h).

Set of Six Preludes and Fugues (dedicated to Sir Herbert Oakeley).

Set of Seven Preludes and Fugues (dedicated to the Hon. Miss Rushout).

Set of Eighteen Preludes and Fugues.

Set of Six Short Preludes.

Set of Three Andantes.

Two Preludes and Fugues (contributed to *The Organists' Quarterly Journal*).

Two Sonatas (the first one was composed for the opening of the new organ, by Willis, in the Sheldonian Theatre, Oxford).

Voluntary for Christmas-tide (No. 8 of *Original Compositions for the Organ*).

Voluntary in F (No. 9 of *Original Compositions for the Organ*).

Overture to the oratorio *Hagar* (arranged by B. W. Horner).

March from the oratorio *St. Polycarp* (arranged by Langdon Colborne).

Andante Expressivo (published in George Cooper's *Classical Extracts for the Organ*—Cocks & Co.).

(h) As a player of extemporaneous fugues, Ouseley, like S. S. Wesley, was almost unrivalled. This branch of the divine art is now rapidly becoming a lost one ; but an able exponent is still left to us in the person of Dr. G. B. Arnold, the organist (since 1865) of Winchester Cathedral. Many quiet hours were spent by Ouseley and his friend, Dr. Arnold, in the Winchester organ-loft ; subjects of extemporisation being mutually given and worked out. Dr. J. C. Beckwith and Dod Perkins, the respective organists of Norwich and Wells Cathedrals early in the present century were noted fuguists. The former would sometimes pour forth four extempore fugues on one Sunday.

265

LIFE OF SIR F. A. G. OUSELEY

WORKS EDITED FOR CHURCH USE.

———

A Collection of Cathedral Services by English Masters of the 17th and 18th Centuries (folio, Novello, 1853) (*i*).

CONTENTS.

Aldrich in G (*Sanctus and Gloria*).
Childe in A minor. (M. C. E.) (*j*)
Church in F. (M. C. E.)
Creyghton in B flat. (M. E.)
Farrant in D minor. (M. E.)
Foster (*Gloria in Excelsis* for Gibbons in F).
Kelway in G minor. (E.)

Kempton in B flat. (M. E.)
Ouseley (*Gloria in Excelsis* for Rogers in D).
Rogers in E minor. (M. C. E.)
Rogers in F (*k*). (M. E.)
Tomkins in C. (M. with *Venite*, C. E.)

The Sacred Compositions of Orlando Gibbons (folio, Novello, 1873).

Containing Prefatory Memoir, two Sets of Preces, two Services, eighteen Anthems, and six Hymn Tunes.

A Collection of Anthems for Certain Seasons and Festivals (2 vols., folio, Cocks and Novello, 1861–66).

Containing compositions by—Leslie, Gilbert, Greatheed, Stainer, Goss, Hayne, E. J. Hopkins, Haking, Rev. H. E. Havergal, Steggall, Oakeley, Sterndale Bennett, Armes, Allen, G. J. Elvey, Wintle, Dykes, E. G. Monk, Macfarren, E. J. Ottley, Barnby, Chawner, Colborne, Sullivan, and the Editor.

An old Anthem, "Hear my prayer," by Thomas Wilkinson, edited by Sir F. A. G. Ouseley and Dr. A. H. Mann, from the ancient choir-books of Peterhouse, Cambridge.

(*i*) None of these had ever been printed before, except Tomkins' Service, in Warren's edition of Boyce's *Cathedral Music*.

(*j*) M. = Morning ; C. = Communion ; E. = Evening.

(*k*) The *Sanctus, Kyrie, Gloria Tibi, Gratias,* and *Credo* belonging to this Service, which were not given by Ouseley, are in an ancient MS. organ book once belonging to John Bishop, organist of Winchester Cathedral and College (died 1737). Another copy is in an oblong quarto volume in score, containing the complete Church compositions of Benjamin Rogers. This is in the handwriting of Dr. Philip Hayes, Professor of Music in the University of Oxford, 1777–97, and organist of Magdalen, New, and St. John's Colleges. Both volumes are in my possession.—J. S. B.

266

APPENDIX D

Anglican Psalter Chants—Single and Double, edited in conjunction
with Dr E. G. Monk (4to, 1876).

The Psalter Pointed for Chanting, edited in conjunction with
Dr. E. G. Monk (various sizes).

Tallis' Preces and Responses, arranged for the use of the
Shropshire Choral Union.

Final Amen.—This very beautiful and touching little piece of
music—one of Ouseley's last compositions—was composed for
use in Winchester Cathedral, where it is constantly sung at
the close of Evensong on Sundays.   It was printed in the *Lichfield Choral Festival Book* for 1889.

II.

SECULAR.

N.B.—Music under this section has been published only where mentioned.

INSTRUMENTAL MUSIC.

Overture in D for a full orchestra.
Overture in D minor   ditto.
Overture in F   ditto.
Concert March in C   ditto.
Concert March in D   ditto.
Minuet and Trio   ditto.—published by Lafleur.
String Quartet in C (*f*) } published by Augener.
String Quartet in D minor }
String Quartet in A   } MS. property of the Rev. J.
Fugue in 4 parts for Strings } Hampton.
Minuet and Trio for a very large orchestra.

A set of unpublished "Songs without Words," written between
the years 1839 and 1849.

(*f*) The slow movement from this Quartet was arranged for the organ by
George Cooper, and printed in his *Organ Arrangements.*

VOCAL MUSIC.

GLEES.

Ah, why should nature (A.T.B.).
Gem of the crimson-coloured Even (A.T.T.B.).
Go, lovely rose (A.T.B.B.).
Go, tuneful bird (S.A.T.B.).
O Memory (A.T.B.).
Sweet Echo (S.A.T.B.B.)—composed 1845; published by J. Vincent, High Street, Oxford.
The Water Sprites (S.A.T.B.).
The Spirits of the Wood (S.S.A.T.B.).
Though I may never more behold (S.A.T.B.).
When o'er the silent sea (S.A.T.B.).

MADRIGAL.

Your shining eyes (S.S.A.T.T.B.).

PART SONGS.

Place the helm on thy brow (S.A.T.B.) ⎱
War, wine, and harmony (12 parts) (*m*) ⎰ lithographed only.
Life (S.A.T.B.)—Novello.

SONGS.

Set of Six—for Sunday use—(words by the Rev. Richard Wilton) —published by Novello, containing :—

    1. " Oh, where."
    2. " Under the snow."
    3. " Home."
    4. " The Sparrow."
    5. " Apple Blossoms."
    6. "The resting-place."

    " How beautiful is day."
    " The Skylark."
    " The ploughshare of Old England."
    " Zephyr, should'st thou chance."
    " Old Bells."

(*m*) This was written at Cambridge as an ἐπίδειξις of what Oxford could do.

APPENDIX D

III.

THEORETICAL AND OTHER WORKS.

A Treatise on Harmony (8vo, Oxford, 1868).

A Treatise on Counterpoint, Canon, and Fugue, based on Cherubini (4to, Oxford, 1869).

A Treatise on Musical Form (4to, Oxford, 1875).

"History of Music," by E. Naumann, edited by Sir F. Ouseley (2 vols., Cassell, 1882).

The Choral Worship of the Church—a Sermon preached at Derby (8vo, 1861).

Jerusalem at Unity—a Sermon (8vo, 1863).

Secular Education—a Sermon (8vo, 1869).

Essay on "The Education of Choristers in Cathedrals," being No. 9 of the series of "Essays on Cathedrals," edited by Dean Howson of Chester (8vo, Murray, 1872).

Papers read before the Musical Association by Sir Frederick Ouseley, President from its formation in 1874 : —

1. "Contributions on the History of Ecclesiastical Music of Western Europe," January 3, 1876.

2. "On the Early Italian and Spanish Treatises of Counterpoint and Harmony," March 3, 1879.

3. "On some Italian and Spanish Treatises on Music of the Eighteenth Century," February 6, 1882.

4. "On the Position of Organs in Churches," February 1, 1886.

These have all been published in the Association's Papers (Novello).

Paper on "Organs," read at the Musical Institution, Sackville Street, April 3, 1852.

Papers on Church Music, read at the Church Congresses at Manchester (1863), *Wolverhampton* (1867), *Leeds* (1872), *Brighton* (1874).

*The following works are in Manuscript in the Library of St.
Michael's College, Tenbury :—*

" Let tears fall down" (ode on the death of the Duke of Wellington, 1852)—scored for full orchestra.

" Now let us praise famous men " (ode on the Installation of the
Marquis of Salisbury as Chancellor of University of Oxford)—for
soprano solo, five-part chorus, and full orchestra. November 1869.

"Peace Ode" (after the Crimean War)—for soprano solo, five-
part chorus, and full orchestra (1855).

———

In the library at St. Michael's College, Tenbury, is also pre-
served a small volume $9\frac{1}{2} \times 5\frac{1}{2}$ inches, containing 243 compositions,
showing the extraordinary precocity of Ouseley's genius. Many
of these were composed at the age of five years (chiefly waltzes,
marches, and melodies), for his parents, Queen Adelaide, Madame
Pasta, Madame Weiss, Lady Denbigh, Lady Fitzgibbon, Hon.
Miss Jervis, and others. The earliest example is dated November
1828, when only three years and three months old.

At the age of seven and a half years he composed an opera, the
MS. of which consists of 53 pages of six lines each, but it has no
distinguishing title ; and when about eight he wrote another, with
Italian words, entitled, *L'Isola Disabitata*, which was noticed in
the *Musical Library* of September 1834. About the same time
he composed a duet, " *Vanne a regnar besnomio*" *per Soprano e
Contralto*. This was printed by Novello, and favourably reviewed
at the time of its appearance.

In a book entitled *Original Compositions in Prose and Verse*,
published by Edmund Lloyd, of Harley Street, Cavendish Square
(1833), appeared a March in C and an Air in A flat, both composed
at the age of six.

In the eleventh volume of *The Harmonicon* (1833) appears
another March in C.

INDEX

INDEX

INDEX

MORRISON AND GIBB, PRINTERS, EDINBURGH.